J.J. RUSSELL

Bite Me

The Artemis Necklace Series, Book 2

Contents

Chapter 1

"This place looks like it's straight out of *House of Wax, Jax.*" I stared apprehensively at the Victorian house. Ramble made a dog-like sound of agreement. We stood outside the car, staring up at the creepy house. Though the dark swallowed the outline of the house, I could still see the two upstairs windows watching me like dead eyes from above a front door that looked like a mouth waiting to swallow us whole.

I shifted my weight so that my thigh came into contact with Ramble's shoulder. As a hellhound, he's a little taller than the average dog. He also has glowing red eyes, bat-like pointed ears, and weird prickly fur. Not that any of that matters since I'm the only one who can see him. One of the few perks of being the descendant of a weird vampire hunting family was apparently being able to see hellhounds. And ghosts.

I shivered at the thought of the potential ghosts inside the Victorian house.

Get a grip, Vianne, I told myself and zipped my dark red fleece all the way up against the chilly upstate New York night air. My imagination was definitely running away from me. Maybe it was because we were almost a week away from Halloween that made everything seem so sinister and out to

1

get me.

Or maybe it was because I knew that a horde of vampires sent by their terrifying vampire patriarch was trying to find me and kill me.

So, yeah. I might have been a little paranoid.

In the dark, it was difficult to make out Jax's facial features, but I could easily imagine the look he threw at me.

"You've been bitching for days about how we're always moving from motel to motel and that you don't have the chance to 'figure out the necklace.' Since we can't stay in a motel for too long without being noticed, this," he waved to the house, "is the answer to stopping somewhere long term."

And without being caught by vampires, I mentally added.

I couldn't exactly argue with him, but I wouldn't call it "bitching" to complain about the constant traveling. We'd been on the move for days after being chased by Morvalden (the aforementioned patriarch of vampires) into Between (a weird kind of dimension with multiple portals to places all over our world).

It had felt like we'd been traveling through the misty world of Between for weeks, but it stood a little outside reality and had its own screwed up idea of time. In fact, the first time we'd gone into the Between, we were only there for a day but lost a month of time in this world. This last time we'd gone into Between, we'd stayed for several days in the hopes that the longer we stayed inside and kept moving, the further away we'd end up from Morvalden and his fanged cronies. Instead when we'd emerged, it was only hours after we'd entered. The only positive outcome of going into the Between was that when we reentered our world, we were in a national park in Massachusetts which was a long way from where we'd last seen Morvalden in Indianapolis.

It had only been a few weeks since I'd learned that vampires and other supernatural creatures were real. I just wished things in this weird world of monsters would make a little more sense. At this rate, I'd need a manual to figure it out.

After risking my life to get my hands on the Artemis necklace which was a magical artifact apparently handed down through the female line of my ancestors, I thought I'd be on a little firmer ground with all this supernatural stuff. I'd hoped that possessing the necklace would clear things up, but though the necklace had initially seemed quite chatty, that had quickly turned into a wall of silence.

Now I only got the occasional vague feeling of doom from it. Super helpful.

When I didn't answer Jax, he nudged me then thrust something metal into my hand. "Here."

I quickly realized he'd handed me a sharp blade. "What do I need this for? I thought this house was abandoned?"

I could tell from Jax's body language that he was debating on whether to answer me or not. He must have realized that I would only continue asking questions if he didn't answer because he quietly growled, "Better to be safe than sorry. Could be other squatters here."

I looked again at the ramshackle house. Half of the front porch was falling in and, though I couldn't really tell without better light, it looked like the place had been battered by the elements so much that it had lost virtually all its paint. It seemed highly unlikely that someone else would look at this house and say, "Perfect! Let's stay here for the night!"

I considered saying as much to Jax but realized he would only call it "bitching." Whatever. What he saw as me complaining, I viewed as being the voice of reason.

As much as I hated to follow this hunter of supernatural monsters around, he did have his uses. Jax had a knack for procuring cars, cash, and weapons. Still, it didn't make up for what I saw as betrayal. I had a hard time completely trusting him since learning that he'd been working with Morvalden's lover or wife or whatever. Jax and Constancia had been in cahoots the whole time to get the Artemis necklace into my hands. While that should have been a good thing, it meant that he'd been a big reason that my life had suddenly been turned upside down.

The worst part was that he hadn't just come out and told me all this. Instead he'd strung me along and only fed me bits and pieces of information as he saw fit. The lack of information had almost led to me being killed by a group of vampires. So, yeah, we still weren't exactly pals.

I gripped the knife harder in reflexive anger. Punching him when we were in Between had felt great and, since I'd been wearing the Artemis necklace at the time, it had been quite the wallop. Still, it didn't make my anger go away and did absolutely nothing to make me trust Jax. Which was a problem because it meant that I couldn't tell him what I really thought was going on with the necklace.

While wandering Between, I'd noticed that the voice and the power coming from the necklace faded with each passing day. I thought at first that maybe it had something to do with being in the strange world of Between. Now, outside Between and back in our normal world, I thought there was something else going on. Something way worse.

I'd hoped that stopping for a little while would not only let me figure out why I could no longer seem to use the Artemis

CHAPTER 1

necklace's powers, but would also give me time to figure out if Jax was trustworthy enough to share my theory with about why I thought the necklace wasn't working anymore.

Looking back at the knife in my hand, I couldn't help but ask Jax one more question. "If you think someone else might be inside, shouldn't we have guns instead?"

"We won't need guns." Jax struggled to keep his voice neutral as he explained, "I looked it up. The house was foreclosed on and nobody's lived here for a long time."

"Then why do we even need the knives if no one's inside?"

There was a moment of silence while Jax swallowed his anger and put a stranglehold on his reply to keep it even. "Because it never hurts to be cautious. Now, come on."

He moved away from the car which was parked off the road and partially hidden from the house by overgrown bushes and a copse of pine trees. I followed him, carefully feeling the knife to get an idea of how long it was and its weight. The one good thing about being around Jax was that he'd been teaching me to defend myself with a variety of weapons. I still didn't think I'd have a dog in the fight without the Artemis necklace backing me up with its powers, but at least I was better at hiding knives on my person now and could keep from shooting myself in the foot with a gun. Always a plus.

Beside me, Ramble quietly crept with me toward the house. I still couldn't believe my luck that I'd somehow made a deal with the hellhound when I'd freed him from a cage. It meant that, had I realized I'd made a deal with him and known anything about deals with hellhounds, I could have ordered him around. As in: "Hey hellhound, protect me from the bat-shit scary vampires who are trying to kill me."

But according to Jax, I'd screwed up when I'd given Ramble

5

his name. Apparently naming a hellhound is really bad. (Again, a supernatural manual would be great.) By naming him, I'd granted Ramble freedom from our initial deal. Rather than immediately eviscerating me though, Ramble had stuck by my side and helped me escape more tight spots than the human hunter had.

Ramble quietly padded alongside me up to the house. He blended into the darkness so well that, were it not for his glowing red eyes, I might not have realized he was even there. I should probably be nervous having a hellhound at my side, but his presence made me feel a lot braver. Maybe it had something to do with the fact that he was invisible to everyone else and could breathe fire. Yeah. That might have had something to do with it.

The creepy house loomed overhead as we drew closer. I couldn't help staring at those empty windows. I expected that a ghost or something would materialize in one of them. I was not looking forward to sleeping in a house that was so clearly haunted.

Especially since I could occasionally see ghosts.

I glanced down at the knife in my right hand and whispered, "Is this silver?"

Jax paused long enough to give me what I assumed was a dark look before sneaking around to the back of the house.

I guess that was a yes—which made alarms go off in the back of my mind. I didn't need a magical necklace to tell me that something was up.

Question: Why would I need a silver knife instead of a gun to scope out a house that was clearly abandoned?

Answer: Because Jax didn't actually think the house was abandoned and whatever he thought was inside was immune to bullets but not to silver.

Shit.

I followed Jax around the back of the house while mentally reviewing some of the lore Jax had taught me so far. Let's see, silver is a good weapon against werewolves, dark faeries (whatever those are), ghouls, shapeshifters—I had to stop. I was seriously getting creeped out. It was one thing to deal with hellhounds and vampires. I'd even met a powerful witch who could reshape living trees to her will. And, though I hadn't actually seen her, that witch's sister had sent a swarm of bugs to attack me and my companions. I wasn't ignorant anymore that there were other supernatural creatures out there, but it was a bit overwhelming to name them in a list as possible creatures that might be lurking in the dark corners of this house waiting to attack me.

I looked up at the creepy house and pictured a party of werewolves waiting inside for us. *Wonderful way to psych yourself out, Vi.*

Ramble gently nudged me to keep me moving.

The backside of the house was less imposing than the front, but I still felt watched by something behind the dark windows. Similar to the front, there was a short set of stairs leading up to a backdoor but the porch was still intact. Jax started up the stairs but I caught his arm.

"Is there something inside that I need this for?" I whispered and waved the knife in the air.

"It's just a precaution. Now be—"

The rest of his admonishment was drowned out by a scream from inside the house.

I jerked my head at the sound and sucked in my breath. "Sounded like a girl's scream, right?" I whispered.

Jax immediately reacted by shaking my hand off his arm. He charged up the rest of the stairs and plowed into the door shoulder first. It groaned but surprisingly didn't break. I sped up the steps behind him and, before he could pull back to ram the door again, I reached out and twisted the doorknob. It turned easily in my hand and Jax shoved the door open and rushed into the house.

It was even darker in the house than it had been outside. It took my eyes a moment to adjust. We were in an empty kitchen. It was devoid of anything that would suggest people lived here. No coffeemaker. No refrigerator. If I hadn't heard the girl's scream from outside, I would have thought that Jax was right and that the place was abandoned.

There was also a musty smell of decay permeating the house. As if a rat or a mouse had crawled into one of the heat ducts and died.

"No!" The muffled shout came from upstairs. Ramble's glowing eyes tracked up to the ceiling. "Please! Just let me go!"

It was the girl again. I didn't hear anyone answer her, but they may have been speaking too quietly.

"Upstairs," I whispered to Jax.

The hunter immediately went into what I thought of as his "stealth" mode, sinking down a little and turning side-on, his right hand holding the knife a little out in front of him. He crept forward, leaving the kitchen and turning a corner.

Swallowing, I copied his posture and tried to remember all the fighting techniques and defensive moves he'd been shoving down my throat for the past few days. I left what felt like the safety of the kitchen and followed Ramble's glowing eyes as he rounded the corner. Jax was already on the other side of a dark hallway which ended in a partially broken window. A set of stairs led up to the left and I hurried to catch up to Jax as he started up them.

Even on the inside, the house looked completely abandoned. Dust lay thick on the floor making me want to sneeze. As I started up the stairs, I noticed that there were more than just Jax's set of footprints going up them. It was hard to tell, but I thought there were at least two other sets there.

My thoughts and movement skittered to a stop behind Ramble halfway up the stairs when another scream sounded above us. I sucked in dusty air and tried to overcome the fear that threatened to freeze me to the spot by telling myself, *Maybe we can help save this girl!*

It was enough to kick my brain back into gear, but I had to ignore the low thrum of foreboding from the Artemis necklace as I followed Ramble up the stairs, his long claws clacking on the wooden risers.

Jax had already reached the landing and was looking around as if he didn't know which way to go. The smell was stronger on this floor.

"No!" The girl's voice came from an open door at the end of the hallway, but she sounded lost now. Like she was protesting but knew that it wouldn't make any difference.

She was wrong. We were going to get to her in time. We were going to save her!

Jax still stood looking around the upstairs hallway. Why wasn't he moving to help the girl? Was he stopping to plan or something? The girl didn't sound like she had that much time left. We needed to move! I shoved past him and headed for the open door—

—and something slammed into me from the left, bashing

me *through* the right wall. The attacker rode me down to the ground and my head slammed into the wooden floor while at the same time my right side went numb. My ears rang and I braced myself for the pain that would inevitably replace the numb feeling in my side.

My attacker sat up enough to roughly roll me onto my back. With no windows in this room, I could only vaguely make out his shape.

"Filthy human!" The words were garbled, like he had marbles in his mouth.

Or lots of teeth, my brain helpfully supplied.

A low pulse came from the Artemis necklace... then it fell silent again. So much for magical assistance. I was on my own here. Which was not great since I'd managed to drop the knife while getting shoved through the wall.

My attacker suddenly darted his whole upper body toward me. I tried to get my hands up to fend him off but he was too fast. I felt his hot breath seconds before several somethings punctured the skin below my collarbone. I cried out as a burning sensation lit up my senses where he'd latched onto me.

The teeth in my skin didn't feel like a vampire's, but my attacker was definitely more than human. If the weird feel of his teeth didn't give him away as something other than human, the fact that he'd called me a "filthy human" definitely did.

I shoved my hands at his face, trying to find an eye to poke or a nostril to yank on, but it didn't phase him and I couldn't seem to get any purchase.

A menacing growl made the hair on the back of my arms and neck stand up. It wasn't coming from the thing on top of me. My fight or flight response said that it would be worth it to run away from whatever had made that noise even if it meant dragging my attacker with me.

I cried out when my attacker's teeth were suddenly ripped painfully out of my skin when someone yanked him off me. My savior, Ramble, didn't give the creature time to regain its footing before tossing it in the corner and leaping after it. A weird, human-like squeal pierced the room before dying down to the meaty sounds of tearing flesh and chewing. I lay there for a few moments, my stomach roiling at the noises coming from the corner. If I hadn't been so dazed by the attack, I think I would have hurled.

Before I could think about moving, sudden light blinded me. I flinched away and raised a hand to shield my eyes.

"Did it work?" Jax's gruff voice came from behind the light on his phone.

"What?" I was still trying to get my wits together. What was he talking about?

A scream from another room made my heart leap into my throat. The girl! I'd totally forgotten about her in the attack. Some savior I was.

"No! Please! Just let me go!"

It sounded like she was just down the hall. I rolled to my knees and searched through pieces of the wall scattered around the floor for the knife. I saw a glint of light in the debris when it reflected Jax's phonelight. I snatched up the knife and, feeling a little more energized by the need to help the girl, was able to push to my feet and shove past Jax.

"The girl still needs our help! There must be another one of those things up here!" I shouted over my shoulder as I ran down the hall.

Jax must have turned to follow me because light from his

phone spilled down the hall. I was thankful I didn't have to go running through the dark anymore as I neared the room where I thought the girl was.

The smell of rot near the open doorway was strong enough to make me want to gag. Whatever the smell was coming from was definitely in this room. I paused, gathering the courage to step forward and look inside. I didn't know what sight would await me. A sob from the room gave me the courage to move, knife first, through the door.

The room had two adjacent windows, and luckily, the clouds outside chose that moment to part and let some moonlight into the room. It was just enough to illuminate the scene inside.

"Please," the girl pleaded from the dirty floor where she sprawled face up. She had jeans on, but her shirt was ripped open, exposing the bra underneath. An odd, circular wound the size of my palm marred the skin just over her left breast. She tried to shove weakly at an invisible assailant as her head fell back, eyelids fluttering, struggling to stay awake. No, to stay alive.

As I watched, her cheeks sucked in, as if she was rapidly losing weight. Her chest began to do the same, making her bra several sizes too big. Her skin shriveled up like a raisin.

Something was sucking the life out of her.

I jerked forward at the realization and, reacting more than thinking, crossed the room in three quick strides to slash the invisible assailant and get the thing off the girl.

The knife passed harmlessly through the air.

Behind me, Jax let out an annoyed huff and leaned against the door frame. "There's nothing there, Vânători."

"What?"

The girl writhed on the ground before me while the life was sucked out of her. Suddenly, she let out a small gasp and then disappeared.

I jerked back and turned to Jax who was staring at me like I was an idiot.

"She disappeared," I said.

His eyebrows drew down. "That's because she's dead."

A scream split the air making Ramble and I both jump. Jax jerked as well, but only in reaction to our surprise. The girl appeared again, healthy and with her shirt intact, standing between Jax and I while she backed away from the doorway.

Understanding trickled its slow way through my brain as the girl backed away from an invisible attacker.

"She's just a ghost," I breathed to myself as reality sank in.

"No! Please! Just let me go!" The girl continued to back up, moving toward Ramble and I without ever acknowledging our presence. I hastily moved out of the way and Ramble followed just before she would have stepped through us.

I'd only recently started seeing ghosts and the only other ghost I'd encountered so far had been completely silent, opting instead to stare at me until I'd figured what he wanted. When I'd touched his hand, I had been transported to the moment of his death, experiencing it firsthand from inside his mind.

It seemed I wouldn't have to touch this ghost to see how she'd died—which was good because I really didn't want to experience what was clearly a pretty horrible death.

"What's it doing?" Jax asked. Though he was looking at the spot where the girl was slowly having the life drawn out of her, his eyes weren't tracking anything.

"*It* is a she and *she* looks like she's repeating her death over and over."

Though Jax made a living killing supernatural things and occasionally saved people, the saving people part was just a happy accident. He seemed to have no empathy for others and didn't bat an eye if some random bystander got in his way or was killed by the monsters he hunted.

He put his knife away and flicked a finger at the scene to indicate he wanted more information about what Ramble and I could see.

The girl looked to be about sixteen or seventeen. Her hair was dark, but in this light it was difficult to tell if it was black or just a really dark brown. Her makeup had been applied with a liberal hand, making her look older. Her shirt was a silky thing with a plunging neckline you usually didn't see outside a club. The whole ensemble made me think that maybe she'd been dressed up for a date.

Jax watched me as I tracked the ghost. He wouldn't care about any of those details.

"A young woman is being attacked. Her shirt gets ripped open and it looks like something starts sucking the life out of her. Her body shrivels up and then disappears when she dies. Then it starts all over again."

He nodded. "Ghosts that relive their deaths are usually stuck and won't be able to tell you anything."

"So there's nothing we can do for her?" I asked, wincing as the ghost's back reached the wall. She'd trapped herself between the wall and her invisible attacker. Her hand was batted down and she let out another scream, the same one I'd heard earlier, as her shirt was torn open. She tried to shove something off but that round wound suddenly blossomed on her chest.

My hand involuntarily moved to where my attacker had

bitten me earlier and I craned my neck to see it. It was the same shape as the girl's wound. Shit. Had that thing almost sucked the life out of me? I was lucky Ramble had my back.

"No!" She moaned. Slowly, the attacker lowered her to the ground, putting her in the same spot her ghost had been in when we'd entered the room.

Her protests became weaker, her head lolled back, eyelids fluttering. Her skin did its liposuction trick again until her face looked like a grimacing skeleton. Then she winked out of existence.

"What can we do for her?" I asked again, this time looking at Jax.

He shook his head. "We already killed the lamprey. If that didn't set her free…" He shrugged. "There are different kinds of ghosts. Some interact with the world. Some are stuck in their own death loop."

Stuck in a death loop? That sounded…horrible.

Ramble sniffed the air and made a beeline for the other side of the room to stare at something in the corner. Now that I stopped to notice, the rotten smell was definitely coming from whatever he was looking at. It was a darker shadow against the blackness of the room, but there was also a lighter colored piece of cloth there.

It didn't help to alleviate the smell, but I put a hand over my nose and mouth anyways before moving closer to the corner. I had a feeling I already knew what it was..

Seeing where I looked, Jax moved his phone-light and my gut feeling was proven right. The attacker had left the girl's body curled up on itself in the corner like a piece of trash. Her skin had shriveled up like a dry husk. It was as if when her attacker had sucked the life out of her, it had also sucked all the moisture from her body.

The girl's scream pierced the room again and sent my heart into my throat once more. She flickered back into the world and I watched helplessly as she stumbled backwards. She went through the whole thing again, and when her shirt was torn open and the wound appeared, a realization hit me.

Jax had specifically armed us with silver knives. He'd known that something was in this house. No—not just something. A lamprey, whatever the hell that was. The name conjured images of an eel-like fish thing with teeth, but clearly the thing that had attacked me was more than that.

And Jax had known it was in this house.

"You made sure we both had silver knives." I held up the knife to him as evidence. "You knew there was a lamprey thing in here, didn't you?"

My brain chose that moment to catch up to something he'd said earlier.

"Wait, you also asked me something before." I had to stop and try to remember exactly what he'd said. I'd still been dazed by being shoved through a wall and then attacked. When I remembered his words, my mouth dropped open.

"You asked me if 'it' had worked." Now I pointed the knife at him in accusation. "Did you think the necklace would somehow magically start working if we were in danger, Jax?" I bit off his name. Ramble caught my anger and let out a quiet growl.

The hunter was silent for a moment, obviously weighing his options to not answer, before he finally said, "There were rumors of attacks in a cluster of towns nearby." His gaze dropped to the body at my feet. "A few bodies were found like this one—shriveled up like the life had been sucked out of them. No wounds though."

I opened my mouth to yell at him. To tell him that maybe if he'd let me in on the fact that we were actually investigating a monster, that maybe I could have helped rather than be dragged around and left in the dark. But his last statement threw me off.

"What do you mean no wounds? She had a great big bite on her chest!" I pointed to my own bite which was starting to throb now that my adrenaline was wearing off. "Just like this!"

Jax tipped his head in thought. "Some monsters have healing properties in their saliva. It lets them feed on prey multiple times then close the wound after they feed."

"Seriously?" That was... horrifying. "So this creature could feed on someone, heal them with their spit, then come back for more later? And the person would have zero evidence they'd been attacked?"

Jax shrugged. "How do you think vampires keep themselves secret? They bite you, heal up your wounds, then mesmerize you to forget they were ever there. It lets them keep you around as a snack longer."

"Why didn't mine heal up, then?"

He shrugged again and I realized I was beginning to hate that shrug. "Probably the lamprey got pulled off you before it could heal the bite. Or it didn't bother because it didn't expect your body to be found. Why bother with the extra step of healing you if it's not gonna keep you around to feed on?"

Without another word, he turned and used the flashlight to make his way out of the room.

"Where are you going? We can't just leave her here." I motioned toward the body on the floor. The ghost had just flickered out again which meant there was a short span of quiet before she would pop back into existence with a scream. I didn't want to stick around for that, but we couldn't just leave. Surely someone out there was missing her and wondering what had happened.

"What do you want me to do about it? Bury her?" He didn't let me get a word in before he rolled on, "We don't have time for that. If we stopped to bury every dead body in this line of work, we'd never catch the monsters." He strode off down the hall taking the light with him.

I couldn't help but follow him, which was good because at that moment the girl's ghost popped back into existence. Leaving the room cut down the volume of the girl's scream, but not by much.

"I'm not staying here if there's a body in that room and a ghost that's going to keep me up all night screaming and living out her last few seconds."

"We're not staying here," he said over his shoulder as he descended the stairs. We made our way back to the first floor, through the hallway, and back into the kitchen. Ramble stayed at my side as I put on a burst of speed to get in front of the hunter and stand between him and the door so he couldn't leave the house.

"So, you lied about us staying here, too?" I demanded. "This whole thing was just about putting us in danger to see if the damn necklace would work?"

At the mention of the necklace, I felt a light pulse from it. *Not the time!* I wanted to shout at it.

When he didn't answer, I put my hands on my hips, knife still clenched in one hand, and stared at him. "Well?"

He shrugged and I wanted so badly to punch him in the

face. Again. Of course, I'd had the strength of the necklace behind the blow before. Now all I got from it were feelings of foreboding. Super.

"You led me in here just so you could see if the necklace would start working when my life was in danger?" I thought back to the moment when I'd been attacked. "You didn't even bother to try and help me in there, did you?" I shook my head in disbelief. "If Ramble hadn't been there, I would be just as dead and shriveled up as that girl in there!"

"The necklace—" he started before I cut him off.

"The necklace isn't working!" I threw my hands in the air. I was sick and tired of this. I'd told him a million times that something was wrong with the necklace. It wasn't like when I'd first put it on. For some reason, the necklace's power had faded over a short period, and I'd tried everything I could think of to make it work again.

Okay, almost everything.

"It will work if the wearer needs it to," he sounded so sure of himself.

I pointed to my wound below my neck. "Clearly it doesn't!"

A taunt silence fell between us. I took a deep breath and tried to regain control of my anger. Screaming isn't usually the best way to convince someone of your point. It was hard to let go of the anger though. I mean, this idiot was going to get me killed!

I tried for a calmer tone as I said, "Couldn't you have at least told me about the lamprey? I mean, it wouldn't have made it any less dangerous."

"I wasn't sure if it would work if you knew you were walking into danger."

"I knew I was facing freakin' vampires the last time it

19

worked. Why would now be any different?"

He grunted as if to concede my point, then got a thoughtful look on his face before slowly saying, "Maybe you have to know about the danger and do something to activate the necklace to make it work...."

I opened my mouth to protest but stopped and forced myself to consider it. Minus the part about needing to know that danger was imminent, his theory sort of lined up with mine which was that the necklace only worked when I drank vampire blood.

It hadn't taken me very long to come up with the theory. After all, I didn't start seeing ghosts until Jax forced me to take vampire blood—which doesn't make Jax sound so great. Especially when I add that he kidnapped me, tied me up in a motel room, and *then* forced me to drink the vampire blood. On the upside, he did save me from a vampire that was about to kill me. So, there's that.

Then, after finally getting the necklace, the crazy vampire who gave it to me also forced me to drink her blood. Only after drinking her blood while wearing the Artemis necklace did I hear the voice of Artemis and suddenly gain superhuman strength and speed.

But here was the problem: I couldn't tell Jax any of this.

Though he had cooperated with a vampire to get the necklace into the hands of the next Vânători (ahem, moi), he also *hated* supernatural creatures. He did have a weird cooperative relationship with the aforementioned witch, the Lady of Woods... but even then, he didn't talk about her like he would a person. And if given half the chance, I knew he wouldn't hesitate to kill Ramble.

I was afraid that if I told him my theory about the vampire

blood and the necklace, that he might no longer think I was human enough to continue breathing. I mean, sure, he thought that the Vânători family weren't quite human, but as far as I knew, none of the other Vânători had needed to drink vampire blood in order to use the necklace. I wasn't sure what that made me, but I was afraid Jax would think it meant I either wasn't human enough or Vânători to continue breathing.

I took another deep breath before I responded to Jax. I tried to choose my words carefully so as to get my point across.

"Regardless of why the necklace isn't working, keeping me in the dark about a dangerous creature doesn't make the situation less dangerous. When you pull a stunt like this, it makes me trust you less than I already do."

"Tough shit. I'm all you've got, so you'll just have to get over your trust issues and stop whining about every little thing like a little girl."

Whining like a little girl? I'd just gotten shoved through a wall and been bitten by a life-sucking creature! If he thought I wasn't going to complain about that or that I wouldn't speak up when he lied to me, he was gravely mistaken.

"This isn't working." I turned and shoved the door open, making my lamprey bite twinge, and strode back into the chilly night air. Of course, now that things weren't scary any-more, the clouds had decided to part and let some moonlight through. Ramble walked beside me like a lithe nightmare panther.

Jax followed right on my heels. "What? Did you think this would be easy?"

I spun around. "No, Jax! I didn't think this would be easy." I threw my hands in the air. "I'm the descendant of some weird hunter lady and have a magic necklace that is supposed to help me hunt supernatural creatures like vampires! Of course it's not going to be easy! It's going to be weird and scary and completely unbelievable!" I dropped my voice and stepped forward to get in his face. "But you know what? I thought we had a deal that you would quit keeping stuff from me. And then you go and do this," I pointed behind him to the house.

I had to close my eyes for a brief moment and dig deep to find the patience to keep myself from screaming at him. All I'd done lately was follow him around in the hopes that I'd learn more about how to be a hunter. He'd shown me a few things here and there, but it was only when I pried it from him with excessive questioning that I actually got any real information about the world of hunting supernatural creatures. A perfect example was the whole thing with some creatures' saliva having healing qualities. That seemed like something I should have learned before now.

"I thought we had a deal," I sighed. "You were supposed to be open about everything and teach me what I needed to know in order to be a hunter. No secrets, remember?"

Not that I didn't have a secret of my own.

Something must have sunk in because he was silent for a moment before saying, "I know. I'm not used to working with other people."

I waited for more. Maybe an actual apology.

Who was I kidding? I was more likely to get struck by lightning.

"I don't think I'm the right person to train you," he said and started walking toward the car.

"Wait, what?" I rushed to catch up to him. "That's not what I'm saying…"

"No, you're right. This isn't working. Something is wrong with the necklace." We crossed the yard at a quick clip and before I knew it, we were back at the car. He popped the trunk and pulled my bag out. "I thought I could help you figure it out," he continued, "but it looks like my part here is over. I got you the necklace. Now you have to do your part to become the Vânători."

He shoved the backpack at my chest and let go, forcing me to grab onto it. It took me a moment to recover as he slammed the trunk closed and walked past me toward the driver's side of the car.

"Wait, you can't just leave me here. You're supposed to help train me and figure this out!"

Shaking his head, he got in the car, but I dropped the backpack and grabbed the side of the door before he could close it.

"Jax, we're in the middle of nowhere and I have no idea how to fix the necklace."

He stared at me until I let go of the door, then slammed it shut as soon as I did.

Shit! My brain screamed. What was I supposed to do now?

Before I could go into a full-blown panic attack, Jax flipped on the car's dome light, leaned over, and popped the glove box open. He pulled out a small handgun, set it on the passenger seat, then fished out a familiar leather book. It was where he kept all his fake credit cards and extra cash. After a second of flipping through the book, he drew out a card.

He rolled down the driver's window and shoved the card at me. "Here."

I still held the silver knife and had to shift it to my left hand to take the card. Before I could make out the writing on the card, Jax shoved the gun at me too, forcing me to almost drop the card to accommodate the weapon.

"You're a shit shot, but it's better you have this than nothing." After a moment, I started to hand him back the silver knife, but he waved me off. "Go to that address and ask for a witch named Rosalyn. She might be able to help you figure out the necklace."

For someone who hated what he dubbed "monsters," Jax sure did have a lot of friends who were supernatural. Maybe I should have trusted him with my theory after all. Maybe he wouldn't have tried to stake me or bury me alive.

"You're sending me to a witch? I thought you hated all supernatural creatures. And why don't I just go to the Lady of the Woods instead?"

"Asking Moira or any witch for too much help puts you in their debt. Trust me when I say that you don't want that. In my book the only good witch is a dead witch, but some witches, like Moira and Rosalyn, are too powerful for me to put in the ground. If I can't take them out, I might as well make occasional use of them."

Alright then. I guess I was right in not trusting him with the whole blood-drinking thing.

"Besides, I've already tried to contact Moira and haven't gotten a response."

He started the car, an old sunbird with flaking teal paint that had seen better days. For once the engine caught right away, dashing my hopes of diving into the car before he could drive away.

"Wait!" I yelled, panicking that I was about to be stuck in the middle of nowhere in front of a scary house with a creepy ghost and a dead lamprey. I fumbled to hold up the card Jax had given me. "How will I get here without getting caught by police or killed by vampires?"

Did I mention that I was in trouble with the law for breaking the terms of my parole and leaving the city? Not to mention that I might have had a hand in killing two vampires and burning down their house before I left town. Okay, technically Ramble had done most of the killing but I'd been the one who dumped gasoline all over the house. Ramble had just ignited it by breathing fire on it.

"Follow what I've taught you about laying low and get to that address." Jax pointed at the paper, then looked up at me. "You'll be fine, Vânǎtori. You've got the hellhound." He waved in the general vicinity of where he thought Ramble was (though he was completely off) before looking back at me with a more serious expression. "I wish you luck in figuring out the Artemis necklace and becoming the hunter you were meant to be."

And then he drove off and left me standing alone on the side of a back road in the middle of nowhere.

Shit.

Chapter 2

J ust like that I was once again alone in the world. I mean,
I'd been alone before. Heck, after my short stint in
jail for too many DUI's, none of my old friends had
wanted much to do with me, especially since I wasn't into the
drinking scene anymore. Trying to kick alcoholism will do
that. At first it had been hard to cope with the sudden lack of
a social network, but eventually I'd grown to sort of enjoy the
independence that not having close friends or a significant
other brought. I'd gotten to choose my daily activities without
having to consult with anyone else and could change my mind
about things at the drop of a hat without having to apologize
for the sudden shift in plans. Looking back on that point in
my life, being alone hadn't been so bad.

But things were different now that I had the weight of the
supernatural world bearing down on me. Not to mention that
Morvalden and his minion vampires were trying to kill me.
In this new world of supernatural creatures, being alone felt
like I was gripping the ledge of a giant precipice with the tips
of my fingers. At any second, I might let go and plunge down
into the depths of panic.

Ramble chose that moment to sidle up and hip check me
with his shoulder. I stumbled to the side a little, but the blow

wasn't enough to knock me down.

"Hey! Not cool, Ramble."

The hellhound stared at me with his glowing ruby eyes and gave a pointed huff.

As much as I hated to admit that Jax was right about something, he had a point that I still had Ramble.

What does it say about my situation that realizing I had a fire-breathing hellhound by my side made me feel a little better? I might have been abandoned by the guy who was supposed to be teaching me to be a hunter, but at least I wasn't completely alone.

"You're right," I said to Ramble before retrieving my backpack.

I checked the gun to make sure its safety was on before stowing it in the bag. It was the Glock 19 that Jax had been training me to use, so at least I had some experience with it. As much as I wanted to grumble about Jax, his training on the safe use of basic weapons was one good thing I'd learned from him.

I stared at the silver knife trying to decide if I wanted it within easy access or if I should just tuck it into the bag. After a second, I wrapped the blade up in a random sock and shoved it in the bag while still leaving the handle easily accessible. I wasn't really worried about getting accidentally stabbed by it since I had a small laptop in the padded section of the backpack between the knife and my back, but wrapping the knife in the sock made me feel a little more reassured about avoiding such an incident. If we ran into any trouble along this road, I trusted that Ramble would be able to buy me enough time to pull off the bag and grab either the knife or the gun.

I spun the backpack around and unzipped the front pockets

to see what resources I still had. Inside was one throwing knife (I sucked at using), a small medical kit, a half-charged cell phone and its charger, seventy-four dollars in cash, one fake ID with the name Violet Mason (courtesy of Jax), and one credit card with that same name. It meant I could use Vi as a nickname and not have trouble remembering to answer to it. I sincerely hoped that the name and credit card weren't actually connected to a real person's social security number. I didn't want to be one of those identity theft jerks who always seemed to get away with screwing up some innocent person's credit.

I pulled the medical kit out, unzipped my fleece, and set to work doctoring up the bite from the lamprey. I would have preferred to do it with running water and soap to really clean the wound because who knew what kind of bacteria lamprey had in their mouths? Hell, who even knew what a lamprey was? Instead, I settled for using alcohol wipes then covered up the bite with a big gauze pad. It would have to do for now.

Shivering, I carefully zipped the fleece back up—not that it would do me much good against the cold with a big hole in it— and put the kit away.

I'd been thinking about my current situation while playing doctor. Unfortunately, I didn't think seventy bucks was going to get us very far. Still crouching, I pulled out the card Jax had given me and tipped it to catch enough moonlight to read the address.

"Shit." I looked over at Ramble. "We're gonna need a lot more than seventy bucks to get to Maine."

I stuck the phone in my back pocket, zipped the bag up and, with a sigh, donned the backpack just as a light breeze ghosted through my ripped fleece and made me shiver. Winter would be here in full force soon and I would definitely need a real jacket if we were going to head up to Maine…but first, we needed to get out of the middle of nowhere and find a car before I could start thinking about a shopping spree.

I briefly considered going back to the house to try and open a door to the Between, but that seemed like a bad idea. Not only was I unsure if it would actually work, but Between was a fickle place. We could end up even further away from civilization than we already were.

No. It was best to stick to this world.

I stared at the road and let out a sigh, "I guess we're walking." Now that the adrenaline had worn off from the attack and the fight with Jax, my body decided to remind me just how much abuse it had sustained. It was gonna be a long walk.

Ramble let out a huff.

"What?"

The hellhound jerked his head in the direction Jax had gone.

"Oh, come on. You were sick and tired of his crap, too. I might have learned a few things from him, but he couldn't help us with this." I gripped the Artemis necklace where it lay outside the fleece against my collarbone. It was a gold-colored, coin-like talisman with a square hole punched out of the center. I was still using the rusty chain it had come with just in case it needed to stay a set, but I worried that wearing it all the time might wear out the chain and I might accidentally break it at some point.

I slid the necklace back under my fleece and t-shirt as Ramble snorted and rolled his eyes. I could read his message loud and clear.

"I know you wanted me to tell him about the vampire blood, but I just didn't think I should. Who knows how he'd react?

He was likely to see me as a monster and cut off my head."

The hellhound raised an eyebrow.

"I know you could protect me from him, but the whole point is that you shouldn't have to. How can I learn from someone if I can't trust them not to behead me when you're not around?" I looked around trying to decide which direction to go. "Besides, none of that matters now. He's gone and we're on our own. ...and apparently heading to Maine."

I slid the phone from my back pocket and tried to open a map app. Yep. We were definitely in the middle of nowhere because my phone was not going to find a real signal anytime soon.

"Crap." I looked at Ramble, "Do you think you could lead us in the direction of the closest town?"

This time I got a grumbly whine from the hellhound, but he dutifully started walking down the road in the direction we had come from in the car earlier. It was the opposite direction that Jax had driven off in, which suited me just fine.

I put the phone back in my pocket and followed the hellhound down the gravel road. Maybe I shouldn't have been so abrupt with him. After all, it wouldn't do to alienate all my allies in one night.

In the silent walk, I couldn't help but think about the poor ghost we'd left in the abandoned house. The thought of her ghost being murdered over and over in a horrible loop was really bothering me. If I died, I wouldn't want to be stuck like that.

I silently promised that I would at least try to alert the proper authorities about her body. Maybe if they discovered her remains and laid her to rest, she'd be able to stop repeating her death.

Hours later, we finally made it to the edge of a small town. I found a seedy motel and woke up the young receptionist by smacking a little bell on the counter a few times. It didn't take long to talk him into letting me stay well past the check-out time.

I think he gave in mostly because he was freaked out by my ripped and bloody fleece and just wanted me out of the office. Or maybe he just wanted to go back to sleep. In the mildewy-smelling room, I locked the door behind us, dropped my backpack, and was asleep seconds later.

* * *

I woke feeling out of place—which lately had become a normal feeling. I'd gotten used to waking up in a strange hotel room every morning. Was this how rock stars felt while on the road? Only, you know, waking up in much cleaner hotels?

Snippets of a dream hovered just around the edges of my foggy brain. Something about arriving at a fancy dinner party but not being appropriately dressed. Ugh. Why did dreams always make you live through the most horrible social foibles possible? I couldn't tell you how many times I'd had the dream about studying hard for an important test only to forget to wear clothes to school. Gah. Dreams sucked.

On the plus side, while wearing the necklace, my dreams were no longer filled with Morvalden trying to kill me. So I guess I should just appreciate having normal dreams again.

I turned my head and found myself staring into the glowing red orbs of a hellhound. The wisps of the dream I'd remembered disappeared. Ramble had gotten into the habit of sleeping on the same bed as me, but usually he woke well

31

after I did.

"What's wrong?" I mumbled, blearily rubbing my eyes.

He stared at me for another minute then snorted, spraying me with hellhound snot.

"Ugh. C'mon, man." I sat up, wiping my face. I guess snot was better than being singed by fire. It was only then that I remembered I hadn't just woken up. Something had nudged me awake.

"Did you wake me up?" I asked the hellhound around a yawn. Ramble gave a curt nod, then put his head back on his front paws and closed his eyes.

If he was going back to sleep, then that meant he hadn't woken me up for anything that required my immediate attention. Perhaps he'd just nudged me to wake me up from the crappy dream.

"Thanks, I guess?" I patted the hellhound on the head and earned a dark look. He didn't much care for being treated like a domesticated dog.

A glance at the nightstand clock told me it was almost noon. Good. That would give me time to shower and do a little research on ghost girl. I was sure I would find a picture of her among a list of local missing persons. Then I could just make a phone call, drop a tip about an abandoned house with suspicious activity, and the authorities could take it from there. Hopefully having her body laid to rest would be enough to release her from reliving her death over and over.

I savored being lazy in bed for another moment. It couldn't last though. If I wanted to get anything worthwhile done while I had access to wi-fi in the motel, then I'd need to get a move on. I gave a dramatic sigh that Ramble steadfastly ignored by keeping his eyes tightly shut.

CHAPTER 2

"Lazy dog." I rolled to the other side of the bed and levered myself up. The minute I moved, the muscles on my right side protested to remind me that I'd been shoved through a wall the night before.

I let out a moan but managed to stay on my feet. Still ignoring me, Ramble stretched and repositioned himself right in the warm depression I'd just vacated, completely unsympathetic to my pain.

I slowly trudged to the shower, carefully undressed, and surveyed the damage. My right side was a mix of black, blue, and green bruises. It looked (and felt) like my right shoulder and thigh had taken the brunt of the fall. I was somewhat surprised that my head didn't hurt more where it had smacked the floor. Maybe the rest of my body had padded the fall enough that it didn't take more damage.

I peeled the bandage away from the lamprey bite. The edges looked raw and red—hopefully not an infected red. There wasn't much I could do about that except to keep it clean and replace the bandages.

A half-hour later, I was feeling a little better from the hot shower and sat perched on the end of the bed with a cup of absolutely terrible coffee, balancing a cheap laptop on my thighs. One good thing about running around with Jax was that I'd talked him into getting me my own computer. It was kind of exciting actually. I hadn't had my own computer since college. After getting out of jail, I'd scrounged every penny just to make rent and keep food on the table. There wasn't exactly any money left over to blow on fancy electronics.

It took all of twenty minutes to find out who the ghost girl was. Her name was Samantha Frank. She was a seventeen-year old high school student and had gone missing in late

September. One of her friends admitted that Samantha had gone on a date with a strange guy and that's when she'd disappeared. So far authorities didn't have any leads on who the guy was.

I stared at the picture of Samantha. It wasn't fair that this girl had gone on a date with a guy who'd turned out to be a monster. Then again, there were plenty of human monsters out there and, if I was being honest, there were probably a lot more of those kinds of monsters out there than the actual kind that ate people as snacks.

I found information about how to report a missing person and saved the contact info for later. "Next up," I said, grabbing the card with the witch's address—and immediately got a jolt of foreboding from the necklace. There really wasn't any other way to describe it. One second I was fine and the next it felt like I was about to jump into a pit of vipers.

"Alright then."

Ramble cracked an eyelid.

I waved my other hand at the necklace. "It apparently isn't too keen about the witch."

The hellhound lifted his eyebrow as if to say, "And?"

I let out a breath of exasperation and lay back on the bed while one hand kept the computer from sliding off my lap. Staring at the grimy ceiling, I asked, "How am I supposed to figure out the necklace if Jax can't help me and the necklace itself doesn't want me to follow the only lead we have?"

Honestly, what was the necklace expecting me to do here? Okay, yes, during the short period that the necklace had actually worked, it had told me I should keep Jax around to train me. But then the necklace had gone silent other than the random burst of emotions I felt from it. Which, so far, had not exactly been helpful.

Unfortunately, it wasn't exactly an option to just throw the necklace away and try to live a normal life. Not only did the necklace somehow protect me from my own addiction to alcohol, it was also my only hope against the vampires who were coming for me. If only I could make it work again.

"What do you want me to do?" I asked the necklace, tucking my chin down against my chest so I could glare down where it lay beneath my t-shirt.

My question was met with silence.

I rotated my head to look at Ramble. He was sprawled half on and half off the pillows across the top portion of the bed. I reached up and poked his foot with the card. "What do you think we should do?"

He jerked his paw back and picked up his head to give me a glare. I glared right back.

"Well? Should we go to Maine and talk to this Rosalyn witch lady? Or should we try to find Jax again and take our chances with him?"

Ramble looked like he was weighing the options—or perhaps deciding if it was worth it to burn me to crisp. Finally, he leaned forward and nudged the card with his nose.

"Alright then. Witch hunting it is. Well, not like that, but you know what I mean," I said and sat up, opened a new internet tab, and typed in the address from the card. A few seconds later, I stared at the picture of a Tudor style house set back a few feet from the road with a tidy garden out front. This was the house attached to the address. I guess I'd expected it to be a rickety shack or something more like the house we'd been in last night. Instead, the place looked like it belonged on the front of a magazine. The lawn was well-manicured and the small garden was bursting with vibrant flowers.

I really needed to update my expectations when it came to supernatural beings. I'd only met one other witch so far and she'd lived in a cute cabin in the middle of the woods. Never mind that she could rearrange the structure of her home like some people rearranged furniture. I should have learned from Moira's house that witches weren't going to conform to Hollywood's expectations.

The site of the cheerful looking house gave me hope that maybe Rosalyn would be willing to actually help me. I ignored another twinge from the necklace. If it wasn't going to help me figure out another path forward, then it didn't get to have a say.

Ramble was still sitting up behind me, so I twisted around on the bed to show him the picture of the house. "This is where we're going."

He looked at the picture, then at me, and gave a small, "Whuff." I translated that to mean, "Okay." Then he pointedly licked his chops.

Who needs words when you can understand dog body language?

"You're hungry? Me too. Let's go get something to eat. Then we'll find a ride and start our little road trip."

I did a quick search and found a fast food joint two streets over we could go to before we left town. Satisfied with my plan, I powered down the laptop and shoved everything back in my backpack before toting it with me into the bathroom. I swiped the shampoo, conditioner, and the unopened bar soap and threw them all in the bag. You never knew when you might end up staying somewhere without amenities. It paid to be prepared.

After doing a quick walkthrough to make sure we hadn't forgotten anything, I pulled the "do not disturb" placard off the outside of the door, tossed it onto the bed, and we left. I'd left the keycard in the room as well so we wouldn't have to make another stop in the office. The less people who saw my face around town, the better. Especially since once we finished eating, I was going steal a car.

A few hours later, we cruised down the Interstate in an ugly gold Ford Taurus I'd hijacked from the back of a grocery store parking lot. I had to admit that I'd learned more in the short time I'd spent with Jax than I'd originally thought. It had only taken me thirty minutes to break into the car and hotwire it. It was new enough that I didn't think it would break down on me but also old enough that it didn't come with a Lojack or Onstar system that could be used to track us down. Getting arrested for stealing cars would definitely put a cramp in my hunting career.

Then again…

"I wonder if I would actually be safer going back to jail," I mused.

Ramble didn't bother responding from where he was sprawled in the front seat looking completely dejected. His pathetic mood was attributed to me not letting him keep the window rolled down so he could stick his head out. It was fine for the first five minutes of the ride, but as the day wore on and we drove further north, the air had gotten decidedly colder.

Since I was getting crickets from the hellhound, I decided talking to myself was the next best thing. "Then again, Morvalden could just send a vampire into the jail to mesmerize the security guards and I'd have no way to escape."

Yeah... I definitely needed to avoid going to prison.

Of course, it would help if I hadn't completely thrown myself into this life of crime. On top of stealing the car, I'd also used the fake card to get the maximum amount possible from two ATMs at different gas stations. I hoped to avoid using the card again for a while since the less I used it, the less likely I would be to get caught.

The only other stop we'd made was a fast food drive-thru. I made sure to pick one that would have wi-fi, then we parked next to the building to eat while I used their internet to create a fake email account and fire off a tip about finding Stephanie Frank's body in the abandoned house.

Fueled by caffeine and terrible fast food, we were making pretty good time on our little road trip north.

Beside me, Ramble let out a put-upon sigh. If he were a regular dog, you would have thought he'd just lost his favorite chew bone.

"Oh my god—fine!" I rolled down the window. Ramble immediately leapt up and shoved his head through the opening. Apparently, hellhounds found the wind in their hair to be the height of bliss. Who knew?

I managed to one-handedly zip up my fleece against the cold October air rushing through the now open window. I made a mental note that I seriously needed to buy a real jacket to replace my shredded fleece. Otherwise this was going to be a long, cold trip.

Chapter 3

About three hours from Ricketts, the town where Rosalyn lived, I decided to stop in the last big city before we went practically off the grid in the western Maine wilderness. It was a lot easier to hide a stolen car among other tourist's vehicles—not that there appeared to be many tourists in this part of Maine during October.

Mostly I stopped because I was exhausted. I'd been driving with a few breaks for about eight hours. I really wanted some sleep before I approached Rosalyn for help. Moira, the only other witch I'd ever met, had played a lot of psychological games. She'd also tried to poison me as some sort of sick test. So, yeah, my experience with witches thus far didn't exactly make me super trusting.

Once again I was dragging myself to a shady motel. Gah. The lady behind the front desk was in her early fifties and so engrossed in a bodice-ripping romance novel that she almost didn't notice me. Taking my cue from the book in her hands, I told some story about driving all day to get to my grandma and grandpa's fiftieth wedding anniversary, then I sold it by spinning a tale about my fake grandparent's forbidden romance. This earned me a free breakfast coupon for the café across the street.

Lying had its perks, even if they were only in the form of a free meal coupon.

A little voice at the back of my mind tried to make me feel guilty, but I told it to shut the hell up and come back when it had something useful to say. So far, lying had kept me a few steps ahead of the vampires and garnered free swag here and there. Okay, yeah, maybe I felt a little guilty at some of the more outrageous lies or the ones that deliberately tugged at someone's heartstrings, but it wasn't like I'd *chosen* this lifestyle. And it wasn't like running from vampires paid good money. Or any money for that matter.

Once in the room, I shucked off my shoes and stared longingly at the bed. Ramble had already taken up more than his half of it and now lay with his eyes closed.

"Do you do anything other than sleep?" I tiredly asked the hellhound before hauling my backpack to the bathroom. I forced myself through the new routine of taking the bandage off the lamprey bite before taking a shower. The bite was still an angry red color and it was tender to the touch, but I figured that was to be expected when a damn monster bit you.

After showering and redressing the bite, I messily braided my hair then laid on the small portion of bed Ramble had left me and tried to sleep. "Try" being the key term here. Though my body was exhausted, my brain was still riding high from all the caffeine I'd consumed. I was having trouble shutting it off.

When I still hadn't fallen asleep thirty minutes later, I forced myself up and grabbed the laptop. Might as well look up where we were going tomorrow.

There wasn't a ton of information about Ricketts. It was a smallish town in the northwest part of the state with about

1,000 residents. There was exactly one local motel which didn't have a website (swell) and a few shops on the main street.

A newspaper article that mentioned Ricketts proved to be quite a bit more interesting.

Apparently, there had been three recent deaths which the local police were classifying as fatal dog attacks. Autopsies of the three bodies suggested that the victims had all died from wounds caused by the teeth and claws of large dogs. While that might be believable for two of the deaths, one occurring in a park and one in a vacant field, I had to agree with the newspaper that something was a bit off about a third death.

"'Though the victim was found within the parking lot of a busy apartment complex,'" I read out loud, waking the dozing hellhound, "'it appears that there were no eyewitnesses to corroborate the cause of death which authorities report are consistent with the two recent deaths in town.'"

Tests on the victims remains had come back negative for the rabies virus, so whatever killed them was unlikely to be rabid. The article continued on about how to stay safe in the case of a wild dog attack but continually reassured readers of the unlikelihood of such an event.

I stared at Ramble after reading the article. "What do you think? Werewolves, right?"

It wasn't a huge leap of faith to believe in the existence of werewolves when I already knew that vampires, witches, and ghosts were running around. I knew Jax had hunted his fair share of werewolves since I'd seen some of the files on his computer where he'd saved information about deaths classified by police as "animal" or "canine-related." The descriptions in those articles and the one from Ricketts were too similar for the deaths to not be from werewolf attacks.

It was one thing to deal with an unknown witch who might be friendly but adding werewolves to the mix made it a whole different situation.

Ramble just looked at me, unfazed. Maybe werewolves didn't scare him, but they certainly scared the crap out of me.

I needed more input about what I could expect to find in Ricketts.

Grabbing my phone off the bedside stand, I found the number I needed and hit the call button before I could change my mind. I let it ring a few times and was just about to disconnect when Jax picked up.

"You still sitting at that house whining about life not being fair?" It sounded like he was in a car with a throaty engine, which meant he'd already ditched the sunbird in favor of a different ride.

"What? No, I…" I forced myself to stop. I would not let him bait me into an argument. I'd called for a reason, dammit. "I needed to ask you a question about this town Rosalyn lives in." The hunter didn't say anything, but I could still hear background noise, so at least he hadn't hung up. "Local newspapers say there have been some sort of attacks there. Looks like werewolves or something like it. Is there anything else you can tell me before I go up there?"

"There are always 'some sort of attacks' in that area. It's the middle of nowhere Maine. Do you think Lovecraft was just making it up when he wrote about all the monsters up there?"

"What?" I wasn't sure what was more surprising—the fact that Jax knew who H.P. Lovecraft was or that Jax thought the monsters in his stories were real.

"Maine, the northern part anyways, is full of monsters.

Been that way for years. There's word that some of them are teaming up to keep hunters from trying to clear them all out. Most hunters just steer clear of the whole state."

I wanted to ask him why the hell he'd sent me up here by myself then but decided that he'd take that as a complaint and hang up before I could ask more important questions.

"Okay, so how do you kill a werewolf? Is all that silver bullet business real or just made up bullshit?"

"That's real enough," he paused just as the sound of the engine in the background died. He must have pulled over somewhere and turned the car off so he could hear me better. I took it as a good sign that maybe he would actually give me some useful information and reminded myself to try not to interrupt him.

He cleared his throat, then said, "Werewolves are severely affected by silver, but it's similar to vampires with sunlight: the older a werewolf, the less effect silver has on them."

"Okay," I said, wishing I had a pad of paper to take notes on. My motel was too cheap to even offer the complimentary pen.

"The werewolves I've encountered were lone wolves. Most of the time werewolves live in the same area as a pack. Each pack has a hierarchy with an Alpha werewolf as the leader. I guess having a pack helps the werewolves retain their humanity or something because the ones without a pack seem to lose it pretty quickly and go on murderous rampages before ending up with a silver bullet to the brain, courtesy of your friendly hunter."

I'd have commented on the whole "murderous rampage" thing, but this was the most I'd ever heard Jax utter at one time. I didn't want to break whatever spell this was and potentially

43

miss out on important information.

Instead I said, "The newspaper says there have been three fatal animal attacks in different parts of the town. Do you think they'd be from a lone werewolf?"

The line was silent while Jax thought for a moment. "Maybe," he finally said. "Were the attacks all in one day?"

"No, I they were spread out across a few days."

"Huh. Seems unlikely it's one wolf going berserk then. Usually in those cases you end up with a lot of bodies all at one time. Then the wolf calms down or turns back into human and the killings stop."

"These were just one body at a time." I thought about what I'd read and compared it to Jax's information. "And one was even in an apartment parking lot," I said slowly, feeling hopeful that maybe I wouldn't be dealing with werewolves after all. "So, if it was a berserk werewolf, it seems like it would have gone after other people as well, right?"

"If there were other people around, sure," Jax agreed.

His words deflated my feelings of hope. There hadn't been any eyewitnesses to the attack, so it was unlikely anyone was in the parking lot at the time.

Jax must have sensed my change in mood. "Look on the bright side, Vânători, if it were a lone wolf or some other creature on a rampage and there was a pack in the area, the pack would have taken care of it by now.

"So... that means there's unlikely to be a pack of werewolves in the area." That was good, but why did I feel like I was waiting for the other shoe to drop?

"That or the killer is too strong for the pack to eliminate. Or the pack is actually the one behind the attacks."

Well, shit. I had hoped to get an easy answer from Jax

about what I might expect before I drove the last few hours to Ricketts, but his input had made the situation even scarier.

"So, what am I supposed to do if I get to this town and there's a werewolf running around killing people?"

This earned me a sigh of annoyance. "Just keep your head down and go to the address I gave you. Talk to the witch and figure out the necklace. You'll be in and out of town before anyone even knows you were there."

He disconnected.

"Great," I said to myself before turning around to glare at Ramble. "Not only are we in a state that's full of creatures who might want to kill us, we're going directly into a town that might have a 'murderous' werewolf problem."

Ramble huffed and put his head down, clearly unconcerned. I guess I wouldn't be scared either if I was a big, scary supernatural creature who was invisible and could breathe fire.

Whatever.

* * *

I sat at the end of a ridiculously long table with a heavy white linen tablecloth set for a lavish dinner party. Crystal glasses sparkled from the light of a chandelier and each porcelain plate held a carefully folded white linen napkin in the shape of a bird.

At the other end of the table were two figures, but they were too far away for me to make out their features. A glance down revealed I was wearing jeans and a torn t-shirt. Embarrassment at my outfit made me blush. How could I not have bothered to dress up for this fancy party?

I opened my mouth to apologize for my rudeness, but something

45

on my plate grabbed my attention. Was the napkin-bird moving? As I stared at it, a deep crimson stain blossomed on the white linen exactly where one of the bird's eyes would have been. Was it weeping blood? I felt a twinge of sadness for the bird. Why was it crying?

The stain grew larger, engulfing the linen bird's head. Suddenly my sympathy for the bird became terror. Why was the napkin bleeding?

"Vânători," a voice whispered from the other end of the table.

A cold, wet sensation touched the back of my neck. I jerked my head up—

—And woke to a puddle of my own drool on the pillow. Lovely.

I'd fallen asleep on my stomach, which always made my back stiff, so it took me a moment to roll into a more comfortable position on my back. It wasn't until I tipped my head to the left that I noticed Ramble was staring at me from his place on the bed beside me. When it was clear that I'd seen him staring, he put his head down and huffed. I realized that I had a wet spot on the back of my neck.

It took me a moment to remember my dream. What had happened? Something about a dinner party and a napkin shaped like a bird. Or maybe it turned into a bird? Dreams were always weird so who could tell.

"Did you wake me up, buddy?" I mumbled.

A soft grumble confirmed my suspicion.

The dream, Vânători.

I jerked into a sitting position as the necklace's voice spoke directly into my head. She seemed far away, which was weird since it wasn't an auditory sound but was actually coming from inside my head. My sudden movement caught Ramble's attention and now the hellhound was giving me a look as if to ask, "What is your problem?"

I waited for the necklace to say something else. When nothing happened, I pointed at the necklace so that Ramble would know who I was addressing before asking, "What about my dream?"

We waited in silence together but nothing else came from the necklace.

"Apparently that's all it wanted to say," I told Ramble.

He ticked up an eyebrow. Clearly he wanted me to explain.

"I dunno. I had a dream about a dinner party or something. There was a napkin that turned into a bird and scared me, I think." It sounded ridiculous when I said it out loud. Especially when I should be more afraid of real things like vampires and werewolves. "Was I making noises in my sleep or something? Was that why you woke me up?" I asked.

Ramble gave a brief nod.

"When I woke up, the necklace spoke to me. It hasn't done that since I first put it on. But it wasn't as loud this time. It was like it was speaking from a long way off or something."

I tried to remember anything else I could from the dream, but all I got was the memory of feeling embarrassed for not being dressed appropriately for a nice dinner party, something about a napkin becoming a bird, and then a sudden feeling of fear before I woke up.

So why had the necklace suddenly spoken now when it had been silent for weeks? Especially since compared to some of the dreams I'd had after being attacked and almost killed by the vampires, this dream had been a walk in the park.

Since my brain wasn't serving up any other pieces of the dream and the necklace was decidedly not going to offer any further enlightenment, I decided it was time to get up and get moving.

I sincerely hoped that sending me to Rickett's wasn't Jax's sneaky way to put me in danger again in a ploy to wake the necklace. I didn't really see any other options though, so north it was.

Chapter 4

Rickett's was certainly nothing to write home about. The town center was a roundabout with a courthouse in the middle, complete with a fountain and the statue of some notable local. I didn't look too closely, choosing instead to drive past and get a brief layout of the area.

Four main roads shot off from the roundabout—though I'm not sure you could call them "main" roads. The center line paint had worn away long ago and the road itself was pockmarked with potholes that were impossible to avoid.

Heads turned as I drove past a local café, a second-hand clothing store, and a laundromat. Apparently this wasn't a tourist town because my out-of-state tags were getting some attention.

It felt a little like I'd just traveled back in time to a bygone era where soda fountains and going steady were still a thing. I was suddenly happy that I'd decided to get moving so early and reach the town in the middle of the day. With any luck, Ramble and I would meet the witch, get the information we needed, and then could high-tail it out of the state before any local monsters noticed us.

I'd also been hearing a lot about an incoming front of freezing rain as we'd driven further north. It wasn't supposed to hit until early the next morning, though, so I wasn't too worried about it. I planned to be long gone from Maine by then.

Using my phone to navigate, I took several turns that led us away from the heart of town and to a quaint little suburb where the houses were a little older and had actual lawns.

"You have arrived at your destination!" The GPS chirped.

I pulled over and parked in front of where the GPS said the house should be.

"Something must be wrong. Maybe I put in the wrong address?" I double-checked the address I'd typed in against the one Jax had given me. It all matched up.

I looked back out at the empty lot where the cute Tudor house was supposed to be. I turned to Ramble. "What the hell?"

He put a paw against the glass and, realizing he wanted me to roll it down, I complied. He shoved his whole head out the window and took in halting breaths like he was sniffing for something. After a moment of this, he pulled his head back in and gave me a soft, "Whuff."

It wasn't the first time I wished I spoke hellhound. I'd have to play twenty questions to figure out what he wanted to tell me.

"You smell something?"

Ramble gave me a little air-whuff of agreement which was his way of saying yes. It was sort of like a bark without sound, which meant it didn't draw attention when we were out among people who couldn't see him.

"Do you think it's the right address?"

Another air-whuff.

"Huh." I looked at where the house was supposed to be.

Only then did I notice that the little garden I'd seen in the picture online was there, but the plants that would have been closest to the house had mostly been burned away. Those that were further away had survived but were blackened and curled at the top.

I blew out a breath, then looked back at Ramble. "There was a fire and the house burned down."

He gave another, "Whuff," then sat in the front seat, waiting for me to make our next move.

The problem was I had no idea what that would be. My only lead had freaking burned down. Now what?

My first instinct was to try and contact Jax. As much it sucked to keep running to him for help, he was the only person I could talk to about this supernatural stuff.

"Put on your big-girl pants, Vi," I mumbled to myself and hit the call button.

After letting it ring and go to a voicemail box that wasn't set up, I realized Ramble and I were on our own.

"Okay," I said, turning to the hellhound. "We can't just sit in front of the house." My stomach sank as I realized what we'd need to do. My phone signal wasn't strong enough to handle a heavy internet search and I hadn't seen any businesses that looked like they might offer free wifi, which meant…

"Let's find a motel and see if we can do some sleuthing online about what happened to the house. Worst case scenario, we don't find anything and we have to go out and ask some of the locals. It's a small enough town, most people will probably know what happened here." I waved to where the house used to be.

Ramble agreed by immediately sticking his head out the window before I could roll it back up.

"Really?" I said and got a sideways smirk in reply.

Jerk.

It was an easy thing to navigate to the one motel in town. We'd passed it on our way to the witch's house. I hadn't gotten a great look at it, but it hadn't struck me as any better or worse than any of the other places we'd been staying. I would have chosen to stay in a bigger city so the out-of-state plates wouldn't be as noticeable, but Ricketts was over an hour from the next biggest town. That seemed like a long way to drive if I had to stay more than one night.

The local motel wasn't as far out of town as Jax normally would have chosen, but it was close enough that I'd be able to walk if the weathermen were right and it started getting nasty outside with freezing rain.

Walking would also mean that I could leave the stolen car at the motel where it was less likely to draw the attention of local law enforcement. Since I had plenty of cash, I was unlikely to have to use the credit card here. The less I used it, the less likely I was to get caught.

After getting checked into the motel by a dour looking woman at the front desk and finding the room, I decided to do some laundry. Then I'd be able to start searching online for what happened to Rosalyn's house while the wash did its thing. I left Ramble in the motel room and took the bundle of clothes out to the back of the building where the coin-operated machines were.

Since I was trying to be efficient and cheap, I started a load going with every piece of clothing I owned and just wore a tank top, a pair of boxers (I usually slept in them), and the torn fleece. I needed to wash the fleece, but I was afraid that it would get ripped apart if I ran it through the wash before trying to mend the tear in it.

Covered in goosebumps from the cold, I retreated to the relative warmth of the motel room to do some sleuthing. Unfortunately, there wasn't much actual research to do. I only found a single article on the fire from three months ago and it basically just said the house had burned down and stated that the reason for the fire was unknown. The only useful piece of information was that there hadn't been any deaths, so at least that meant I might still be able to find Rosalyn.

I tried to search for Rosalyn online but couldn't find anyone by that name in relation to the town. Maybe it was a fake name that she only used for the supernatural world or something. Or maybe she just kept a really low profile. Actually…

I went back and reread the article about the fire. It hadn't listed who the owner of the house was. Didn't they usually include that kind of thing? Maybe my second guess was more on the mark and Rosalyn just kept a really low profile.

Or maybe she'd moved away years ago and Jax had given me an old address.

Further attempts to find more information on her were a dead end. Without much else to do, I decided to learn more about the local animal maulings.

"Huh. Look at this," I said mostly to myself because Ramble, laying on top of the table, ignored me and continued to stare out the window. "Okay, or don't look. But listen, 'Samuel Vance was found outside his apartment where he had apparently been mauled by a wild animal. Authorities believe a bear might have been responsible.'"

The article I'd read yesterday had been from a bigger paper in another town. This one was from the local paper and seemed to have a few more details.

Ramble grunted. Apparently he didn't see what was so impressive.

"But he was found in the parking lot of his apartment complex—look here's a picture." I turned the laptop around so the hellhound could see.

He glanced at it then stared at me, clearly unimpressed.

"Well, it's not a picture of the body, but it shows the apartment's parking lot. Whatever killed him managed to do it in the middle of a parking lot *without anyone even noticing.* Isn't that weird?"

Ramble yawned.

I ignored his lack of enthusiasm. "I know we already knew that, but I just think it's weird. I mean, if you're getting mauled by an animal, you make noise, right? You scream or call for help or something…" I chewed on a fingernail, staring at the picture of the parking lot. "Unless the animal—or werewolf—slashed his throat first. I guess he wouldn't have been able to cry out then."

I scanned the article again. This had actually been the second mauling. The first had been of a guy named Tony Duluth and the third was another guy named Joseph Kleinman. Both Kleinman and Duluth's deaths were a little more believable as animal attacks since Kleinman's body was found in a field and Duluth's was discovered at a local park.

I let out a sigh. It wasn't much to go on except that Vance's death was somewhat odd because of its location. What if these men really were just victims of animal attacks?

"Let's see something…"

I checked to see how many animal attacks usually occurred in Ricketts. It seemed unlikely, but my search results suggested that these three attacks were the only ones to occur since the

1940s. That was quite a stretch for a town on the edge of a big forest.

As a comparison, I ran a search on other towns nearby. There weren't many attacks within about a thirty-mile radius of the town, but once you got outside that area, low rates of animal attacks cropped back up again. However, they were just attacks and almost none of them resulted in death.

Which meant the attacks in Ricketts were definitely odd. Either this was something supernatural or it was a normal animal that had suddenly moved into the area and was really good at killing humans.

The latter option seemed unlikely. This thing seemed a lot smarter than a regular animal. After all, no one ever saw it. Even in the apartment parking lot, no one had seen any animals lurking around before or since the attacks.

I rubbed my eyes which were tired and dry from the long drive and from staring at the computer for so long.

"I'm gonna switch the laundry over."

Ramble sighed to show he'd heard me but continued to stare out the window. If he'd been visible, anyone walking by would have had a heart attack when they came almost face to face with him

I shoved my sockless feet into tennis shoes. "If you hear screaming, come kill the animal attacking me."

This earned me a genuine eye-roll. So glad to amuse him. I was kind of serious though. I even left the door open a crack just in case he had to get out in a hurry.

The washing machine and dryer were in a little open room at the back of the building. There wasn't a door, making it a bit chilly to be wearing as little as I was. Whoever set up the laundry room clearly wasn't female because the washing machine and the dryer both faced the door—which meant you had to turn your back on the open doorway when using them. Not cool. But then again, I wasn't expecting the vampires to find me anytime soon and if there were any other supernatural creatures in town, it seemed unlikely they'd even know I was here. If jumped by a human, I'd just yell for my invisible hellhound.

The little voice at the back of my mind kept reminding me that I was putting my back to the open doorway, but I ignored it and started pulling sopping wet clothes from the washing machine. It looked like the damn machine's spin cycle was just about broken because I had to wring out each piece of clothing before putting them in the dryer. The process took a lot longer than usual with the extra step and by the time I was almost done, my fingers were starting to go numb from handling the cold wet clothes.

Someone cleared their throat behind me and I almost jumped out of my skin.

Spinning, I dropped the wad of wet clothes to the dirty concrete and put my back against the cold metal of the machine. A broad-shouldered man leaned against one side of the doorway with his meaty arms crossed over his chest. He wore a light flannel jacket and tight-fitting jeans. If my heart wasn't thudding so hard in my chest, I might have found his bulging muscles attractive. As it was, I was busy assessing him for any signs of danger.

His eyes—a grayish blue—suggested that he would be all kinds of danger if I let him. But I wasn't in a harlequin romance and this guy was effectively blocking my means of escape if he turned out to be a threat.

We stared at each other for a few awkward seconds. When

it was clear that the guy wasn't going to say anything, I finally got my thundering heart under control and managed to ask, "Can I help you?"

The man tilted his head forward a little, glaring at me. "This is my territory. You should leave."

"Excuse me?"

Who was this jackass to tell me where I could be? Screw him. I crossed my arms over my chest, mirroring his pose, but I couldn't quite pull off intimidating in my boxers. "I paid to stay at this motel. If I want to wash my damn laundry, I'm going to wash my laundry."

He left that hanging in the air for a minute while something danced in his eyes. Was that amusement? Was I somehow amusing this pushy beefcake? So glad I could make his day more fun.

The glint of amusement disappeared and his eyes became more intense. "I said, *leave*."

Suddenly I was reminded of staring into a vampire's eyes—which is usually a bad idea by the way. They have the ability to sort of mesmerize you.

This was different though. Rather than feeling sucked into this guy's gaze, it was as if he was willing the opposite. I got a brief flash of feeling, as if I was a rabbit who should be running from prey.

Who the hell was this guy?

I fought the urge to flee, then dropped my arms, letting my hands rest on my hips. I might not be able to use the necklace's magical powers, but I knew how to deal with intimidating bullies like this from jail. It didn't matter how many times you let them get one over on you with their bullying antics. They always came back again and usually they upped the ante each time.

The best thing to do with them was to stay off their radar or not let them bully you in the first place. Since it was too late to avoid this Gold's Gym wannabe, I opted for option two.

I laughed at him.

The reaction was immediate. His head jerked back like I'd smacked him in the face. I hadn't expected that much of a response, but maybe this guy had never had anyone defy him?

Well, there was always a first.

"Who died and made you king?" I asked but didn't give him the chance to even draw breath to answer. "Like I said, I'm going to finish my laundry because I *paid* to do so. Also," I added, my voice rising as I built up steam, "since I just spent about ten minutes wringing out sopping wet clothes because the damn washer didn't drain correctly, I am going to dry them *no matter how long it takes for them to dry.* Got it?"

He opened his mouth, floundering for how to handle this situation. Clearly things were not going the way he'd intended.

"Then…when you're done, you *will* leave." His voice got louder as he finished his demand, as if he was regaining face by making a show. Jackass.

I thought about it. Not the leaving part, but telling him that I'd leave just to placate him. I mean, he was a *lot* bigger than me and I'd stupidly left all my weapons, including my hellhound, in the motel room. Ugh. Live and learn I guess. Er, well, hope to live.

Before I could make a decision, a growl came from the left of the doorway. I couldn't see him from my vantage point, but I knew that growl.

Ramble to the rescue!

The man jerked his head toward the sound and froze his entire body like a living statue, all except for his nose, which flared repeatedly as he took rapid, shallow breaths.

Ramble growled again.

"Don't move," the man quietly cautioned.

Wait. Was he talking to me?

"There's a predator near...but I can't see it." He flicked his eyes toward me and then back in the general direction of the sound.

I couldn't help the smile that tugged at my lips. Suddenly the big tough guy was nervous, huh? Well he should be. Jerk.

"I can see him just fine." Okay, technically I couldn't right then because the wall was blocking my view, but Beefcake didn't know that. "You see, that's my pal and he doesn't like it very much when people try to bully me."

The man's eyes came back to rest on me though his body remained taunt and ready to respond to an attack. "I wasn't bullying you. You're clearly here to interfere in Pack business. You should leave before you get hurt."

Well...shit.

It looked like there was a werewolf Pack in town after all and I'd gone and managed to get off on the wrong foot with one of them.

Great job, Vi, I chided myself.

"You're... a werewolf?" It felt like a stupid question, but come on! I had to ask!

"And you're a Vânători. So glad we could establish that. Now call your hellhound to heel."

This time my laugh was genuine. "I can ask him not to rip you to shreds, but Ramble is not the kind of canine you 'call to heel.'"

59

The werewolf's mouth dropped open. "You named your hellhound?"

This conversation was getting old pretty quickly.

"Yes. Jeeze. It's really not that big a deal. And besides, what was I supposed to call him? Hellhound? Spawn of hell? You can't exactly say that in public without getting a lot of attention, you know."

"Do you even have control of him?"

Ramble decidedly did not like this question. His growl became quite a bit louder and somehow more feral.

"We have more of a mutual agreement to work with each other." Okay, that was sort of a lie. I'd had no idea what I was doing when I'd named Ramble. I just didn't want to call him "boy" or "hellhound" anymore. Besides, he seemed to like the name. I'd had no idea that naming him was the equivalent of giving a house elf a sock. I'd essentially released him from any obligation he had to me from our deal. Then again, I hadn't even realized I'd made a deal with him in the first place.

So far, my experience as a hunter was a lot of trial and error.

Luckily, Ramble had chosen to stick with me even after I'd named him. He'd fought and killed vampires to keep me safe and I really had no complaints about him. Well, okay one complaint: he had really bad morning breath...but maybe that was because of the whole fire-breathing thing.

"How about you step back and stop blocking the doorway," I suggested when the werewolf found himself at a loss for words. "I think that would make Ramble feel a little better. Plus, I can't exactly leave if you're blocking the exit, can I?"

"If you were human, you would have pushed past me and run away like a rabbit."

Huh. So that flash of feeling earlier was some sort of

compulsion thing. I'd have to ask Jax about that later if he ever bothered to answer my calls.

"And if you had simply introduced yourself politely instead of trying to intimidate me, we wouldn't be in this stand-off," I glowered.

He glared at me for what felt like an eternity before he finally decided to cooperate. "Fine." He stepped back two paces and put his hands out, palm up. "Look, no weapons." His voice held a little too much sarcasm, making me think that he didn't actually need weapons.

Whatever.

The moment the door was no longer blocked, I stepped through and found Ramble out of the corner of my eye. I moved to the left so that I was nearer to the hellhound but made sure to leave him a straight shot at the werewolf if he needed to attack.

Okay. So there was a local werewolf Pack and now they knew I was here. *And* they knew I was a Vânători. I had no idea how they knew that, but I wasn't about to ask and make myself look like any more of an idiot. I needed to fix this situation, otherwise I might as well pack it in right now and look for answers on the necklace somewhere else.

I put on my best professional voice. "I'm just here to speak to a witch named Rosalyn."

"If you're just here to talk to Rosalyn, why are you here at the motel and not talking to her?"

I opened my mouth to retort but didn't really want to admit that I didn't know where to find her. Before I could come up with anything else to say, his face screwed up in anger.

"I knew it! You're not here to see the witch. You're a Vânători and you're here to hunt werewolves for the murders, aren't you?" He leaned forward like he might attack me. "The Pack had *nothing* to do with that, so you can pack your shit and leave right now."

I guess that cleared up whether the three deaths were animal attacks or something more sinister.

If I wanted to stay in town long enough to find and speak with Rosalyn, then I needed to salvage this conversation quickly.

"You're right that I'm a Vânători, but I'm not here to hunt anything." I held up a hand in a placating gesture. "I didn't even know there'd been murders here before I got to town." Not quite true, but he didn't need to know that. "I'm really just here to speak with Rosalyn and get some information. The address I have for her is to a house that burned down. If you can point me in her direction, I can speak with her then be on my way."

The werewolf continued staring at me. I tried to put myself in his shoes and realized it wasn't that difficult. He thought I'd come here to kill him just for being a werewolf—similar to how the vampires had hunted me down for being a Vânători.

Maybe I just needed to be honest with him. After all, the whole Vânători-thing seemed to be pretty common knowledge, so maybe it was also common knowledge that I'd only recently become a hunter. He wouldn't know that the necklace wasn't working.

"Look, my name is Vianne. As you might have guessed, I'm pretty new to this. You're the first werewolf I've met—"

"You mean, I'm the first werewolf you've met that you didn't kill on the spot."

I frowned. This guy was trying my patience. "No. I didn't misspeak. You're the first werewolf I've met. Period." I took a deep breath in an attempt to regain some composure. "Now, you know my name. What's yours?"

There was another beat of silence and I almost started talking again when he finally said, "I'm Donavon."

Getting his name was a small thing, but it was a start to not having my throat torn out. I was kind of partial to it.

"Great. Nice to meet you, Donavon." This wasn't a handshake sort of situation, so I forged ahead. "Like I said, I'm just here to get some information from Rosalyn, then I'll be on my way."

This earned me a suspicious squint. "You'd just get in your car and leave town when people are being murdered? That doesn't sound like the Vânători stories I've heard."

"Well," I shrugged, "I'm not like the other Vânătoris."

He gave me a once-over before saying, "Clearly."

I suddenly remembered how ridiculous I must look in my torn fleece, thin t-shirt, and boxers. My face flushed red but I ignored his judgmental comment and pretended I wasn't freezing my butt off.

Though he wasn't wearing a real jacket, he didn't seem bothered by the cold air. Maybe werewolves had a higher metabolism or something and were better able to keep warm? Or maybe he just had so much muscle that the cold had a hard time getting through.

Down girl, I chided.

"This sounds like it's werewolf business. If you don't want me investigating, then I won't. Point me in Rosalyn's direction and I'll be on my way."

Also, I had no intention of investigating anyways. Even if the necklace was working, this wouldn't be my choice for a first solo hunt. I'd had the chance to work with Jax on researching and hunting down some supernatural creatures who were causing issues in other towns, but nothing that killed three people. Hunting something in a werewolf Pack's territory—something that might actually turn out to be one of the werewolves—didn't seem like a great idea even for a novice hunter..

He mulled over my statement before making a decision with a jerky nod. "I have to talk to my Pack about this. You are free to stay the night. I'll have an answer for you in the morning."

He turned as if to leave, but paused when I held out a hand and said, "Wait, an answer for what?"

"For whether you'll help us investigate these murders."

"What? No, that's not what I was saying—"

"You said you need information. Well, the Pack needs someone to find this killer before we get blamed for it. Who better than a Vânători? You help us get this killer and we'll introduce you to the coven so you can talk to Rosalyn."

"Five minutes ago you thought I was here to take out your Pack." I used the same emphasis he did for the word. "Now you want me to help you?"

He shrugged and amusement tugged at his lips as he looked at my outfit again, "Like you said, you don't seem like other Vânătoris." Just as quickly, he dropped the amusement and was all business again. "Plus, you need information and we need a neutral party to help us see what we're missing in these murders."

I would get torn apart without the necklace's powers if I tried to hunt whatever this thing was, but I couldn't tell the werewolf that the necklace wasn't working. That seemed like an invitation for *him* to tear me apart.

Ramble was no help and gave no indication of what he

thought I should do.

Shit. Now what?

"Um, okay."

"Great. I'll get back to you tomorrow." He pointed at the ground and added, "Also, you might want to pick those up before they freeze to the ground."

I looked down and realized that the clothes I'd dropped when Donavon had startled me were two pairs of underwear and a bra.

Great—hey werewolf! Take a look at my underwear!

My face turned red again but when I glanced back through the doorway, Donavon was gone.

Chapter 5

When Ramble and I got back to the room, I practically dove under the covers to get warm, pausing just long enough to yank the window curtains closed. Both the curtains and the bedding were of a higher quality than any of the other motels we'd stayed at. They also held a faint vanilla scent which was a nice change from the usual stale cigarettes and vomit smell.

I couldn't help but wrap myself up in the soft blanket as I mentally ran through my conversation with the werewolf.

Ramble hopped on the bed before pointedly looking at me, then at the silver knife I'd left on the table, then back at me.

"Fine. I get the point," I huffed. "I should have brought some sort of defense with me when I went out, but how was I to know that the werewolves would find me within a few hours of getting to town? How did they even know I was here?"

Ramble leaned his head forward and gave me several loud sniffs as if he was smelling me for something.

Oh.

"You think they smelled me?"

I got a small air-whuff in answer to my question.

"Well damn. I didn't even think about smell. Do I smell different because I'm a Vânători?" This got me an "of course, stupid" look.

I guess I'd need to start taking into consideration that some supernatural beings would be able to tell I was a Vânători just from the way I smelled. That also explained why all the vampires always knew who I was.

I'd also noted in the conversation with Donavon that he'd mentioned a coven of witches, not just Rosalyn. I wasn't sure how the witches felt about Vânători but hopefully it wasn't the same way the werewolf felt about me. Otherwise I'd either end up dead or conscripted into a job with them.

Which reminded me…

"How am I supposed to help investigate these murders?" I asked Ramble. "I mean, I don't really know what I'm doing and the necklace doesn't work, which means I'll just end up getting chewed up and spit out by the killer if we catch it."

The last statement earned me an offended raised eyebrow.

"You're right," I amended. "It probably wouldn't get past you, but you know what I mean. I'm in over my head here. The plan was to speak with Rosalyn about the necklace, then get the hell outta dodge."

Warm now, I tossed off the blanket and walked back over to the window, lifting back the curtain to peer out. The clouds were rolling in and it was already starting to precipitate. Was that regular rain or freezing kind out there?

Great. Just what I needed: to be stuck in a town full of werewolves, witches, and a killer.

"I need a drink."

As soon as I said it, I realized it was true.

Shit!

Was the necklace not working at all anymore? I still had it on, right? I frantically, dug under the fleece, fumbling to find the Artemis necklace I had almost died to retrieve.

I breathed a sigh of relief when my fingers grasped the circular pendant, but the relief was short-lived. If I still had on the necklace and I craved a drink, then that meant the necklace was either not working at all or had lost the ability to shield me from that need.

And I really, *really* needed a drink. Right now.

Okay, you can handle this, Vi, I told myself. *You managed this before you had some dumbass magic necklace. You can handle it again. First, assess the situation. HALT: Hungry, Angry, Lonely, Tired. Feeling any of those things right now?*

I was definitely tired from the drive but my hunger was a much more pressing need. And, if I was honest with myself, I was also a bit lonely. Having Ramble around helped, but there was only so much conversation one could have with yes or no answers.

Okay. First thing on the list, food.

Of course, the rain chose that moment to pick up and I amended the plan a bit.

I sighed and glanced back at my companion. "I guess if we're going to be here for a bit, I might as well go buy a real jacket and then we can grab dinner."

Ramble licked his chops in agreement and in one leap was off the bed and standing beside the door.

I guess someone was hungry.

* * *

There were a few more cars rolling through downtown Ricketts than there had been when I'd first driven through. Probably people going home from work after a grueling day at some nine to five job. Cars zipped past as I made my way down the sidewalk huddled in on myself to stay warm. It had taken me about five steps to determine that it was freezing rain after all when I almost busted my butt on the frozen sidewalk.

My jeans, now soaked from walking in the rain, made things even colder. I'd layered several shirts in an attempt to keep the heat in, but couldn't bring myself to wear the torn and bloody fleece as the final layer. Instead, I'd donned my only flannel shirt and hoped that, combined with the layers underneath, it would be enough to keep me warm.

It wasn't.

Unfortunately, freezing was not the best way to distract from wanting a drink. Hollywood had done only too good a job in convincing us that a stiff drink would warm you right up when you're cold. I knew it was bullshit. Knew the science that drinking alcohol actually made your body colder...but I wanted a drink all the same.

And, dammit, here I was thinking of alcohol again. Longing to swallow a shot and get that wonderful sensation of burning warmth as it hit the taste buds...

A growly-whine rose from hip height on my right. Ramble looked up at me, his glowing eyes a little more pronounced now that the sun was starting to set.

"I know buddy," I murmured quietly in case we passed someone. I didn't want them to hear me talking to something invisible. "I'm not going to drink. I just...really want one."

Instead of the huff or a snort of response I expected, Ramble just silently padded along beside me.

I switched my line of thinking to take it off alcohol. Since I didn't want to get picked up for fraud by using the fake credit card in town, I'd need to make my cash stretch. I had enough money for about a week in the cheap motel as well as meals. If I was really stingy with the meals, I could also get a better jacket. I sighed. It seemed like money—or lack of money—would continue to be an issue for me.

It wasn't that I'd ever been rich by any means, but my parents had always made sure that I'd had enough. Even in college, before my parents died, I hadn't really had to deal with going without something since my parents had always been just a phone call away. Until their car accident. Then I had no one.

I'd already been drinking and having fun like a normal college student, but when my parents died, drinking became less about socializing and more about forgetting my pain. It hadn't taken long to spiral out of control. A semester of missed classes and a string of DUI's later, I'd not only been kicked out of college, I'd also landed in jail. When the judge had told me she was doing me a favor by sending me to the slammer for a year, I'd thought she was out of her mind.

But she'd been right.

I mean, don't get me wrong. Jail was a horrible experience. I'd been bullied, almost beaten up, and was afraid all the time, but I hadn't had access to alcohol. That was the thing that really saved me.

Okay, that and mandatory mental health counseling as well as AA meetings once a week.

I shook my head again, trying to shed the familiar weight of my alcoholism as it settled on my shoulders. I needed to stop thinking about all this. It was just making me want to drink more.

It hadn't looked like a long walk to get to town from the motel, but much of the way was down a road between two open fields where there was nothing to break the icy wind. We picked up the pace, hunching against a particularly strong gust that promised imminent wintry weather.

The first building to make up the town center on this side of the street was the second-hand clothing store I'd noticed on our drive in. A jacket from there should cost half the price of a new one. At least, I hoped it would.

Nearing the second-hand store's entrance, I jumped when a black cat suddenly darted away from the door and bolted across the street. Hopefully all that superstition about black cats being bad luck wasn't as real as hellhounds or werewolves. Ramble kept an eye on the cat and when I tried to urge him to come inside with me, he refused.

"Fine," I said under my breath, "but don't complain when you freeze your tail off out here."

Ducking inside, I was surprised at the lack of the all-too familiar scent of used clothing in bulk. Instead, the store smelled like lavender incense. Huh. Maybe that's why Ramble didn't want to come inside. He seemed to have a pretty sensitive sense of smell. It was possible that he'd smelled it from outside and decided not to expose himself to a stronger dose.

"Hi! Anything I can help you with?"

I jerked around. I hadn't noticed the woman on a step stool dressing up a mannequin in the window. She looked to be in her mid-fifties with once black hair that had gone mostly gray. Silver rimmed glasses somehow gave her both an endearing and studious look. There was a glittering intelligence in her eyes.

She gave me an apologetic smile. "Sorry, I didn't mean to startle you."

"That's okay. I was in my own world." I smiled back. "Can you point me toward the ladies coats?"

Her eyes swept quickly over my hodge-podge outfit, taking in my permanently stained jeans and the tennis shoes that let in too much air for a Maine winter. Her mouth screwed down into a barely-there grimace.

Stepping down from the stool, she ushered me toward the back corner of the store. A rack of jackets all marked with sales tags stood slightly off on its own.

Was it really that obvious that I could only afford the clothes on sale from a second-hand shop?

"You must not be from around here," she said, tossing me a glance before dutifully focusing her attention on the jackets. "Here are some coats that are more suitable to the winters we get up here. There are a few women's coats, but mostly we have a lot more men's and children's jackets to choose from. You have a small frame, though," she reassured me with a smile, "so you could probably fit into a boy's large or a men's small." She pointed to the corner. "There's a mirror over there if you'd like to try anything on."

"Thanks."

The woman returned to the front of the store then paused, almost as if deliberating on whether or not she should say anything else. Finally, she turned back to me. "And, dear, there are boots over there." She nodded in the direction of the opposite wall. "I hope you don't mind me saying so, but while I was in the window, I saw you walk up here and those shoes of yours aren't likely to stand up against Maine weather if you're going to walk everywhere."

I wasn't offended, but I felt a little embarrassed that I was both inept at dressing for the weather and obviously too poor to even afford second-hand items that weren't on sale. I'm sure I turned red, but managed to mumble a thank you. Anything to make her stop looking at me that way.

Thankfully, she returned to dressing the mannequin in the window and didn't make any other suggestions while I perused the coats. It quickly became obvious that she was right. There were only two women's jackets on sale and both were two sizes too large.

I briefly wished I'd thought to stop and get out more money before finding my way to this town. Blowing out a quiet sigh, I moved to the men's sales rack and resigned myself to perusing the jackets there.

* * *

An hour later, I sat in a café booth with Ramble underneath the table sniffing at my slightly used boots. The shopkeeper had insisted that I wear the new boots and the jacket that was slightly too large when I left the store. My tennis shoes now sat in a shopping bag on the seat beside me…along with an extra pair of jeans I'd splurged to buy.

I'd justified the purchase by telling myself that I could afford it if I was going to be walking everywhere in this town. Just think of all the gas money I was saving! Okay, not really, but if the weather was going to continue being crappy, then I'd need the extra jeans to change into when these ones got soaked.

Like they were now.

Though I appreciated the warmth of the new jacket imme-diately upon leaving the store, it wasn't cut for a ladies frame and hung awkwardly, leaving me looking bulky in all the wrong places. It did, however, earn some redeeming points by having one of those internal pockets on the left hand side. There was just something cool about secret pockets. Why did men's clothing always have the cool stuff while women's clothing had annoying things like pretend pockets?

I would never understand fashion.

When I'd entered the café, I wasn't sure if it was the oddly fitting jacket or the fact that I was a stranger in a small town that had all the patrons craning their necks to get a good look at me. The middle-aged waitress introduced herself as Cheri and, though I got the feeling she was curious about me, she didn't seem overly chatty.

Good. I wasn't feeling in a very chatty mood.

Staring at what seemed like a pricey menu for a small town café, I thought about how I might have to drive to another town and take out more money. The boots and jacket hadn't been expensive, but they'd definitely taken a dent out of my living expenses.

The waitress returned to my table with the water I'd ordered. First rule of saving money: cut out unnecessary expenses like soda.

"Do you know what you want to order?" Cheri asked, her tone suggesting anything I ordered would be discussed with others at length.

Was there really nothing else to do around here? Or was I just being a judgmental ass and reading more into the waitress's tone because I was jonesing for a drink?

The front door chimed and everyone looked to see who'd decided to dine at the café this evening. I found myself automatically doing the same and was surprised to lock eyes with Donavon, the angry werewolf.

Shit.

I pulled my attention back to the waitress and opened my mouth to give her my order, but she was already walking away. She moved to intercept Donavon who had been heading in my direction.

"Hey Don! Want your regular booth?" She asked warmly with a lot more enthusiasm than she'd shown me.

Hmm. Either they were an item, had been an item, or she just really wanted some of that. Not that I could really blame her. Donavon was a very handsome guy, er werewolf, with intense eyes that held dark promises. Of course, knowing he was a werewolf, those promises seemed to be more about turning into something furry that sported sharp teeth rather than a night of fun between the sheets.

"No, thanks, Cheri," his voice rumbled in his chest. "I'm meeting someone."

I looked up to watch as he smiled at the waitress and slipped past her to head toward my booth.

Dammit.

"Keep it together, Vi," I murmured to myself. "You're not about to get chewed on by the scary werewolf in such a public place."

Donavon sank down on the opposite side of the booth. Though the smile stayed on his face, it was clearly a mask since his eyes had lost their warmth.

"Vânători," he greeted me quietly, aware that all eyes were now on us. He kept the fake smile on his face as he continued in a low tone, "I thought I made it clear to stay at the motel."

My eyebrows shot to my forehead of their own volition. "Excuse me? You did no such thing."

Donavon glanced around at the other customers. Faces immediately looked away, suddenly busy with inspecting their own food or staring out the windows into the night. He opened his mouth to argue further, but I cut him off.

"You said I could stay the night. You didn't mention anything about staying in the motel the entire time. Was I supposed to sit in my room like a good little girl and starve without supper?"

His eyes grew darker. "You do not have permission to go around town."

I leaned forward, "I don't need your permission, *Fido*. It's a free country and I'll go where I please."

A quiet snort came from under the table just loud enough that only Donavon and I could hear.

Donavon's face tightened. "What was that?"

"My invisible friend." I smiled sweetly. "He's hungry, too."

Donavon's eyes got wide and I thought I saw a little flash of white before we were saved by the waitress.

"Do you two know what you want?" Her demeanor had completely changed. She'd gone from politely curious to faintly pissed and was only addressing Donavon now.

"I'll have my regular," Donavon said without even looking at her.

That only seemed to piss her off more.

"And for you?" She didn't look at me, choosing instead to glare at the notepad in her hand. It suddenly hit me that she must think we were on a date. Well, shit. If she had a thing for Donavon, then I was definitely going to end up with spit in my meal. I'd planned on having a burger, but that would be all too easy to sabotage.

Dammit.

"I'll have the chicken finger basket with French fries, thanks." I tried to stay cheery, but nothing would help me now. Cheri

76

walked away without saying anything else. Ah well. At least the chicken fingers would be a lot more difficult to mess with.

A tiny whine rose from underneath the table.

"I know, but no burger tonight, buddy. It's too crowded for you to eat here, anyways."

A dejected sigh was my only answer.

"You can't just… just go around town with a hellhound," Donavon spluttered but was careful to keep his voice down.

"Why not? You go around town as a werewolf."

He jerked and looked around to make sure no one had heard me, but I'd been careful to pitch my voice equally low to match his.

Score one point for me. I'd just learned something new: people in town didn't know that they lived in the midst of a werewolf Pack. I suppose it wasn't that surprising that the werewolves kept their existence a secret, but up to now, I hadn't been sure that the whole town wasn't in on that secret.

"Look, you can sit here and chastise me all you want, but it's not going to change the fact that I'm not in the motel. How about we have a nice meal and try to keep it from looking like a date so your number one fan doesn't lose her shit and spit in my food?"

"What are you talking about?"

I jerked my head toward the kitchen. "Cheri, the waitress. She's definitely into you."

"It's not like that at all. Cheri's like my little sister. I've known her since she was a baby."

Donavon maybe had five years on me, which put him in his mid to late twenties. Cheri, I was pretty sure, was in her mid to late thirties. There was no way he'd been around when she was a baby. Unless…

I must have worn an expression of disbelief because Donavon felt the need to explain his previous comment.

"I'm not as young as I look." This time his smile was genuine—genuinely smug, that was. He was a little too full of himself in my opinion. It wouldn't hurt to take him down a few pegs.

"I never said you looked young."

There was that flash of white in his eyes again. If nothing else, at least I was learning how to push this guy's buttons. It was kind of fun. Unless it ended in him wolfing out and ripping me apart. Might not be so much fun then.

I decided to change the subject. Keeping my voice low so we'd be the only three to hear, I said, "Since we're not on a date, that means business. If I'm gonna help you out with your problem, it would be nice to know a little more about what's going on than what's been in the papers."

Now that the necklace was failing to even protect me from my alcoholism, I was willing to put my neck on the line if it meant getting connected to Rosalyn who might be able to figure out what was wrong with it. That meant I needed to take this whole hunting thing more seriously in order for Donavon to keep his side of the bargain of introducing me to the coven.

His meaty arms automatically crossed over his chest. "There's no point in discussing it since the Pack hasn't decided whether they'll let you help or not."

I rolled my eyes. "What could it hurt to tell me what you've got so far? You're clearly watching me, so you know I won't go haring off on my own to look into things."

His lips remained sealed.

"Oh come on. It can't possibly hurt anything. Unless," I

tapped my finger on the table in thought, "you don't have anything to go on in the first place." I made a show of thinking about that possibility, then nodded. "Yeah, that must be it, huh? You don't want to share because you don't have anything *to* share, right?"

"Do you think I'm going to fall for something like that?"

I smiled and held out my hands in a placating gesture. "Hey, you don't have to play stupid. I get it. I'd be embarrassed too if something was wreaking havoc in my territory and I didn't know squat about it or how to stop it." I paused, deciding on whether to continue or not. What the hell. It was unlikely that he would attack me in such a public place if it was a secret that he was a werewolf.

"Plus," I leaned in, making sure only he could hear me, "it would be *really* embarrassing if one of my own was the one wreaking the havoc."

His eyes lashed entirely white. The effect sent a shiver down my spine all the way to my groin. I inhaled a little in surprise.

Holy shit. Was I attracted to the big scary werewolf?

Donavon's nostrils flared and, though his eyes stayed white for another moment, a tiny smile tugged at the side of his mouth.

Oh godammit. Could he tell—smell maybe— that he'd just gotten me aroused?

Luckily, I was saved by the now thoroughly pissed Cheri. She slid Donavon's "regular" onto the table. It was a mouth-watering bacon cheeseburger with a side of chili-cheese fries. Without even a glance in my direction, she dropped my chicken fingers basket in front of me, sending two fries toppling out.

"Anything else?" She pointedly asked only Donavon.

Though there was no longer any trace of the werewolf in his eyes, his voice still held a little warmth as he answered. "No, I think we're good. Thanks, Cheri." His smile was the same one he'd just been directing at me, so I knew the warmth was actually lingering amusement at my body's reaction to him.

Jackass.

"Great." Cheri gave me a withering look and stalked off.

"Told you she's into you," I tossed out there, trying in vain to change the subject

"Looks like she's not the only one," he retorted, still smiling.

It was time to change the subject before I had to ask Ramble to bite him and wipe that smile off his face.

"So, what do you know so far about these attacks? Is there any possibility they really could just be animal attacks and not murders?"

He sighed at the change in subject, but I could tell I had him now. "First, they definitely aren't attacks from a normal animal. Dangerous animals don't tend to come into Pack territory." He smiled and there was that flicker in his eyes again, "We're a bigger threat as a predator."

That flicker of otherness hadn't done more than make the hair on the back of my neck stand up this time, which I took as a good sign.

"Could it be someone like you who doesn't belong to your Pack?" I didn't think anyone could hear us, but figured it would be best not to talk too openly in such a public space.

He shook his head while and inished chewing a bite of burger. "Highly unlikely," he said when his mouth was clear. "The method of attack is totally different than if…someone like that had perpetrated the attacks." He lowered his voice a little more before adding, "And if it was *someone* who lost their control, then it would have been during a full moon and none of the attacks match up to that kind of timeline."

I ate some fries while I thought that over. So werewolves only Hulked out and lost their control when there was a full moon. I wasn't sure about the method of attack part. Did werewolves attack their prey in a certain way? I didn't want to ask and make myself look too ignorant, otherwise Donavon might decide I was too green to be of any help and would rescind the offer to introduce me to the coven.

"Did you know any of the victims?"

He nodded and a shadow of sadness seemed to settle over him. You didn't get that kind of pain when someone who was just an acquaintance died. I had a feeling I knew the answer to the next question but felt I needed to ask it anyways.

"Were any of the victims a part of your Pack?" I again kept my voice pitched so it wouldn't carry past our table.

It was another beat before he nodded his head. Patting his mouth clean with a napkin, he said, "Only one of them. Samuel Vance."

"He was found in the apartment parking lot, right?"

Donavon's eyes were darker when he nodded.

"I'm sorry," I said. I had no idea what being Pack meant, but it was clear that Donavon had been close to Samuel.

The werewolf went silent for a few minutes while we ate and I couldn't tell if it was a don't-ask-me-any-more questions kind of silence or an I'm-thinking-about-it kind of silence. When the quiet became too awkward, I finally risked another question.

"Can you tell me about him? About Samuel?"

This earned me a hard stare before Donavon's eyes flicked

around the room, indicating the other patrons. "Not here. Somewhere quieter. Let me drive you back." He glanced outside. "It's sleeting anyways. Not great weather for walking."

I hesitated. I mean, I didn't really know the guy and he could turn into a predator. Did I really want to get into a car with him by myself?

Seeing my hesitation, his lips quirked into that sly smile again.

"What's wrong? Afraid the big bad wolf might eat you up?" His eyes swam with that white light that suggested he was more than human. This time it sent tingles from my stomach to my toes...and wasn't the least bit unpleasant.

Oh boy. If I was going to ride in a car with this werewolf, I needed to work on minimizing my body's reactions to him. Otherwise it was going to be a very embarrassing ride.

Chapter 6

Getting into Donavon's small, somewhat sporty Subaru with my hellhound companion proved to be interesting. I'd expected him to drive something a little more posh, maybe a BMW or an Audi, but the all-wheel drive Subaru made a lot more sense for Maine winters.

Once Ramble was settled in the back seat, I gave him my leftover chicken tenders and fries. He scarfed them down while Donavon watched in open wonder as the food disappeared into what he saw as thin air. I, on the other hand, could see Ramble fully enjoying his meal.

"I can't believe you have a hellhound—a named hellhound," he said, glancing at me.

I shrugged, struggling out of the overlarge jacket. Apparently the seat had a heater in it because the car was almost immediately too warm. "I can't believe you're a real werewolf."

He gave me a dubious look. "You don't think I'm a werewolf?"

"No, that's not what I mean. I've just never met a werewolf. I kind of can't believe you exist."

"Well, if it makes you feel any better, my people kind of can't believe a Vânători exists again. Your kind have been gone for years."

My kind. Interesting way to phrase it.

"Well, here I am."

"Yes. Here you are." There was that white flash again.

In the small space of his car, I could smell his pleasant scent just under the chicken and French fries smell. It made me not want to keep my hands to myself. Especially when he kept letting whatever that white flash was flick into his eyes. Every time he did, it gave me a little thrill.

Down girl, I chided myself.

"You smell...funny," the werewolf said, his nostrils flaring.

My mouth dropped open a little and I could feel my face turning red. "Wow. Thanks a lot."

"No, I mean..." He ran a hand through his perfectly cut hair, making me even more aware of my own, unstyled hair that I'd messily pulled into a ponytail. At least he was floundering a little to explain himself, which made me feel a little better. "I mean, I— you smell like the witches."

"...Okay."

"It's not a bad thing," he hastily explained. "It's just...weird. You didn't smell like that before at the motel." He leaned over and took a quick whiff of the jacket in my lap, making me jerk back instinctively. He immediately pulled back.

"Sorry. I—it's the jacket I think. It smells like the witches."

"Really?" I pulled the jacket up to my nose and sniffed. All I got was fading lavender and an underlying scent of clothing that hadn't been washed in awhile. I wished I could have washed the thing before wearing it, but I needed it against the cold and it wasn't like it was actually dirty.

Donavon laughed and I gave him a dark look. Was he just messing with me or something?

"Sorry, sorry." He laughed again, then got control of himself.

"I don't think you'll be able to smell it." He tapped his nose. "Werewolf sense of smell, remember?" His eyes slid back down to the jacket. "Where'd you get it?"

"I picked it up at that second-hand clothing store—Second Chances, I think it was called."

He nodded. "That explains it then."

I waited for him to elaborate but apparently he thought that was the only explanation needed.

"Getting my jacket from a second-hand shop explains why it smells like witches?"

He looked puzzled for a moment before his features straightened out again. "I forget that you don't know about our town. That shop is owned by a witch."

Shit. The spectacled woman with graying hair from the shop was a witch? I could have asked her about the coven and saved myself the trouble of this whole investigation thing! I suddenly remembered that Ramble hadn't wanted to go into the shop. I turned my head and fixed him with a glare. Had he known that the woman in the shop was a witch?

I gritted my teeth but tried not to blow my top at the hellhound. We would definitely be chatting about this later. For now, I changed the subject and focused on the reason I was sitting in this warm car with a muscle bound werewolf.

"So, can you tell me about Samuel Vance now?" I asked.

The mood in the car immediately shifted as Donavon looked away and out the window. He was silent so long that I thought he was going to refuse to answer the question.

Finally, while still looking out the window, he said, "Sam was young for a werewolf. He'd just been Turned four years ago and he was only twenty-five then. He had a good head on his shoulders, which was why the Pack let him be Turned."

I assumed that when he said "Turned," he meant being turned into a werewolf. I had questions about that, but nothing relevant to the attacks, so I just nodded.

Donavon fell silent again and I realized I'd have to keep asking questions if I wanted information. What were the right questions to ask though? I hadn't actually seen Jax talk to anyone while hunting. His method of investigation mostly consisted of online research, then showing up in town and guessing where the monster might be.

I decided to fall back on my years of watching police procedurals. What would they ask on something like *Law and Order* or *CSI*?

"Did Sam have any enemies? Inside or outside the Pack?"

This got me another dark look from the werewolf. "Pack aren't enemies. We're more like a family."

"Okay…but every family has its little bit of drama."

He stared at me for another few seconds then finally away again. I realized I'd been holding my breath against that stare when I let it out with a whoosh.

"Sam was a likable guy. Got along with everyone and didn't try to Challenge anyone."

"What do you mean, 'Challenge' anyone?"

Now I had his attention again. "You really don't know much about werewolves, do you?"

I felt a little embarrassed at my lack of knowledge, then decided that it was stupid to be embarrassed. It wasn't like I'd been told I would one day be a hunter and had years to study up and get ready.

"Nope. I wasn't lying when I told you that you're the first werewolf I've met."

He shook his head a little in disbelief and glanced back at

Ramble when the hellhound let out a contented sigh after finishing off the last of the food.

"This is very strange. Vânători are legendary. Yet here I am, explaining to one of them the very basics about werewolves."

I tried not to get annoyed. "I'm new. So sue me. What do you mean by Challenge?" Now that I'd asked the question, I couldn't back down without an answer. Doing so would set a precedent for him not answering any future questions he didn't like.

"There's a hierarchy to a werewolf Pack. At the top is the Alpha." He raised his hand high in the air. "Underneath the Alpha are the other werewolves with the strongest or smartest at the top, just underneath the Alpha. Then the next strongest underneath that werewolf and so on and so forth." As he spoke, he put his other hand below the first, then moved the first below that hand to indicate a kind of invisible chain.

"Got it. And you Challenge someone to move up the chain?

He nodded. "A Challenge is a fight. Sometimes, but not usually, to the death."

I nodded. "Okay. So where was Sam in the Pack hierarchy?"

"Not quite here," Donavon dropped his hand way down, "but maybe more like here," he put his other hand a few hand spans up from the bottom.

Now I was confused. "If he didn't Challenge anyone, how did he move up to that spot when he was a relatively new werewolf? Did the Pack Turn other people into werewolves after him?"

Donavon shook his head. "No, he was the last person we Turned. Becoming a werewolf is a very serious act. We only Turn people who we think will get along with the Pack. Sometimes we go years without Turning anyone. It's almost an instinct for who would make a good werewolf. It's the same with the Pack hierarchy. There's an instinct for just knowing where one belongs in the chain."

"An instinct?" I asked a bit skeptically.

He leaned over the console and very slowly so as not to startle me, brushed a finger down my arm. I felt the touch as if I wasn't wearing the long sleeved flannel and Donavon had run his finger over bare skin.

It sent a thrill racing through my whole body. I stifled a gasp.

Silence hung in the car for a moment before he broke it.

"An instinct."

Though his sly smile was back, the expression in his eyes was more that of an animal-like hunger.

My body echoed it with a pang of need.

I closed my eyes and pulled back from him. I was *not* going to have sex with a werewolf. Clearly my desire for a drink was manifesting as this feeling of lust for Donavon. *Get it together, Vi. You're here to do a job.* I took a deep breath and ignored how his earthy scent was stronger now.

"I see," I said, opening my eyes. I tried to kick-start my brain again. "What about outside the Pack? Do you think Sam might have pissed someone off enough to kill him?"

The need in Donavon's eyes winked out as I brought up his dead friend. I almost felt bad for it but we needed to stay focused here.

"No. I told you, he got along with everyone and everyone got along with him."

"Huh." Well that was a dead end. "What about the other victims? Did they have any ties to the Pack?"

"No. I mean, it's a small town, so we all knew them, but

none of them knew about the Pack." He hesitated, then said, "we don't think the attacks are necessarily connected to the Pack."

"Really?" I couldn't help the tone of disagreement. "Even if the other victims weren't Pack, wouldn't it have been difficult to hurt, let alone kill Sam if he was a werewolf?"

"Werewolves aren't invincible."

"No, but…" I struggled for a way to express my thinking, "you're strong, right? I mean, whatever could kill a werewolf would have to be stronger. Which means it's not likely to just be some regular serial killer making it look like animal attacks."

"No, this isn't a serial killer. Not a human one at least."

I shivered at the terrifying idea of a supernatural creature who was also a serial killer. Then again, wouldn't vampires be classified as serial killers?

Not really something to think about right now.

"Anything else that might give some insight or suggest who did this?"

"No. Nothing—and we have our best trackers on it, too. The killer doesn't even leave a smell.".

"Huh."

I couldn't think of any other questions to ask. Sensing this, Donavon reached out and started the car. "I'll take you back to the motel."

We drove in silence. I was glad that Ramble wasn't begging for the werewolf to roll down the windows so he could stick his head out. Apparently the hellhound was too dignified when in the presence of a werewolf to ever do something so frivolous.

The little town receded and the buildings were quickly

replaced with empty fields on both sides—except now they weren't empty.

There was a man jogging in the field. I could only make him out in the dark because he had on a light colored shirt.

"Do people regularly go for a jog around here when it's sleeting?" I asked.

Donavon gave me a strange look so I pointed out the window at the jogger. "The man there. See him? He's—" As I spoke, the man had whipped his head around, looking over his shoulder. It suddenly hit me that the man wasn't jogging—he was running from something.

"Stop the car!" I yelled.

Donavon slammed on the brakes. I had to brace myself against the dash to keep from slamming into it. The moment the car came to a stop, I flung open the door and ran after the man, forgetting the jacket in my lap as it tumbled to the ground. I heard Ramble leap out of the car behind me.

The man was still running across the field, stealing looks over his shoulder at an attacker I couldn't see. Now that I was out of the car and closing in on him, I could hear him making strangled, high-pitched noises like a trapped animal. He threw a glance back again and another sound escaped his lips. It was the sound of a scream from a man who didn't have the breath to spare for a real scream as he ran for his life.

I've never been much of a runner, but Jax had been making me do drills when he was "training me." I wouldn't win any marathons, but I could be quick in short spurts when I needed to be.

I poured on speed and Ramble easily kept up with me.

The man suddenly lost his footing on the uneven dirt. He went to a knee, scrambled to get up, lost his balance, and fell again. I was only about thirty feet away and gaining when the man screamed, "No! I'm sorry!" and threw his arms over his head in an effort to ward off an attack.

I still couldn't see what was attacking him but there was definitely something there because something bit and clawed him, leaving wounds in his neck and shoulders. His face froze in a silent scream a split second before his body rose up from the ground and was violently shaken like a rag doll.

I slid to a stop. Whatever this thing was, it was invisible, it could pick up a grown man, and I had no idea how to fight it.

I forced myself to move forward again. I had no plan on what I was going to do once I reached them, but I felt I had to help. The man wouldn't last much longer in the jaws of that thing.

It happened so fast I would have missed it if I'd blinked.

The man was suddenly thrown roughly to the ground. There was a loud CRUNCH before the man went limp.

I picked up my pace and raced over to him, hoping the invisible monster wouldn't come after me next—but the man had vanished.

The ground where his body had landed was bare. There wasn't even any sign of a struggle. I looked around. Maybe I'd somehow run to the wrong spot? Or the monster had picked him up and flung him somewhere else? I didn't see anything else in the field except for Ramble standing beside me. Donavon closed on us quickly.

Maybe the man had gone invisible for some reason?

"What are you doing?" Donavon wasn't even panting when he reached us.

"Looking for the man who was just attacked!"

The werewolf looked from me, to the ground around us,

91

and back to me again. "There's nothing here."

"He might be invisible!"

This got me a definite this-lady-is-crazy look, but instead of backing away from the crazy lady, Donavon asked, "What did you see?"

"There was a man running from something. Then he fell and the thing attacked him. But I couldn't see what was attacking him."

The werewolf watched me for another heartbeat. Somehow I had a feeling I knew what was going to come out of his mouth before he said, "This is where one of the victims was killed."

"He was a ghost." I realized the truth as I said it. "Shit."

I suddenly became aware of how cold and wet I was. My jeans were soaked through and splotched with mud from the calf down. As the adrenaline wore off, my body started to shake and my teeth chattered.

"Do you still see him?" Donavon asked.

I shook my head and forced myself to stand. "I think...I think he disappeared when he died." Steam puffed from my mouth as I spoke. I wrapped my arms around my body in an effort to keep warm.

Donavon took one look at me and pointed back the way we had come. "Back to the car. You're freezing."

If he hadn't been right, I might have argued with being bossed around. As it was, my ears, nose, and fingers were going numb. My legs from the knee to ankle already felt like blocks of ice. At least my feet were warm thanks to the new boots.

I had to force myself to put one foot in front of the other. What is it about the cold that seems to slow everything down in the body? Except for the shaking that was. My entire body was jerking uncontrollably in an effort to restore warmth.

My brain wasn't sluggish though. I had just seen a man—a ghost—run across the field and get shaken to death by a monster I couldn't see.

"W-w-as that m-m-man, Kleinman?" I managed to stammer out past my chattering teeth when we reached the car

Donavon nodded as he picked up my jacket from the ground and wrapped it around me. I felt a deep gratitude to the witch at the second-hand store for convincing me to go with the men's coat rather than the thinner women's one I'd been eyeballing.

"I think you just witnessed Joseph Kleinman's murder."

Chapter 7

I sat in one of the chairs in the motel room, teeth chattering and body still jerking with cold as Donavon cranked up the heater. It had been less than a two-minute drive from the field to the motel, so we hadn't been in his car long enough for me to warm up.

I'd initially protested that I would be fine if Donavon just dropped us off, but after watching me fumble the key when trying to unlock the motel room door, he'd gotten out, taken the key, and sort of taken over from there. I hardly had the energy to protest.

Ramble, who had shaken himself off outside, was still dripping wet, too. He looked as miserable as I felt.

"Can you bring me a bath towel?" I asked Donavon. I hated to ask for help, but I felt so drained all I wanted to do was curl up in the vanilla-scented blankets and go to sleep.

He brought me the towel and I held it out to Ramble. This earned me a sour look from the hellhound.

"Well, you can be cold and wet all night or you can let me dry you off a little. But wet hellhounds don't sleep on human beds. Your choice."

Donavon glanced from me to a wet spot on the floor that was slowly growing damper under the hellhound's dripping body. I guess it would be kind of weird to watch water dripping from nowhere.

With a huff that made Donavon jump a little, Ramble prowled over like a drowned, angry cat and let me rub him down with the towel.

"Do you want me to—?" Donavon stopped talking abruptly when a small growl emerged from seemingly empty air. "Alright then."

The werewolf lowered himself onto the bed and watched me dry off the invisible hellhound.

When Ramble was as dry as he was going to get, I set the soaked towel on the table. The heater in the room was running full blast and I was feeling a little more comfortable. At least my teeth had stopped chattering. Maybe I could just sleep right here?

"You should take a hot shower," he suggested. "It's important to get your core temperature back up."

I nodded at Donavon's suggestion, suddenly feeling too sleepy to actually answer.

A second later, I jerked awake at the sensation of hands underneath me. I blinked and watched as the room seemed to sail past. Suddenly I was in the bathroom, sitting on the toilet lid and looking up at Donavon. He'd taken off his flannel jacket at some point. Now he only wore a tight, gray t-shirt that showed off his arms. His jeans were nice and tight, too.

"Come on, now," Donavon said and lifted me to stand. I didn't complain since I was now leaning against his warm, muscular frame. In one smooth move, he pulled my t-shirt up over my head and gently eased my arms out.. "We'll get you into a nice warm shower—" His voice cut off as he maneuvered me away from his body and stared down at my chest.

95

I guess werewolves are into boobs just as much as the next guy, I thought before looking down and realizing that he was staring at the bandage just above my bra. Oh yeah. I'd forgotten about that.

The bandage was so drenched that it was coming away from my skin. Donavon carefully peeled it the rest of the way off, revealing the circular bite mark from the lamprey that was still raw and angry at the edges.

"What happened?" Donavon gently touched his finger to the wound and I winced a little. It didn't hurt as much as it had, but it was still a little sore.

"Lamprey. Ramble took care of it though," I mumbled.

He leaned forward and gave the wound a sniff. "Not infected. That's good."

I was still too fuzzy brained to call him a weirdo for sniffing the bite. Who does that? Instead, I simply enjoyed it when he pulled me against his chest again to free his hands up in order to turn on the shower.

"I'll rebandage that later. First, we need to get you warmed up. I think you're getting hypothermic from the cold." His voice was smooth and gentle, like he was talking to a child.

Here's the thing, when I'm struggling not to drink, I tend to make some bad choices. My counselor called it "addiction replacement" and explained it as replacing one need with another. Maybe that was why I stood on tiptoes right then and gently laid a kiss in the crook of Donavon's neck.

He inhaled sharply and froze.

Touching him was even better than just looking. I let my hands find his chest then trail down to his stomach where I could feel his muscles tighten underneath the thin t-shirt. Only when I slipped my hand under his shirt to touch his warm skin did he take another breath.

One of his hands lifted from where it had been on my hip, brushed past my breast, then moved to slip one bra strap off my shoulder. His other hand trailed slowly down my mostly naked back, over my hip, and then came to rest on my butt before pulling my hips into his.

My brain tried to interfere and give me an image of how awkward it would be to work with Donavon after a one-night hook-up, but I told it to shut up as his hand slid under my bra. His thumb brushed my nipple and something electric lit up my synapses. I gasped and he pressed me harder against him. I could feel through his jeans how much he wanted this, too.

I slid my hand back down his tight abs and was just fumbling for his zipper when his phone rang.

Just ignore it, I thought and tried to draw his attention back to the moment by tasting the skin of his throat while pushing my body harder against him. He lowered his head and put his lips to my neck while at the same time he gently squeezed my breast. I might have moaned a little before redoubling my efforts to unbutton his pants.

The phone rang again. This time he stopped what he was doing.

I let out a sigh and pulled myself away from him.

"Go ahead and get it," I said a little breathlessly.

Now that we'd pulled apart, I could see his eyes shimmered with that white ethereal glow again. I stifled a shiver, wondering what I might have gotten myself into by coming onto a werewolf. He pulled his phone from his back pocket and stepped outside the bathroom.

"This is Donavon."

I had to stifle my disappointment as I slipped my bra strap

back up, but I also had to admit I was a little relieved that we'd been interrupted. We were supposed to be working together, after all. What was I going to say when he came back in that wouldn't sound lame?

I heard Donavon end his call before he stepped back into the open doorway. His look of disappointment was easy to read: whatever he'd heard on the phone would keep us from getting any more intimate.

"Another victim was just found."

* * *

We arrived at the crime scene about twenty minutes later. I'd only gotten a quick shower and ended up just slapping another bandage on the lamprey bite. At least I'd had the chance to throw on some dry clothes. I was very glad I'd splurged on the extra pair of jeans at the witch's second-hand store.

The drive over had been marginally awkward, but only because Ramble kept whuffing his unhappiness from the backseat because we had to go back out into the cold. Unfortunately, Donavon could also hear the hellhound's unhappy noises and I got the feeling that the werewolf was taking it as disgust at our near tryst.

On the bright side, at least the freezing rain had stopped. Now there was just a fine mist drifting lazily in the air.

The newest victim had been found at a gas station. When we pulled in, I immediately spotted a sheriff's car in the parking lot with its blue lights on.

"Shit," I said under my breath. I don't know what I had expected, but I hadn't thought we'd be talking to any kind of law enforcement.

Donavon paused in the act of exiting the car to look at me. "What?"

I opened my mouth but nothing came out. I couldn't exactly tell him I was wanted for skipping parole (among other things).

"Oh," he said as if perfectly understanding my predicament, "your car—it's stolen, right?" He smiled at my slightly panicked look. "I had a friend on the force run your plates. Don't worry. He won't call it in."

I wanted to ask him how he knew this cop would go against his ethical code and not call in a stolen vehicle, but before I had the chance, Donavon had already gotten out of the car.

I sighed. It would be more suspicious if I just sat in the car. And more importantly, I'd come here for a reason. If I could see Kleinman's ghost, then I might be able to see the new victim's ghost too. I figured it was worth a try.

A second later I caught up to Donavon. Ramble was already ahead of me, trailing the werewolf.

Yellow crime scene tape cordoned off the front entrance to a brightly lit gas station where the automatic door had been propped open by a block of concrete. Even from far away, I could see blood on the white tile just inside the door.

Two uniformed Sheriff's Department personnel waited just outside the tape. One of them was older with brown hair and a bit of a beer belly. The other was younger and when he turned, I could see the faint hopes of a mustache that gave him the unfortunate look of a pedophile. He seemed awfully young for a job in law enforcement.

Donavon made a beeline for them, so I swallowed my fear of getting caught, and followed the werewolf. Ramble split off and went immediately to the crime scene itself, slinking under the yellow tape and sniffing around so quietly no one

99

even knew he was there.

"Whoa there, big guy." The younger deputy held up one hand while his other hand moved toward his hip. I couldn't see it from this angle, but I was sure he had a sidearm there. "Just stop right there. This is Sheriff's business."

The older deputy—the sheriff, I realized as I noted the title on the breast of his jacket—turned quickly, ready to back up his younger counterpart. On seeing Donavon, he immediately dropped the tension in his shoulders and smiled.

"Donavon," he greeted the werewolf. "Glad you could make it." There was a wry sense of humor behind that statement. "This is the guy we've been waiting for, Ken."

Ken, the younger deputy, didn't look convinced but he dropped his hand from the butt of his gun.

"Who's your friend?" The sheriff asked. He appeared friendly on the surface, but underneath that I could see him wondering if Donavon had brought a girlfriend to a crime scene. Maybe to impress me.

"She's a friend of the *family*." Donavon's emphasis on the word family was just slight enough that Ken didn't seem to notice, but the sheriff raised an eyebrow. I guess that meant he knew about the Pack.

"Must be a real *special* friend to bring her out for this."

Donavon nodded instead of answering him and then turned to me. "This is Sheriff Bart Allen."

The man waved away the title. "Please, call me Bart. And you are?"

I decided to stick with the information on my fake license, that way if the sheriff or his trigger friendly deputy asked for ID, I'd be okay. I stuck out my hand. "I'm Violet Mason—but please, call me Vi. Everyone else does."

The sheriff shook my hand then jerked his head toward the younger deputy. "This is my newest deputy, Ken Smith."

I smiled. "Nice to meet you, Ken."

"It's Deputy Smith, miss. We're on official business."

"Oh. Got it." I gave him a smile but thought, *Deputy Asshole it is.*

Donavon's mouth turned down in an effort not to laugh at the deputy. The sheriff, however, shot his newest deputy a look that seemed to suggest the young man was being a prick, before jerking his head toward the front door of the gas station.

"Let's get this over with."

We followed the sheriff under the police tape and fanned out around the door. Ramble was inside, still sniffing around. I briefly hoped he wouldn't try to help himself to any of the gas station food before my attention was caught by the grisly scene before me.

Blood was splashed all over the white floors with one pool of it larger than the others. The most distressing sight was a lone, bloody palm print on the floor which ended in streaks of blood where someone had obviously been dragged across the floor.

"We won't be disturbing anything will we?" Donavon asked in a neutral voice. There seemed to be some weird, unspoken awkwardness here. I'd been under the impression that Donavon and the sheriff were friends, but now they seemed to be treading lightly around each other. Weird.

"Nah," The sheriff responded. "Forensics has already been out and done their job. Nothing left now but to wait for the clean up crew. Thought I'd let you take a look at it first."

"Nothing on the security cameras?" Donavon asked though

he didn't sound hopeful.

"Nope. Apparently after the last manager left, no one realized that the system was down. So nothing's been recorded for the past two years."

I caught Deputy Smith eyeing Donavon suspiciously. It was pretty obvious that he was trying to figure out why the sheriff was allowing Donavon onto a crime scene. Apparently the newest member of the Ricketts Sheriff's Department wasn't wise that there were werewolves among the townspeople.

Refocusing on the crime scene, I visually followed the trail of blood across the floor to a smudge of it on the frame of the back door. It looked like the victim had struggled hard against their attacker. They'd tried to stop being dragged away by holding onto the doorframe. I closed my eyes for a second against the image of such a terrible way to die. Dragged off and murdered.

"You okay, miss?" Ken—Deputy Smith, was looking at me like he'd wanted nothing more than to see me be throw up.

Though all the blood was making me want to do just that, I wanted to show the deputy that women could be tough, too, so I told my stomach to stop roiling and pointed to the trail of blood that led out the door.

"The victim was dragged outside?" I'd been so focused on the splashes of red against the white tile that I'd completely missed the trail of blood as it led out onto the lighter concrete sidewalk and around the corner of the gas station.

"C'mon." The sheriff, careful not to step in the blood trail, led us through the store and out the back door. Ramble followed but at a slower pace, keeping his nose barely above the blood trail as he sniffed for clues. The trail had been partially washed away by the rain and became even more difficult to follow before it completely stopped at the bottom of a dumpster.

"The guy who called in the murder was a medic. He thought maybe whoever had gotten hurt might still be alive and might be saved." Using a handkerchief, he flipped the lid of the dumpster up.

There was no way the medic would have been able to save the woman in there. Her body was twisted in ways that no human body should be. What had once been a polo shirt and khakis were shredded to the point where I could see her bra and white underwear beneath. Her skin was just as shredded.

But that wasn't the worst part. It looked like something had clamped its jaws around her head and squeezed until her head just popped.

The corpse's eyes snapped open.

I gasped and jerked back. The men all stared at me. I looked from them to the corpse in the dumpster—and found the dumpster was empty now.

I'd just seen another ghost. It was definitely a record for me. Two in one night.

"Are you okay?" The sheriff asked.

Donavon looked like he really wanted to ask me what I'd seen. Ramble was sniffing the ground around the dumpster, making very quiet noises as he tried to take in all the scents. The sound had caught Deputy Smith's attention and he was looking for the source of the noise with a frown.

"I guess…I thought I saw something there." I gave a nervous laugh, trying to play it off. "Nerves maybe."

Donavon continued to scrutinize me but I'd gotten the deputy's attention off of Ramble.

After giving me an odd look, the sheriff glanced briefly

between me and the dumpster. "The body's been moved to the morgue, but I thought you might want to see where she was found."

"Do you know anything about the victim?" I asked.

The sheriff shot a look at Donavon. When the werewolf didn't stop him, he slowly said, "A little. Her name was Sadie Greene and she worked here at the gas station for the past three years. She was a local—graduated from the town high school, moved away for a bit, then came back and took jobs here and there for a few years until she stuck with this job. Mid-thirties, no kids. Mostly a loner from my understanding." He shook his head. "Not much to go on. To tell you the truth, if she hadn't had bite marks on her body, I wouldn't have put her in the same category as the other victims."

Donavon raised an eyebrow. "What makes you say that?"

"Well, other than the fact that this is the first female victim, whoever killed her made this a lot more personal. The other three victims died quickly and were almost clean kills. Sure they were bitten up a little, but they mostly died from broken necks or a ripped out throat. This… this was something else. This woman suffered massive blood loss and stayed alive long enough to be dragged from inside. And her body was…almost mangled."

It was a very accurate description for the ghost I'd just seen.

Ramble left the dumpster and went back around to the front of the store. I followed him when the sheriff stopped talking. The hellhound had slipped inside the gas station again and was staring at a black spot on the tile when I found him.

He looked at me and gave a very low growl before the others caught up to us. He obviously wanted me to take a closer look.

I did my best not to step in any blood and found myself

standing beside Ramble, looking at a spot on the floor that definitely looked like a scorch mark. It was about two feet around but wasn't quite a perfect circle. The tile in the middle of the circle was blackened, melted, and warped.

Something had landed here and been hot enough to burn through tile. I glanced around. There were sprinklers on the ceiling, but nothing was wet. Maybe this wasn't related to the murder?

Donavon stepped up beside me and took a few sniffs in through his nose.

"Witches," his tone was low enough that only I could hear him (and Ramble of course). He glanced at me. "The dumpster smelled a little of witch as well when he opened it."

"You think the killer is a witch?" I kept my voice low, too.

"I'm not sure about the killer. But the victim, Sadie Green, was definitely a witch." The full weight of his gaze fell on me. "And the coven is not going to be happy when they find out one of their own has been murdered."

Chapter 8

We left the sheriff and his deputy waiting for a clean up crew and kept it to ourselves that we thought the victim was a witch. Donavon made several phone calls on the short drive back to the motel but couldn't seem to get anyone to answer. He pulled up outside my motel room and I started to get out.

"Wait."

Uh oh. Was I about to get a good night kiss? Unfortunately, the crime scene and seeing the dead woman—the dead witch—had killed the mood. That and having been given time to think between now and our little bathroom moment earlier, I didn't feel that now would be a great time to hop in the sack with Donavon.

"What did you see back there?" He asked instead.

Oh. Apparently we were just going to forget about what had happened between us earlier. Why was I disappointed if I didn't want anything to happen? *Get it together, Vi!*

"I saw the victim—Sadie Greene. Or her body at least. She was really mangled when they tossed her in the dumpster."

"It could be that the killer had a more difficult time murdering the witch."

I nodded. "Might explain the melted spot on the floor.

Maybe she tried to magic it or something?"

This earned me a faintly amused look. "Magic it?"

I flushed a little. "What am I supposed to say?"

"Cast a spell, maybe?" Donavon suggested.

"Whatever. You get my point. Maybe that's why she lived longer and the killer got mad and resorted to more violence?"

"Could be," Donavon agreed, "or it could have been a more passionate crime. Maybe the killer knew the victim this time. It's possible that the killer is also a witch. It would explain how they were able to take down one of my wolves."

I opened my mouth to add something else and a thought suddenly popped into my head. "Oh."

"What?"

"I forgot. The man in the field—

"Kleinman."

"Yeah, Kleinman. Just before he was attacked, he said, 'No. I'm Sorry.'"

Instead of getting angry that I'd forgotten to tell him (Jax would have been pissed at the omission), Donavon looked thoughtful.

"So we know at least one of the victims, Kleinman, knew the killer. Maybe Sadie Greene did too. Which means there's a good possibility that Sam and the first victim, Tony Duluth, knew the killer, too."

He sighed, suddenly sounding tired. I was right there with him. Sensing this was the end of the conversation, I popped the door open.

"We'll need to talk to the coven tomorrow," Donavon said as I got out and let Ramble out too. "I'll pick you up at eight."

I leaned down to look at him through the open car door. "I thought you had to get permission from the Alpha to introduce me to the witches?"

He grinned. "I am the Alpha," his smile ratcheted up another notch as he enjoyed my surprised expression, "and I give you permission to meet the coven and stay in Ricketts long enough to help find the killer. See you at eight."

I closed the door and he drove off, leaving me wondering how I'd managed to almost have sex with an Alpha werewolf.

"Go big or go home, I guess," I said to Ramble.

Back inside, the room was almost stiflingly hot. I'd left the heater going full blast when we left for the crime scene. Ramble seemed to enjoy it though. He climbed onto the bed, made a show up turning around in tight circles, then flopped down right in the middle with a sigh.

"Don't get comfortable," I warned him. "You're gonna have to share that bed you know."

He pretended not to hear.

* * *

I was back at the long dinner table again. I looked down at myself. Yep. Completely underdressed again. That's me.

For some reason it didn't bother me like it had before. Maybe the difference was because I knew that this was a dream this time around. I felt more awake and could see more details this time, too.

Another difference was that I was no longer alone at my end of the table.

On my right sat Constancia looking just as she had when I'd last seen her. Though she appeared to be in her late sixties, I knew that's when she had become a vampire and her human body had stopped aging. I was sure she was much, much older than that. She wore a silky red dress that dared you not to look at her cleavage.

I managed to avoid looking into her scary, bottomless-void eyes. It was too easy to become ensnared by the vampire magic that could drop me into a paralyzed hypnosis. I carefully kept my gaze just at her jawline.

"Hello, Vânători."

I dipped my head. "Constancia. I see you've decided to join in my nightmare."

Her expression changed but I could only see that the smile had slipped from her face since I was focused on not looking in her eyes. I felt rather than saw her attention flick to the other end of the table where a shadowy figure sat. Invisible waves of nightmare terror emanated from the figure in great pulses.

I didn't have to see him clearly to know who it was.

Morvalden.

Constancia's voice dropped to a whisper, "He's going to find you soon, dearie. I hope you're getting stronger and are ready to fight!" She was trying to sound eager, but there was also an underlying tremor of fear.

Though I was afraid of Morvalden even here in my dreams, I found it difficult to drum up any fear of Constancia. It made me brave enough to boldly ask, "You're scared of him, aren't you?"

Her hand shot out and clamped down on my wrist. I tried to pull back but she was much too strong for me. Her nails pierced the skin around my wrist, making it bleed.

My gaze slid from her jawline and caught in her eyes before I could stop myself. Her expression was one of surprised horror.

"You're not strong anymore, Vânători." Panic tinged her voice. "Use the necklace or he'll swallow the world!"

As she spoke, drops of blood dripped from my wrist down to the white napkin on the table. The moment the first drop touched, a high-pitched screech came from the other end of the table.

109

The shadow man stood up as he screeched and started in our direction. He was coming to get me!

I tried to shove away from Constancia but she had a vice-like grip on my wrist.

"You're going to lose against him, Vânători," her tone was soft. It was as if she was coming to a horrific realization as she spoke. "You're going to lose... and then he'll punish me."

Her eyes darted around until they stopped and landed back on me. "Unless...unless I give you to him." Her grip increased to the point that I thought she would snap my wrist in two.

I cried out and felt a sudden flicker of pain in my shoulder. It came again...

I jerked up in bed. My shoulder felt like it'd been pricked twice by a needle but it was my wrist that drew my attention. It felt like it was on fire. I managed to get the light on and looked down. Five crescent shaped wounds sluggishly bled onto the sheets. I could already see the outline of a bruise there, too.

Ramble whined beside my shoulder. I realized he must have bitten me to wake me up. That's what the pinpricks had been.

Like a Freddy-Krueger nightmare come to life, the vampires were somehow reaching me through my dreams—only this time, they were able to physically hurt me.

* * *

When I stepped outside before eight the next morning, I spotted a black cat on the sidewalk just outside the front office. It seemed unlikely that it was the same one from the second hand store the other day. Then again, a cat could easily walk from the store to the motel.

110

It watched me as I went to the front office for the free breakfast which turned out to be a cup of yogurt, a piece of aging fruit, and a cup of weak coffee. Free was free, though. I'd take what I could get. I got an extra cup of yogurt for Ramble.

The cat was still outside when I left the office. It stared at me as I walked past it to go back to my room, completely unafraid.

Ramble greeted me at the door, ready for his breakfast. He'd been throwing me disgusted looks after I took a longer shower than usual and then took the time to braid my hair. I wasn't primping, exactly, but why not look my best when working with a very hot Alpha werewolf?

Ramble was even more disgusted when all I had to offer him was a cup of yogurt. He ate it anyway, licking it directly from the cup while holding it still with his front paws.

"Did you see the cat outside?" I asked. Look at me having a perfectly normal conversation with my invisible hellhound. I picked at the bandage I'd put over the cut in my wrist. I hadn't gotten any sleep after that nightmare and had just stayed up watching crappy early morning TV. "I think it's the same cat from yesterday. Remember? The one at the clothing store?"

Ramble licked yogurt off the tip of his nose and, leaving the half-eaten cup on the floor, put his front paws on the windowsill. He nosed aside the curtain and looked out for a second before looking back at me with a questioning expression.

Curious, I joined him at the window.

The cat was gone.

A shiver went through me for no reason. *It's just a cat,* I told myself. The whole killer-on-the-loose thing was getting to

111

me. I needed to stop jumping at shadows.

We finished our breakfast and hung out until I heard the light honk of a horn. A quick check told me it was Donavon. I left the gun in the motel room but took my small throwing knife. I was pretty terrible with it but having it made me feel better.

I let Ramble into the car and plopped down on the heated leather seats.

"Morning," I said.

He handed me a cup of coffee and tossed a greasy bag into the back seat with Ramble.

"Oh, man. You might be my new hero." I took a tentative sip. "The stuff at the motel is terrible." I glanced in the back. Ramble tore open the bag and gleefully found unwrapped breakfast sandwiches.

"I know. My brother owns it."

Well damn. Open mouth, insert foot.

I started to apologize but he waved it away. "No offense taken. *I* don't even drink the coffee he makes."

Instead of driving to the second-hand clothing store as I expected, we drove through town then caught a small side road. The houses here were smaller but well-maintained and set back from the road so that they each had a large front yard. I thought we might not be far away from the address with the burned down house.

"A representative from the coven finally phoned last night," Donavon explained as we drove. "We're meeting a few of them today. I was told they might be able to give us some information about the last victim, Sadie Greene."

"Sounds good."

A few minutes later, we found street parking in front of

a light blue house. I got out and pulled the door open for Ramble but he refused to get out.

"What's wrong?" Donavon asked, waiting on the sidewalk.

"It looks like Ramble's gonna sit this one out." I closed the door and joined Donavon.

"Probably a good idea. I've heard some witches have taken hellhounds as familiars in the past." He shrugged. "Maybe your hellhound is afraid of getting leashed again."

"Familiars?" I repeated. "Like black cats and stuff?" My mind immediately thought of the cat I'd seen twice now. Surely I was reading too much into it though. There were probably dozens of stray cats wandering around town. Just because I'd seen a few that looked alike and seemed to be watching me, didn't mean it was some sort of plot, did it?

Sure it doesn't, Vianne.

There were a few ceramic garden gnomes watching over dormant flower gardens in the front yard. Near the front door, a hoop of plastic covered some other plants. I stole a glance through it and thought I recognized peppermint. The plastic was keeping what must be year-round herbs alive in the winter cold.

We reached the front door before Donavon could answer my question about familiars. He shrugged instead and knocked twice. As we waited, I glanced back and felt a jolt. Sitting calmly just to the rear of Donavon's car was another black cat. It was staring at us. I started to point to the cat but was interrupted.

"Just a moment," a pleasant voice said from the other side of the door. There was the sound of a lock being disengaged and then the door opened on the woman I recognized from the second-hand clothing shop.

Well damn. So she had *been a witch after all.*

Her eyes were red-rimmed and puffy as if she'd been crying recently.

"Hello there. Please, come in." She ushered us inside, closed the door, then led us down a short hallway to a dining room table in the kitchen. Two other women sat at the table, each holding a mug of tea. In the middle of the table was a ceramic napkin holder in the shape of a witch's black hat. Someone had a sense of humor.

One of the women at the table had brassy red hair and tear-streaked make-up. She clutched a tissue in one hand and a mug of tea with the other. It looked like she might lapse back into tears at any second.

The other woman had long, straight, jet black hair. She glared at us as we entered the kitchen.

"Can I get you something? Tea? Water?" Our hostess offered.

Donavon and I declined so she skipped straight to making brief introductions. She gestured to the red-haired woman. "This is Cassandra." Cassandra gave us a watery smile as our host next gestured toward the angry woman at the table. "And this is Willomena." Willomena continued her death glare. I started to wonder if she ever blinked. Maybe that was her magical power?

The woman then gestured to herself. "And I'm Rosalyn Chambers, the leader of our little coven."

So not only was she a witch, she was literally the exact witch I was looking for. I was seriously annoyed that I hadn't known who she was the day before. Maybe I could have avoided getting entangled in this whole investigation thing.

I brushed away my annoyance and forced a smile. "We met

yesterday. At your store. The jacket and boots were perfect for yesterday's weather, by the way." I stuck out my hand. "I'm Vianne."

I'd decided to go with my real first name but left off the last name just in case there was some bad blood between the witches and the Vânători line.

Rosalyn looked down at my hand a little surprised. "Oh, I'm sorry dear. We don't shake hands. Sometimes we see a bit more than we should otherwise."

I think this was supposed to make sense, so I pretended that it did and hastily dropped my hand. "And this is Donavon."

"Oh, yes. I know Donavon. Been around for some time, haven't you dear? Hard not to run into each other in such a small town."

Donavon gave a tight smile in agreement.

My time in jail had made me sensitive to the overall feel of a room. So, though Rosalyn was friendly enough and Donavon seemed to be on his best behavior, I still sensed a bit of tension. When things suddenly got tense in jail, you found another place to be. Unfortunately, that wasn't an option here.

"Please, have a seat." Rosalyn gestured to the two empty chairs as she settled into one next to the angry Willomena. "We'd like to hear about what happened to our sister, Sadie Greene."

I took the "sister" part to mean more that Sadie was part of the coven than that she was their actual sister by blood. If Rosalyn was the coven's leader, did that mean she was the most powerful witch here? Much like with the werewolves, I had no idea how a witch's coven was organized.

Donavon followed her request and sat beside Rosalyn. I took the chair between the werewolf and Cassandra.

This was Donavon's show so I let him take the lead.

"We're very sorry for your loss, but we also want to find out who it was that killed Ms. Greene. I also lost a brother—Samuel Vance— to this same killer. Anything you can tell us about Sadie might be helpful in catching him."

"What do you want to know?" Willomena asked in a haughty tone.

"Did Sadie have any enemies?" Donavon asked. "Or anyone she might have angered recently? Or—forgive me for putting it so bluntly—perhaps a jilted lover or ex who might want her dead?"

At the last question, Cassandra burst into tears.

"That was tactful," Willomena spat. "Cassandra was Sadie's girlfriend." She reached out to comfort Cassandra, and her expression softened for the other witch.

Donavon raised his hands. "I'm very sorry, Cassandra. I didn't mean to imply—

Before he could get any further, the dark-haired witch cut him off. "What? That she offed her own girlfriend? That she tore her to shreds and left her in a dumpster? We could almost *feel* it." She snarled in answer to my questioning expression. "We sensed what that *monster* did to her body. If you had any sense, you would be looking at your own people, *Alpha*."

"Willomena," Rosalyn's voice was as crisp as the air outside. The dark haired woman stared at her leader with unbridled anger for at least a minute before finally dropping her eyes.

Rosalyn lifted her hard gaze from the other witch. "My apologies. We are all upset at the loss of our sister in such a violent way." The coven's leader had bags under her eyes and seemed strained. I believed her when she said that she was upset at Sadie Green's death.

"I understand." Donavon swallowed and I caught the emotion in his voice as he said, "Samuel Vance was like real family to me. I want to catch his killer," here his eyes flecked with white, "and make them pay."

I saw the same note of revenge flicker in Willomena's eyes but she stayed silent, one arm comfortingly wrapped around the sobbing Cassandra.

"Please, Cassandra. Anything you could tell us about Sadie might be helpful." Forgetting what Rosalyn had told me earlier about not touching, I laid my hand over the witch's and squeezed gently to lend comfort. She immediately gasped. Her eyes widened as she stared at me, then her focus seemed to go distant, as if she were looking right through me.

"Vânători!" She spluttered, then in a monotone almost hypnotic voice, she said, "The magic of the Vânători line runs thin in you. It will not be enough."

Willomena jerked Cassandra's hand out from under mine. The red head's eyes immediately snapped back into focus. She stared at me with a look of wonder. "You're a Vânători?"

I nodded, not sure what to say other than, "I'm sorry. I forgot not to touch—"

It seemed that I'd inadvertently been the one to push the tension in the room to an explosive snap. Whoops.

"Get out!" Willomena snapped. Light coalesced around her, like an aura, but it was there and gone before I could blink. "Your kind is worse than the flea-bitten werewolf."

Both Donavon and I started to rise, but Rosalyn smacked her teacup down on the table with a clap that echoed through the room with unnatural volume. We froze, halfway standing.

"This is *my* house, Willomena. You will *not* kick guests out of *my home.*" I was suddenly very happy that it was Willomena on the receiving end of that hard glare. I might have melted into the floor if it were me. "If you are having such a difficult time remaining civil in their presence, then *you* may take your leave."

For her part, Willomena met Rosalyn's glare for much longer than I could have. Finally she dropped her eyes. At the same time, she extricated herself from Cassandra and shoved her chair back so hard that it toppled over.

"Consorting and pandering to vermin and murderers is disgusting, Rosalyn. It's beneath us." She looked like she wanted to say more, but something in Rosalyn's face made her decide against it and instead she swept out of the room.

I had to admit I was a little disappointed that she didn't hop on a broom and fly out the window or something. I guess not all myths are true.

There was a moment of silence but at least most of the tension had left the room with the angry Willomena.

"I'm really sorry." I said, looking first at Cassandra, then Rosalyn. "Perhaps we should go." Since I was still half out of my chair, I stood up all the way. Beside me Donavon did the same.

"No, please." Surprisingly it was Cassandra who stopped us. "If you're a Vânători, maybe you really can help us? You're working with the werewolves, right?" She sniffed and gestured to Donavon.

I nodded. Donavon and I retook our seats. Rosalyn flicked a hand at the chair Willomena had knocked over and it righted itself before sliding neatly back under the table. There was a noticeable difference without the third witch in the room glaring at us. Maybe that's what let Cassandra open up a little.

"I'm not sure what I'll be able to tell you that's useful." She sniffed again but made a visible effort to compose herself.

"Don't worry. Anything you can tell us will be more than what we have to go on now."

It was Rosalyn who spoke next. "Sadie was the coven's Evocatorem." This only earned the older witch puzzled looks from Donavon and myself. At least I wasn't the only one left in the dark about witches.

"That's like a recruiter for a coven," Rosalyn explained. "Sadie was very good at identifying people with the gift. Her job was to approach them, explain their abilities, and offer training."

I wondered if that "training" cost money or if the witches just provided it out of the goodness of their hearts. It didn't seem like an appropriate question though so I kept it to myself.

Donavon's line of thinking was much more relevant than mine. "Is it possible that she might have offended someone she approached as a recruiter? Maybe made an enemy that way?"

Cassandra shook her head as she dabbed at her eyes with the tissue. "Sadie was really good at talking to people. She was an empath—that's why she was so good at being able to tell when people had some magical ability. She could *feel* it in them."

"Would she have been able to feel it if someone wanted to wish her harm?" I asked.

"Oh yes," The red-headed witch said but didn't elaborate.

"Did she ever talk to you about anyone like that?" I continued. "Someone who might have wished her harm?"

Cassandra's face turned to an expression of faint puzzlement and she looked at Rosalyn as if for help.

"What you must understand, Vianne," the older witch said,

taking over, "is that witches aren't usually well received by the public. We are lucky that we live in America and don't have to keep it a secret that we are Wiccans. Unfortunately, not everyone embraces a 'live and let live' attitude. There are many people in this town who wholeheartedly agree with 'Thou shalt not suffer a witch to live.'"

"Oh." I wasn't sure what else to say to that. Especially since the only hunter I knew lived by that motto but on a much larger scale and didn't think he should let *any* supernatural creatures live.

Rosalyn saved us from another awkward silence. "Sadie had the unfortunate gift of sensing the feelings of others—even when those feelings were of hatred for what she was."

"That's...pretty terrible. I'm sorry."

It was Cassandra who answered with a watery smile. "Don't be—Sadie liked who she was. Being an empath wasn't always a walk in the park, but she felt like she was making a difference. Helping witches find a place that understood them and let them be themselves." As she discussed her murdered girlfriend, Cassandra's eyes filled with tears and her voice took on an emotional hitch. She pressed the tissue between her mouth and nose in an effort to maintain her composure.

Donavon ignored the woman's emotions. "But there isn't anyone who might have been particularly hateful toward Sadie for being a witch or maybe someone who stood out as being offended that Sadie pointed out a gift they had?"

"Well..." Cassandra lifted the tissue away from her face. "I guess...there's always Miss Gladstone. She was pretty awful to Sadie for being both a witch *and* openly gay."

Donavon didn't look surprised. He quickly explained to me, "Miss Gladstone is the organist for the local Catholic church.

Though Father Beckett is the open-armed, welcoming kind, Miss Gladstone could stop you in your tracks with just a stare at fifty yards."

"I don't think she's the type to go around murdering people," Rosalyn added.

"No. Me neither," Donavon agreed. "Anyone else, Cassandra?"

She shook her head, the tissue once again clutched to her face. Silent tears coursed down her cheeks. I didn't think we were going to get any more out of her right then.

"That's okay, Cassandra," I heard myself say, ignoring Donavon's look. He clearly didn't want to leave yet and, as much as I wanted to push Cassandra for more information, it didn't seem right when she'd just lost her girlfriend to such a violent death.

I did have another question that could be relevant but which I was also genuinely curious about.

"Rosalyn, did you have another house that burned down not long ago?"

Donavon gave me a look that suggested he wanted to know where I was going with this.

"Yes," the coven leader said. "I luckily wasn't home at the time and the insurance payout was enough to put toward this home." She waved a hand in the air to indicate the house we now sat in. "I don't believe that's connected to this, though," she continued. "That had more to do with coven matters. If this was someone specifically targeting my coven, then why start with humans and a werewolf before attacking one of my witches?"

"I'm not sure. It was just a thought."

I really wanted to ask her about the Artemis necklace, but

it wasn't the right time with Donavon sitting right there. No reason to let him know that I wasn't the powerful Vânători everyone thought I was.

I reached out and plucked a napkin from the holder in the center of the table. "If you think of anything else that might be helpful, please call me." Pulling a pen from my purse, I wrote down my cell number and slid it across the table to the crying woman.

Standing, I shot Donavon a look that I hoped translated to "Let's go" then gave a wane smile to Rosalyn.

"Thank you for inviting us, Rosalyn. We appreciate the information."

Donavon led the way to the door and we were almost there when Rosalyn stopped us.

"Oh, let me give you this." She handed me a business card. The front said "Second Chances, LLC." It wasn't heavily decorated, but it was still nicer than the napkin I'd written *my* number on.

"Donavon has my number, but it might be good for you to have it, too." She gave me a warm smile. "If you think of any questions, or need any *other* information, don't hesitate to call me."

I caught the subtle emphasis she lent to the word "other." Hmm. Did she know that I needed information about the necklace? If so, how in the hell did she know? Could she read minds or something?

A dark shadow crossed her face and it took me a second to realize it wasn't directed toward me.

"I want this son-of-a-bitch caught, too," she bit out.

We all knew that there was more to that statement. She wanted the killer caught before they could strike again.

Chapter 9

"We shouldn't have left without getting more information," Donavon complained the moment we were back inside his car where the witches couldn't hear us. "We have even less information now than when we started."

I started to roll my eyes, but thought better of it. The werewolf was actually pretty pissed. No reason to egg him on or downplay his anger. Instead I went for tact.

"She wasn't going to tell us anything else useful today." I swiveled around to the backseat and felt better when I saw Ramble half-dozing where we'd left him. I'd been a little worried about leaving him by himself after seeing the black cat hanging around the car.

The hellhound seemed fine, though. He'd managed to drool all over the leather seats, but since Donavon couldn't see the hellhound, he probably wouldn't notice the drool until later.

I turned to face forward again. "That woman just lost someone she loved. She needs to have a day to cry. We can check back with her tomorrow and she'll probably have thought of something new that can help us."

He wrapped his hands around the steering wheel and squeezed. The plastic underneath the leather let out several alarming cracking noises. "Sitting around and crying about it isn't going to bring her back and it's definitely not going to stop the killer from murdering someone else."

"True." I thought for a moment. We didn't really have any other leads to go on, especially if he and Rosalyn had dismissed the possibility of Gladstone, the church-lady, being the killer. I'd been toying with an idea since early this morning, when I'd been too scared to go back to sleep for fear of having another dream.

"How about we visit Samuel's apartment?"

Donavon's head whipped around to stare at me like he thought I was playing a cruel joke or something. I quickly explained my thinking.

"I can see ghosts, remember? Maybe I'll see something in the parking lot where he was killed." Donavon didn't look thrilled by this idea, so I added, "If you don't want to go, you can give me the address and drop me back off at the motel."

He shook his head and faced forward again, turning the key in the ignition. "No. I'll take you." His voice was gruff and we lapsed into silence during the drive.

The silence let me think about the black cat (or cats) I kept seeing around town. Was it really just one cat stalking me? Or was it actually a few cats and, because I was getting the heebie-jeebies, I was just noticing them more? The cats couldn't be related to the murders, right? Whatever was killing all these people was certainly bigger than a cat. Then again, maybe the cat could turn into something else?

The other thing on my mind were the vampires. So far I knew there were both witches and werewolves in this town, but what other supernatural beings called Ricketts home?

Before I could chicken out, I said, "So…there are werewolves and witches in this town. Are there any vampires?"

"Why do you ask?" Donavon's voice was carefully neutral.

"Well, if there was a vampire here, they could potentially be a suspect. They've got super strength. Could a vampire take out a werewolf?"

There was a long moment of silence during which Donavon pulled into a parking lot. Finally he said, "There is a vampire in town, but he's not the killer."

I opened my mouth to ask him how he knew that, but he cut me off, "Leave it alone." He killed the engine and pointed to a parking spot a few spaces over from us. "It happened over there. Apartment four. …I'll stay in the car. There'll be nothing new for me to smell anyways and my presence might keep any ghosts from coming out."

"Okay." I didn't argue. It was broad daylight and I felt pretty safe here. No reason to drag Donavon out to the spot where his friend had been killed. I got out of the car with Ramble on my heels.

The apartment complex was a one-story affair that looked like it might once have been a motel before it had been converted into apartments. The building itself was made of brick and had definitely seen better days. Similar to the motel I was in now, the parking spaces lined up with the door of each apartment.

My breath misted in front of me as I walked over to the spot Donavon had pointed out. The local news had suggested there might be a snowstorm on the way later in the week. Great. All I needed was to get snowed into this town with a werewolf, a coven of witches, a vampire, and a murderer running around. I hadn't figured anything out about the necklace, either, so even if we found the killer, I'd have to hang back while Donavon or Ramble took care of it.

I pushed these thoughts from my mind. The spot Donavon had indicated didn't look any different from the rest of the parking lot. From the newspaper's account, Samuel had just gotten out of his car and had been heading toward his front door when he was attacked.

A glance told me that I was in front of the right apartment. A tarnished number four was screwed onto the apartment door. There wasn't a car in the parking space in front of the apartment though. I assumed law enforcement had impounded it or something.

Ramble strode lazily over, his nails, longer than the average canine, clicked loudly against the concrete with every step. He stopped at the spot and sniffed the ground. After the gas station crime scene, I'd expected a lot more blood. Here, however, I found nothing. Either the concrete had been cleaned after the police had finished their investigation or there hadn't been blood in the first place.

"Looks pretty clean, huh?" I murmured to the hellhound. He blew out a breath in disgust.

"Nothing?"

A regular dog would not have been able to shrug at me the way Ramble did then. I guess that meant he wasn't getting any scents.

There weren't any ghostly flickerings so far. I walked over to the apartment's front door and turned back around to face the parking lot. Nothing. After a good five minutes of waiting, I decided to pack it in. Even with my new jacket, the occasional gusty breeze was making me cold.

As an afterthought, I tried the door of the apartment and found it unlocked. Ramble, taking the lead, nudged the door open and trotted inside.

What the heck, I thought, *better check it out before Donavon decides to stop me.*

I pushed the door the rest of the way open and blinked, adjusting my eyes to the dark within. There was a lingering smell of stale cigarettes layered under the musty odor of a room left sealed for several days.

Flicking on the light switch, I found I was right. It looked almost exactly like my room at the motel, except that instead of a closet space to stow suitcases, there was a mini-kitchen area. The furniture even looked like it had been held onto and used long after the motel had been transformed into apartments.

Samuel Vance wasn't much of one for keeping things clean. "Bachelor pad" was the phrase that sprang to mind. A pile of dirty clothes cluttered the space between the bed and bathroom wall. A few beer cans graced the TV stand and the bed was unmade. The small table looked like it had been used as a computer desk, with a power cord still plugged in and the other end taped to the top of the desk. The computer was nowhere in sight.

Maybe the cops took that too? Seemed unlikely since they claimed Samuel had been killed by an animal. Didn't seem likely they'd be collecting evidence since they didn't suspect any kind of foul-play.

Ramble nosed around, disappearing into the bathroom then coming back out. He didn't try to get my attention or anything, so I guess there wasn't anything interesting in there. Outside, I heard a car door slam shut. Was Donavon coming to oust us from the apartment? I did a quick walk-thru but didn't spot any giant notes saying, "This is a clue!"

Sighing, I turned to walk back outside and stopped. On the

other side of the TV were two small picture frames propped on the TV stand.

"Huh. Look at this."

One was a picture of Samuel and Donavon, posing in front of a church. Both wore tuxedos and smiled at the camera. Hmm. Best man and groom? I hadn't seen a ring on Donavon's finger, so he must have been the best man?

Looking at the next picture only confirmed my guess. This one was a happy, just married kind of picture of a grinning bride with Samuel as the groom. It took me a second to recognize the bride since she was so out of context here.

It was Cheri, the waitress from the diner.

I stared at the picture until I felt another presence in the apartment. Donavon's large frame blocked the doorway. His eyes fell on the picture frame in my hands so I turned it toward him so he could see the photo.

"The waitress from the café and Samuel Vance are married?" I didn't wait for him to answer since it was pretty obvious from the photo that I was right. "She didn't seem too broken up about his death."

Donavon's brows drew down. Only then did I remember that Donavon had said Cheri was like a little sister to him. So much for tact.

"She would never hurt Sam." His voice was tight and controlled, like he was having a hard time keeping cool.

Great. Good job pissing off the werewolf, Vi.

I took another look around the apartment. There weren't any women's clothes or other feminine belongings laying around.

"Are they divorced or something?"

"Or something," Donavon said. "We should go. The police

probably wouldn't want us in here."

Suddenly I was annoyed. Here I'd been doing whatever I could to help figure out who the killer was and Donavon was withholding information from me. It felt like working with Jax all over again.

"That's a pretty flimsy excuse for wanting me out of here since the sheriff invited you to inspect a crime scene just last night," I barked. "Something tells me he wouldn't mind you looking around an apartment. Especially since Samuel Vance didn't die in here."

Donavon opened his mouth to answer, then closed it again. I wasn't sure if it was because he was too pissed to say anything or because he didn't know what to say.

"So how about you stop keeping shit from me and let me help you? Unless you don't actually want this killer caught?"

That did it. Donavon's eyes flashed white for a few seconds and his chest puffed out. I was ready for it though and it didn't affect me like it had the day before. Ramble, standing between us, let out a very light warning growl.

"I'm not keeping anything from you," Donavon snapped. "You just never asked."

What a lame excuse.

"Well, I'm asking now."

His eyes stayed white for another few seconds as he glared at me. I got that feeling again like I should turn tail and run. Ramble's growl got louder.

"Stop trying to intimidate me. You want to work with me? Then tell me what you know so I can actually help!"

For another heartbeat, Donavon and I continued our staring contest. Finally, he broke eye contact and looked away. He let his posture slump a little and leaned against the doorway.

"Sam and Cheri were married...but when he Turned, she...changed her mind. She didn't want him anymore." At my dubious look, he quickly explained, "It happens sometimes. Someone gets Turned and maybe they don't have the same feelings they did before." He shrugged. "Or they're such a different person that the spouse doesn't feel the same love from before."

I sank a hip against the TV stand to show I was listening.

Donavon blew out a sigh. "For Sam, it was the latter. He didn't really tell me everything, but once he was Turned, Cheri started treating him differently. He still loved her, but she just didn't feel the same way anymore, I guess. He moved out and started living here," he gestured at the sad apartment, "but they never made their divorce official. I think he thought she'd change her mind eventually and take him back."

So Samuel and Cheri had been separated for some time. Still, I would have thought that Cheri might be a little more sad at Samuel's murder. Thinking back to when I'd first gotten to the diner, before I'd managed to piss Cheri off by dining with Donavon, she'd been pretty chipper. Not exactly the emotional state I'd have expected for someone whose legal husband had been murdered.

Donavon accurately read my silence because he added, "She wouldn't have murdered Samuel. Besides, she's not a werewolf and she's definitely not big enough to throw Kleinman around."

I opened my mouth to argue, but he cut me off.

"She didn't do it, Vânători, so drop it." He spun around and stalked off, saying over his shoulder, "Come on. I have stuff to do today that doesn't involve you trying to point fingers at the wrong people."

I shook my head but followed. Donavon might be right. If Cheri wasn't a werewolf then she wouldn't have been strong enough to kill Samuel. I also couldn't imagine her dragging Sadie Green out to the dumpster, but I still had a bad feeling we were missing something about her. She had just seemed way too into Donavon and had been pretty jealous of me having dinner with him. Now that I knew she'd married his best friend, I felt like there was something even weirder going on.

Of course, it could just be that I didn't like the woman.

The ride back to my motel was even quieter than before. This time, when Donavon dropped me off, he did it without a word. As soon as Ramble was out of the car and I'd shut the door, the werewolf drove off.

"Well," I said to the hellhound, "that went about as well as expected, huh?" Turning to go into my room, I caught a flash of something black and furry out of the corner of my eye near the front office. When I turned my head though, nothing was there.

Ramble gave me an impatient look.

"Sorry...thought I saw something."

The hellhound huffed, standing pointedly in front of the door.

"Okay, okay." I unlocked the room and we went inside.

Apparently the maid had been in. The bed was made and I found fresh towels in the bathroom. I laid on the bed and stared up at the ceiling. Ramble climbed up beside me and laid down with his head on his big paws.

"So," I recapped, "it looks like our latest victim was a witch who recruited other witches for their coven. She was an empath, so she could feel other people's feelings. Her

131

girlfriend, Cassandra, said that Sadie didn't have any enemies that Cassandra knew of."

I sighed. It would have been so much easier if Cassandra had said, "I suddenly remembered that Sadie got a death threat from a man that could turn into a scary monster!" That would have made things much easier.

"All we know so far is that this thing is something intelligent enough to only attack when no one else is around and one of the victims seemed to know the killer. The witch might have known him, too, but we can't assume that just because her murder was more violent. Also, Donavon doesn't think the killer is a werewolf."

I looked over at the hellhound. One of his fangs stuck out beneath his lip. His teeth were certainly big enough to leave the same size holes in a person's body as I'd seen on Kleinman's ghost. Obviously, I knew that Ramble wasn't the killer, but...

"Ramble, are there other hellhounds out wandering around? I mean, could a hellhound have done this?

He rolled his eyes then lifted his head long enough to use one paw to tap his nose before giving a negative huff.

"Hmm. You think you would have smelled them at the crime scenes by now. True. We have one more murder site to check out but I think I'll wait until it's a little darker. We're not looking for clues that are visible in daylight. With any luck, maybe Tony Duluth will still be hanging out around his place of death."

Something dug uncomfortably into my hip. I stuck my hand in my pocket and fished out the business card Rosalyn had given me. "The witches number," I explained to Ramble when he whined his curiosity. I—oh."

I'd turned the card over and found a hastily written note on the back.

"Lunch, Flying Pie, 12:30," I read out loud. A glance at the digital clock on the nightstand told me I had about twenty minutes to figure out where the Flying Pie was and how to get there.

"Looks like we have a lunch date to get to," I told the hellhound.

Chapter 10

The Flying Pie turned out to be a mom and pop restaurant outside town close to the Interstate. Unlike the diner from the day before, the Flying Pie was a large farmhouse with a barn attached that had been converted into a restaurant. The parking lot was big enough to accommodate tractor-trailers and RVs as well as smaller vehicles. Smart thinking on the owner's part since it meant they could capture travelers who didn't want yet another bag of fast food for dinner.

Ramble decided to come with me, but I had a feeling it was only because there would be pie involved. According to the Flying Pie's website, they were famous for having over fifteen different kinds of pie available at all times of the day. You could even have a slice of pie for breakfast.

I'm not gonna lie—I was pretty excited about the pie as well.

We pulled into the half-full parking lot and found a spot. Before getting out, I turned to Ramble. "Are you sure you want to come in? I didn't get the feeling Rosalyn would be the kind of witch who would try to turn you into a familiar, but I've only met her once, so who knows."

He stood up and licked his lips. I took that to mean that he was willing to risk it if pie was involved.

"Alright. But if you get a bad feeling, get out of there and wait for me by the car."

He blew out a sigh as if he was a teenager and I'd just asked him to obey curfew.

"Fine. Let's go Mister Huffy-Pants."

Inside, Ramble and I found ourselves in a small foyer plastered with pictures of pie. If my mouth wasn't watering before, it was now. A wooden podium with a "Please wait to be seated sign" stood in the foyer. Behind the podium was a middle-aged man who greeted us with a smile.

"Hello!" The man cheerfully greeted us. Or rather, greeted me, since he couldn't see Ramble. Over the right pocket of his button-up shirt was a worn out pin that said, "Try the Flying Pie!" Below that were several smaller pins which each featured a different kind of pie.

"Dining solo today?" His tone was pleasant and didn't suggest that he felt sorry for someone dining alone.

"Um, actually, I'm meeting someone." I had expected to be able to see Rosalyn from the front of the restaurant, but since the dining room was hidden from the foyer, I fumbled to explain. "Uh, I'm not sure if she's here yet. She's a little taller than me with silver glasses—'"

"Ah, you're eating with Rosalyn, right?"

I smiled, thankful that I didn't need to fumble through any further attempts at a description of the witch. "Yes. Exactly."

"Right this way."

He led us through a door, but instead of veering into what had once been a living room and now seemed to be the main dining room, he made a left and we went up a flight of creaky stairs.

"This is your first time here, right?" He asked, glancing back at me.

"Um, yeah." I was a little distracted because, though he was trying to be quiet, Ramble was making a little too much noise going up the stairs. Since the hellhound was behind me, the squeaking of the stairs noticeably continued a few seconds after the host and I had reached the landing. He looked behind us with a frown, but thankfully pushed on, continuing a conversation that seemed fairly scripted on his end.

"So glad to have a new customer! The Flying Pie is famous for our fifteen different varieties of pie! These are my favorites!" He tapped the buttons fastened to his shirt. "But don't worry—we don't expect you to try all of them on the first visit!"

He threw a canned smile at me over his shoulder and led me down a short hallway and into a small room that barely had space for the three round tables within. Two of the tables were empty and Rosalyn occupied the third one, sitting with her back to the wall. She was sipping tea when we entered the room and quickly set her cup down.

"Rosalyn, here's your lunch partner." He smiled, clearly familiar and friendly with the witch.

"Thank you, Mitchell."

The host, Mitchell, turned his attention back to me. "Can I get you something to drink?"

"Just a glass of water, please."

He smiled and strode off. I was glad that he didn't want to explain all fifteen different flavors of pie. He seemed nice but was a little over the top.

"I'm sorry I'm late," I apologized, slipping off my jacket and draping it over an empty chair. "I didn't see your...invitation until a few minutes ago." Ramble sank down a little to the left and behind my chair.

The witch waved away my apology with a smile. "Not a problem. I'm sorry for the cloak and dagger. I got the feeling earlier that you wanted to talk to me more privately."

My eyebrows shot to my forehead. "You did?"

She laughed a little at my response then put out a hand. "I'm sorry. I'm not laughing at you. I forget that you're maybe not as…experienced as the Vânători myths would have us believe."

"Is it that obvious?" I asked, a little chagrined. Had I made a complete ass of myself at our meeting earlier?

"Don't worry. It's actually a little bit of a relief that you're not some great mythic hero, emerging from the shadows to slay all the evil supernatural beings."

My eyebrows somehow managed to climb still higher while I struggled between feelings of offense or chagrin that I wasn't living up to the expectations of being a Vânători.

"Not that we actually expected you to smite all those before you just by looking at them. Or to breathe gouts of fire at your enemies." She smiled and I decided that I wouldn't be offended or feel embarrassed. …Or mention that the hellhound behind me *could* breathe fire.

"Those are some pretty high expectations to live up to," I said, finally finding my voice. I didn't get a chance to say anything else though because Mitchell returned with my water.

"Here you are. Had a chance to look over the menu yet?"

I opened my mouth to tell him no, but Rosalyn beat me to the punch. "I'll have the grilled cheese sandwich and half-salad, please." The witch's eyes fell on me in a half-squint for the briefest second. "And Vianne wants the half and half

137

combo with a turkey sandwich and a cup of broccoli cheddar soup. We'll both be saving room for dessert, of course."

"Of course," Mitchell echoed, not at all put off that Rosalyn had just ordered for me and pointedly ignoring my half-opened mouth stare at the witch. He disappeared leaving us to ourselves once again.

"How'd you know I wanted soup?" Though I hadn't seen the menu, I had been thinking on the drive over that I wanted something hot and filling but had been torn because I also wanted to save room (and money) for pie.

"It's one of my gifts."

"Being able to order the perfect meal?"

She laughed. "No. Though that would be an interesting gift, it would not be quite as useful as the one I was born with. No, I have the gift of understanding what people want."

"Oh."

"Which is why I invited you to lunch. I felt that you wanted to meet with me alone." She took a sip of her tea, allowing me to digest her words.

"Yes... I did—do want to speak with you." I quickly amended. But I wavered. Now that I had the witch to myself, I wasn't so sure this was a good idea. Would it really be smart to tell her that I couldn't access the Vânători abilities that the necklace was supposed to give me? If I told her about the necklace not working, what would keep her from hexing me or whatever?

The problem was that the only other person I could ask was Lady Moira and I not only didn't have a way to contact her, but Jax had suggested that getting help from a witch more than once would be a bad idea.

It was time to suck it up and trust this witch.

I took a deep breath. "I wanted to meet with you today

because I need some help and it was recommended that I speak specifically with you." I'd decided to leave Jax's name out of this just in case there was any bad blood between him and the coven.

She nodded, indicating that I should keep talking.

"I, well… I seem to be having difficulty using the Vânători magic, or gift, or whatever." I was also having difficulty even talking about the problem. My face grew red and I fought to keep pushing through to explain the issue. It felt like I was revealing a dark, embarrassing secret.

Rosalyn leaned forward and gave me an encouraging smile. "Can you explain a little more?"

I reached below the collar of my shirt and pulled the necklace out where she could see it. Her eyebrows ticked up as she gazed at the circular pendant. To me, it looked like an ancient Asian coin since it had a hole cut right through the middle of it.

"This is the Artemis necklace. It's supposed to give me, I dunno, some kind of magical ability to be a better hunter," I struggled to explain since I didn't truly understand the whole "magic" thing in the first place.

"Ah," Rosalyn breathed, examining the pendant from a distance. "So with the necklace, the wearer takes on the magical abilities."

"Yes, but apparently only if you're of the Vânători bloodline," I hastened to explain.

"Hmm. Has it ever worked for you?"

I took a breath to explain the whole story of how I'd gotten the Artemis necklace, but at that moment, Mitchell walked back in the room, laden down with our food. He leaned over the table to set down the plates, caught sight of my necklace and sucked in a sharp breath.

"Vânători!" Mitchell's tone was filled with the disgust of someone who had just spotted a rat in the kitchen.

He immediately leapt backward to put his back against the wall, dropping the plates and hot soup to the floor with a crash. He stared daggers at me as he reached down and ripped off his Flying Pie button—

—and morphed into a ginormous, green, fur-covered creature.

This new Mitchell-Creature was almost twice as wide and had grown to three times Mitchell's height, forcing him to bend almost in two in order to avoid smashing into the ceiling—which put his face only about a foot from mine.

Now I was staring into swamp green pupils with only the tiniest bit of white at the edges.

"Vwanathori!!" He bellowed with rage through teeth that stuck out from his lips at awkward angles and apparently made it difficult for him to talk.

I didn't need a translation.

Before I could react, Rosalyn waved her hands in an odd, complicated move that finished with her bringing a finger to her mouth in a shushing gesture. My ears popped and I got the distinct feeling that I was now in a bubble.

"Mitchell! Stop it!" Rosalyn yelled at the giant. To me, the witch said, "It's okay—I've deadened the sound so no one downstairs can hear us!"

"What?" Who the hell would come and save us now if they couldn't hear us?

The Mitchell-Monster didn't seem too keen on listening to Rosalyn. It kept its green-eyed glare on me and took a step forward, swinging a fist. I jerked back and scrambled out of my chair just as the monster dropped its meaty hand through the chair I'd just vacated. The poor chair didn't stand a chance. It splintered and pieces went flying everywhere.

I shielded my face against flying pieces of wood while retreating quickly to the hallway with Ramble beside me. Apparently he also thought that it was in our best interest to run instead of fighting this thing. While retreating, I stuffed the necklace back under my shirt and out of sight.

"What the hell is that thing?!" I yelled.

"He's a troll—but he's friendly!" Rosalyn shouted.

"Friendly!?" I screamed as the troll picked up the table and threw the whole thing at me. I leapt out of the small room and into the hall where, luckily, I was able to duck behind the door frame. The table smashed into the frame and fell to the floor.

"How is that friendly?"

The troll now stood between Rosalyn and myself, effectively blocking her escape. I honestly half-expected her to whip out a wooden wand and shout a spell at him. Maybe I was putting too much stock in the fictional version of witches.

"Go out the window!" I shouted at the witch, thinking quickly. "I'll keep it distracted!"

The troll took two uneven strides toward me but Rosalyn shouted, "Mitchell, stop it this instant. Dammit. *STOP!*"

I felt the strange compulsion to stop what I was doing at the authority in Rosalyn's voice. The troll stopped too. He was breathing heavily and still had a murderous look in those green eyes.

Rosalyn picked her way around the broken pieces of chair and table so that she could stand between me and the troll. "You, sir, are interrupting a *business meeting* and making a fool of yourself *and* of your restaurant. If you wish to continue receiving the coven's business, you will change back at once."

I suddenly understood why Rosalyn was the leader of her coven. I sure as hell wouldn't want to mess with her.

Though she looked downright diminutive next to his ginormous frame, she clearly wasn't going to back down from the larger creature. The troll's shoulders slumped in defeat and Rosalyn shoved something at him. The troll reached over and, very carefully, plucked the thing from the witch's hand. In a blink, he was once again the cheerful man who had led me upstairs. Only naked now. And with a lot less cheer.

What the hell?

Mitchell glowered at me and flipped over the object in his hands. It was the worn Flying Pie pin.

I thought back to when he'd changed into the troll and how he'd ripped off the pin to be instantly transformed. Was the pin magic?

He gripped the pin in his fist and shook a finger at me. "She's a Vânători, Rosalyn. Vânători are *murderers* and worse than that." He spat on the floor. "You know what they did to my family in the Old World?"

Rosalyn's face was tight but her voice remained even as she responded, "I have heard stories, Mitchell. But I have also heard stories of what your people did to humans in the Old World. Specifically, to human children." She raised an eyebrow at the man-troll. "Are we going to start doling out punishments for sins from long ago?"

Mitchell's face turned red but he shook his head. "No."

"Good," she smiled and I was surprised that it was genuine, "because I would probably be punished most of all."

Crap. Did that mean I shouldn't trust Rosalyn with info

about the necklace or simply that someone in her family hadn't exactly been Glenda the Good Witch?

"Well," the witch sighed and surveyed the mess around her, "I suppose we'll be taking lunch elsewhere." She returned her attention to the man-troll. "We will still be having pie, Mitchell. Please wrap up a Flying Dutchman Chocolate Mousse pie to go."

He looked at the witch for a long second before finally moving off. He had to pass me to go downstairs and I immediately stepped out of the way so he could give me a wide berth. He glared at me the entire time and I thought I saw a fleck of green still lurking in his eyes.

When he was gone, Rosalyn picked her way over to me. "I would greatly appreciate it if we kept this little, ah, incident between us. Best not to trouble our furry friends, huh?"

I nodded, absently wondering if the werewolf Pack didn't know about the troll or if they knew and would just have a shit fit that Mitchell had gone into Hulk-Smash mode.

"Good. Let's wait downstairs, shall we? And bring your little friend, too. He did a marvelous job of staying out of the fight and not enraging Mitchell more. He definitely deserves some pie."

My friend? My eyes fell on Ramble. The hellhound was patiently waiting, sitting on his haunches in the corner. Great. So my secret hellhound weapon wasn't exactly a secret anymore.

I could swear he had a smile on his face at the prospect of pie.

Chapter 11

Rosalyn suggested we find a quieter venue to discuss the necklace, so Ramble and I retreated to the car then followed the witch in her SUV out to the edge of a small lake. It was too cold to sit outside on the picnic tables, so Rosalyn, Ramble, and I took refuge in her vehicle, which was much roomier than my stolen Taurus would have been with two people and a hellhound.

The pie turned out to be just as amazing as it sounded. After Mitchell's wife, who was also co-owner of the restaurant, heard about our fiasco with Mitchell-the-troll, Rosalyn ended up getting a whole pie for free. Though his wife gave me a dark look before we left, she did provide us with plastic utensils, napkins, and two cups of tea to-go.

Rosalyn handed out slices of pie, even placing a plate with two slices on the backseat for Ramble. We ate in companionable silence, watching the choppy lake's waves slap the shore. I was just scraping my plate clean with a fork, thinking how weird it was that I was eating pie with a witch after having been attacked by a troll when Rosalyn broke our silence.

"Before we start, I must tell you that seeking my advice isn't free."

"Oh." I hadn't expected that. "Um, I don't have a ton of money—"

The witch waved away the notion. "The coven is not in need of money. Instead, I ask that you promise to do everything in your power to find those responsible for Sadie's murder."

"I see."

"Is this an acceptable trade?" She asked.

I'd already promised Donavon that I'd do what I could to help him find the person or thing that had killed Samuel. Since the two murders seemed to have been perpetrated by the same killer, it only made sense to agree.

"Yes. Sounds acceptable."

Rosalyn stuck out her hand, which surprised me since she'd made it clear at her house that touching a witch was a no-no. She saw my hesitation and explained, "We'll shake on it to make it binding."

Binding. Oh goodie. That doesn't sound magical at all.

"Okay." I reached out and shook her hand. Just like in the restaurant, I felt my ears pop. Rosalyn dropped my hand and ignored my odd look.

"Tell me about the necklace, Vianne." She dabbed at the corners of her mouth with a napkin then took a careful sip of tea. "How did you get it? Forgive me for saying so, but you seem somewhat new to the supernatural."

I wiped a napkin across my mouth, giving myself time to recover from being "bound" to our agreement. "I definitely didn't grow up knowing about any of this. A little over a month ago a woman came into the pawnshop where I worked and sold the necklace. I didn't know it at the time, but she was actually a vampire named Constancia."

"Morvalden's…consort," Rosalyn added after a moment of

searching for the right description. She and Morvalden were lovers... or maybe husband and wife. It was a little confusing.

I nodded and realized I'd have to mention Jax to give the whole story.

"For reasons I don't yet understand, she wanted to get the Artemis necklace to me and was even working with a hunter, Jax, to make sure I received it. He's actually the one who suggested I look for you." It was easy to read Rosalyn's surprise that the anti-supernatural hunter would send me to a witch.

Omitting the fact that Jax had kept his collaboration with Constancia a secret from me, I explained how I'd gone from being a recovering alcoholic working a dead-end job at a pawn shop to learning that I came from a family who hunted the dead and other supernatural creatures. I made sure not to leave out any details about being forced to drink blood, releasing Ramble from being held captive by vampires, seeing ghosts, experiencing vivid dreams that helped me avoid getting killed, and finally getting my hands on the necklace.

"The first time I put on the necklace, I felt...powerful. And I didn't just *feel* strong, I *was* strong. I felt smarter too, like I could see a thousand different potential outcomes from a single action. In less than a day, though, the power started to fade. Now, I can't even tell that I'm wearing the necklace at all." I paused, then decided to tell her everything. No reason to hold back now.

"I also noticed recently that my craving for alcohol is back. It was like the necklace was shielding me from it before and now that shield is just gone. Poof."

The witch listened silently until I finished, then tipped her head to the side a little as if trying to see my story from a different angle.

"I think I have an idea of what might be going on, but let me ask some questions first to make sure."

I nodded for her to go ahead.

"When Constancia pawned the necklace, did you have the chance to touch it?"

I shook my head. "I wanted to…but I never got the chance. The first time I touched it wasn't until weeks after I first saw it." It was tricky to gauge the timeline between when I'd first seen the necklace and when I'd actually gotten to wear it since Jax and I had lost a month while traveling through Between. I figured weeks was a good enough description.

"As I thought," Rosalyn said. Her eyes stayed fixed on me, making me want to crawl into a hole. "So… you imbibed vampire blood on that first day when Constanica pawned the necklace. Did you have dreams immediately or were there several days between?"

I hadn't dreamed the night I'd been kidnapped, first by Jax and then by the vampires, but maybe that's because instead of sleeping, I'd fallen unconscious after being drained and hypnotized by vampires. It was only later, after escaping from them with Jax that I'd finally fallen asleep out of exhaustion. That was when I'd had the first dream of a hallway filled with paintings that showed me both past and potential events.

It was also the first time I'd felt Morvalden's presence..

I shivered at the memory of his eyeless face lunging out at me from a portrait, fangs dripping blood and claws reaching for me.

"Yes," I finally answered, then clarified. "The first time I fell asleep normally, I had one of those dreams. And now," I continued, realizing I'd left something out, "I'm having dreams where when I get hurt in the dream, I wake up with that injury."

I pulled up my sleeve and showed Rosalyn the bandages on my wrist. "Last night I dreamed that Constania grabbed me here hard enough to make me bleed. When I woke up, I was bleeding."

Rosalyn's eyes took on a gleam like she'd just solved the puzzle. "I see." She didn't share with the class though. Instead she asked, "Vianne, I may be stating the obvious, but the Vânători line runs through the female bloodline from mother to daughter. I, along with most other supernatural beings, were under the impression that the female line stopped with Gawynna Vânători who had no children."

I nodded. "That's the way it was explained to me too. Apparently Gawynna had two brothers and one of them, um, Fane Vânători, was my great-great grandfather."

There was a moment of silence while the witch thought about this and Ramble eyeballed the rest of the pie sitting on the console.

"So, you have several male ancestors between you and the female Vânători line."

"I guess so. Yeah."

Her gaze slipped down to the necklace for a moment then flicked back up to my face. "That could be the reason why the necklace doesn't work. I'm sorry, Vianne, but it seems that you don't have enough Vânători blood in your veins to make it work on its own."

How many times did I have to prove that I was a Vânători? I opened my mouth to protest but Rosalyn raised a hand to cut me off.

"I'm not saying that you're not a Vânători—merely that your blood is too... distilled to make the necklace work on its own. But," she fixed me with that stern gaze again, "it appears you've already found a way to access the necklace's powers."

I stayed silent, not wanting to say it.

"Vampire blood." Her gaze remained fixed on me. "I have a feeling you already knew that though, yes?"

"Yes," I sighed. "I guess I sort of did." I had hoped Rosalyn might have a different theory for why the necklace didn't work. Now I just felt stupid for traveling all this way for something I already knew. I'd also managed to tie myself up with obligations to both the werewolves and the witches to solve murders being committed by a mysterious supernatural creature who could easily wipe the floors with me.

Would it be weird if I bashed my head against Rosalyn's dashboard a few times?

"I know you're not exactly thrilled at the idea of drinking vampire blood, but from your story, it doesn't sound like you have much choice with Morvalden and his vampires looking for you. You can bury your head in the sand, but without the necklace's power, I fear you're not likely to last long."

Super helpful, I thought but said, "Even if I ignore how gross it is to drink blood, assuming I can kidnap and kill a vampire just to take their blood, doesn't that make me just like Morvalden and the vampires?"

"Yes, but there's no reason you have to kill a vampire. Or even kidnap one."

I made a face. "I don't think any of Morvalden's cronies are going to line up for a Vânători blood drive."

"There are more vampires out there than just those under Morvalden's control."

"I thought he was the 'father of vampires' or whatever. Doesn't that mean all vampires fall under him?" I asked.

Rosalyn looked away from me and out toward the lake as if

considering her answer. "There are many stories about the vampires and where they come from. I can only tell you what I know. Morvalden has fashioned himself as their patriarch," here she looked back at me as if to drive home the point, "and I don't doubt that he is the most powerful vampire out there, but there are certainly others who don't follow his orders."

My mind immediately jumped to the vampire Donavon had said lived in town. If the werewolf didn't think he was a murderer—or at least, not the person responsible for the current slate of deaths in Ricketts—then maybe this vampire could help me?

Rosalyn stared at me, waiting for my next question. I considered asking her about the local vampire, but there was the slight possibility that she didn't know he was in town. If that was the case, I didn't want to give away Donavon's friend and possibly compromise any blood donation relationship we might have. I focused instead on my goal: understanding the Artemis necklace and the Vânători abilities.

"If I have to drink vampire blood in order to, I dunno, activate the necklace or whatever, why is it that I can still see ghosts? Or Ramble?" I waved at the hellhound in the backseat, catching him in the act of moving in on the remaining pie. He jerked his head back and perked up his ears as if he'd been listening the whole time.

Rosalyn also saw the hellhound's sneak attack on the pie. She scooped out another piece for the hellhound while she spoke. "It's possible those abilities could wear off over time, but I think it more likely that the first time you imbibed vampire blood, it triggered or activated some latent magical abilities in you.."

Though only a few weeks ago I would desperately have

wanted these abilities to wear off, now I couldn't imagine stumbling my way through this weird world without Ramble helping me. I mean, I guess he'd still be there even if I couldn't see him, but how much would that suck?

"So," I said, watching Ramble practically inhale the slice of pie Rosalyn set in front of him, "if I want to make the necklace work again and I don't want to be like Morvalden, then I'll need to find a vampire and convince them to let me drink their blood."

Rosalyn nodded. I blew out a sigh that sounded a lot like Ramble.

Lucky me that there happens to be a vampire in town. Now I just had to find him and hope he didn't kill me before I somehow convinced him to donate a pint of blood to the Vânători cause.

* * *

Ramble watched me from the bathroom doorway as I examined myself in the mirror. Was I really just like Morvalden? Gaining power from the blood of others?

We'd come back to the motel shortly after Rosalyn declared that I was a vampire-blood-sucking psycho. Okay, so those hadn't been her exact words...

"Even if we convince a vampire to let me drink their blood," I said to the hellhound, "then there's the issue that I'd actually have to, you know, *drink it.*"

All those other times the vampire blood had been forced upon me. Now I'd have to willingly drink it. And apparently it wouldn't be a one-time thing. The effects of the blood would eventually wear off, just as they had before, and I'd have to drink more to regain them again.

Why couldn't I just be a normal Vânători? It seemed that all the other Vânători women were able to use the necklace without gorging on vampire blood. Why did I have to be different?

Ramble suddenly stirred and gave a small growl while looking toward the motel door. A second later, someone knocked.

I sighed, gave my face one last glare in the mirror, then stomped to the front door to peek through the peephole.

Donavon stood outside, staring at the ground with his arms crossed over his chest. I got the distinct impression that he wasn't in the best of moods.

Though I could still appreciate his body, I realized I wasn't experiencing that same electric zap I'd felt the night before. Good. I didn't need any other complications in my life right now. My hands were fairly full avoiding being caught by Morvalden and hunting a murderer who could kill a witch and a werewolf all while pretending to have special abilities until I could locate a vampire who might give me some of his blood.

So, you know, just your average week before Halloween.

Suddenly Donavon looked up directly at the peephole. I felt a little jolt, but more at having been caught staring than any sort of attraction.

I pasted a pleasant expression on my face then opened the door. "Donavon. Anything new? There hasn't been another murder, has there?"

"No." He gave me a quick once over, seeming almost disappointed at what he saw, then glanced around the motel, flicking his eyes over my meager belongings. "I heard you met up with the witches without me."

"Keeping tabs on me, huh?" I didn't give him a chance to answer. "I told you I came here to speak with Rosalyn, so I spoke with her."

He stared at me and then looked pointedly at my backpack. "And now that you've done that, you're just gonna leave town?"

Glancing at the room, I realized that, with all of my belongings still in my backpack, that's exactly what it looked like. With Jax, I'd learned that I should always be ready to move out. It just hadn't dawned on me that I could unpack my stuff here and spread out a little.

I suppressed the urge to snap back at the werewolf. I was already in a craptastic mood after confirming that I'd have to start guzzling blood to keep the necklace working. I *so* didn't need this shit from Donavon, but I also understood where his anger came from. Instead of biting his head off, I took a deep breath (they're supposed to be cleansing right?) and explained, "I'm not going anywhere. I said I'd help, and I will." I jerked my head to indicate my stuff. "I'm just not in the habit of unpacking."

I considered telling Donavon that I'd also made a deal with Rosalyn to determine who had killed one of her witches, but decided against it. I wanted to like and trust this beefy werewolf, but he made it difficult with his fluctuating moods and immediate accusations.

Donavon clearly wasn't convinced and stood on the doorstep in brooding silence. My temper finally got the better of me.

"Did you come over here for something or were you just checking up on me?"

His eyes narrowed but he accepted the change of subject.

"Do you still want to see the scene of the first murder?" He asked.

I'd mentioned checking out the first murder scene before he'd dropped me off from our meeting with the witches. I hadn't thought he'd really been listening at the time.

I shoved away my annoyance. "Yes. I'd like to go back to Samuel's apartment, too. It's possible I'll only see his ghost when it's dark out."

That got me a grunt in reply. Donavon spun on a heel and strode toward his car. I guess that meant we were going now. Grabbing my jacket, I threw Ramble a questioning look. "You going with us?"

The hellhound huffed but pushed past me to the door.

"I'm so glad everyone's in such a great mood," I mumbled to myself. "This is gonna be a great field trip."

Chapter 12

Though it was mostly dark when we got to the park, there was a concrete walkway with plenty of lighting in the main area. Donavon led Ramble and me away from the better lit areas past a sign that stated, "Moose Lover's Lane, Three Mile Loop."

"I'm surprised the park is open after dark. Don't they usually close at dusk?" I was thinking of the park near my college. I wasn't a runner myself, but I'd had a few runner friends who'd complained that they couldn't get a long enough run in before 8am classes started since they had to wait for the sun to come up.

"This park is different. It's used by humans in the daytime and my Pack at night. Most humans don't come here after dark."

Were there other cities like this where supernatural creatures like witches and werewolves lived side-by-side in harmony, law enforcement was cool with it, and the local park held after-hours just for the non-human residents? It seemed unlikely I'd find a community like this anywhere else, but then again, I'd had no idea that vampires even existed until recently. Maybe there was a thriving supernatural community back in Indianapolis and I'd just never realized it.

The beginning of the side path we took was pretty well lit, but once we left the mouth of the path, it got dark pretty quickly. Perfectly spaced pine trees lining the path gave way to a more natural hodge-podge of oaks, pine, and birch trees as we moved further away from the main area of the park.

It was a lot darker and quieter than I'd expected. If I had to scream for help, I'd be shit out of luck. Good thing I didn't think Donavon was the killer. We'd be totally screwed following him out to the middle of nowhere.

Donavon suddenly stopped at a dark point in the path. Ahead of us, there was a circle of light illuminating a metal bench and trash can. It was like a mini safe haven. Funny how a simple thing like light could give the impression of safety.

I jumped a little when the werewolf said, "This is where Duluth was attacked." He pointed at the concrete path in front of us.

It was too dark to actually see anything. Would I be able to see a ghost if he materialized? I pulled out my cell phone, toggled the flashlight app on, and shined it at the ground.

The concrete here was relatively clean except for some dark spots on the right side. Blood?

"Then he was dragged through the grass this way." Donavon started walking again. I tracked my cell light across the ground but didn't see any telling drops of blood or torn up grass where someone might have fought an attacker. Maybe the sleet and rain from yesterday had erased that kind of thing.

Donavon stopped when we reached the park bench. I flicked off my cell light.

"This is where the body was left."

"Wait, he was attacked in the dark and then his attacker dragged him into the light?" I asked.

Donavon's expression was grim as he nodded. "He was left on the bench."

"*On* the bench?" I paused in thought for a moment. "Do you think maybe he climbed onto the bench after his attacker left?"

"Unlikely. The position they found his body in wasn't natural. His body was definitely placed there."

That seemed kind of... crazy. "Why attack someone in the dark, drag them into the light, and then place that person on the bench?" I asked. "You'd think that would mean this killer wanted the body to be found. But that doesn't match up with the latest attack where he tried to hide the witch's body in the dumpster."

"Right," Donavon said. Then explained, "Tony Duluth worked as a park ranger, so he was walking the park before dawn, checking trails and picking up garbage. The sheriff said a jogger heard the attack but didn't see anything and thought it was a bear or another animal. When the jogger ran to get help, he made a lot of noise thinking it might scare off whatever it was. Maybe the noise interrupted the killer and he dumped Duluth's body on the bench because he panicked?" Donavon stared outside the circle of light as if he might see the attacker waiting.

"Maybe...but then why drag Duluth into the light in the first place? Seems more likely that the killer wanted Duluth's body to be found. It makes me think Sadie Green's murder wasn't planned since he hid her body. Maybe Sadie sensed something was up with the killer when he went into the gas station and the killer's response was to attack her."

"Could be..." Donavon said, then trailed off into silence as he looked out at the dark surrounding us then back to the lit up area. Sudden understanding lit his features just before they morphed to an angry mask. "Kleinman was a jogger."

"That's right!" I said, trying to connect the pieces between this murder and the one of the ghost-jogger I'd seen in the field. "Could Kleinman have been the one who heard the attack and called for help?"

Donavon stared at the ground as he answered. "If so, it seems like something the sheriff would have mentioned."

I grimaced. "If the jogger didn't make an official statement or they didn't get his name, the sheriff might not realize they're the same person."

"Or the jogger could be a completely different person." Donavon pointed out. "Lots of people run in the park."

"True. But Kleinman told his attacker he was sorry. Maybe he said he was sorry for calling the cops after hearing the attack?"

Donavon nodded, slowly. "And maybe he saw more of the attack on Duluth than he admitted because he was scared of retaliation."

* * *

We hung around the spot where Duluth died, but no ghost-Duluth came to give us an encore of his murder. It was getting colder by the minute and I finally had to call off our watch when I could no longer stamp the feeling back into my toes.

"I don't think anything's going to happen," I said, shifting from foot to foot to keep moving and stay warm. The boots were great, but there was only so much they could do if I was standing around on cold concrete.

"Still want to swing by the apartment complex?"

I thought longingly of the warm motel room, but shook it from my mind. I'd agreed with both Rosalyn and Donavon to help find the killer, so I needed to suck it up and do the job. "Yeah, let's go."

Besides, I could warm up on the drive over with his heated leather seats.

Minutes later, we neared the beginning of the path where the trail widened out and was lit once again by overhead lights when Ramble suddenly stepped in front of me and stopped. I stumbled into him and nearly went head over heels before catching myself on his spiky back.

A long, menacing growl unfurled from the hellhound's throat.

Donavon, who had been walking slightly in front of us, stopped and jerked his head around. His eyes darted from me down to where he thought he'd heard Ramble.

Ramble growled again, this time a little louder. I followed the hellhound's gaze to Donavon's car. He'd parked it directly under one of the parking lot lights.

"Someone turned off the lights around the car," I whispered.

Donavon twisted back around to look. Though the rest of the parking lot was still lit up, four of the lights around the car were off, leaving the vehicle shrouded in shadow.

Donavon's shoulders rounded a little and his body shifted so his weight was in the balls of his feet. He seemed to be getting ready for a fight.

Whipping his head to the left, Ramble's ears twitched to catch something my puny human ears couldn't pick up.

Donavon, still staring at the car, put a hand behind him and beckoned us to follow. As much as I wanted to say I could fend for myself, I knew I didn't have the training or the ability without the necklace's help to take on whatever the hell this thing was. Especially since it had already bested a werewolf and a witch.

What the hell had I been thinking leaving my gun in the motel and walking through the park at night when a killer was on the loose?

We were only about thirty feet from the car when a twig snapped in the woods a little behind us on the right. Whatever was following us had switched sides of the path at some point and now moved audibly through the trees beside us. It no longer seemed to care that we could hear it.

Donavon paused just long enough for me to draw alongside him. Grabbing me under the elbow, he hurriedly pushed me in front of him toward the safety of the car.

The thing in the woods got louder as it moved. Whatever this monster was, it was fast. Somehow it had gotten ahead of us.

Without warning, Ramble knocked me to the side, sending me stumbling. The hellhound planted himself between me and woods just as something leapt onto the walkway.

The thing hissed and spit at the hellhound, matching his volume. Ramble's growl suddenly died in his throat. There was a brief moment where he just stood there, staring dumbly at the animal on the sidewalk.

I realized what it was a split second before Donavon pushed past me to put himself in front of me like a shield. "Get to the car—" The shout died on his lips as he caught sight of the animal.

It was the black cat I'd been seeing all over town. It was putting on a pretty good show, hissing and spitting at Ramble while the hellhound stared at the cat if this was all a big joke.

"What the hell?" Donavon finally said. He inhaled in short bursts, catching the cat's scent. His eyes flashed white. "...That is not a cat."

I suddenly remembered that something had turned off the lights over the car just as a long, low snarl came from the path in front of us. The sound sent chills down my spine, triggering an instinct to run away as fast as I could.

Standing directly in the path between us and the car was a canine-like beast that was three times the size of a Great Dane. Its fur was all black and its eyes must have been, too, because all I see against that dark fur were its big, white, sharp teeth.

It snarled again, lifting one massive paw to take a step forward in a jerky manner. I was just thinking that it was oddly ungraceful when the cat let out a yowl. I jerked as something hit my back.

Twisting around, I found myself yanking the black cat off my back. It hissed and clawed at me, but could only score on my hands since the jacket protected my back and arms. I managed to get a grip on the cat and threw it away from me and into the woods.

A human roar that slowly morphed into an animal growl caught my attention. I spun around just in time to see Donavon's face elongate into a muzzle. His ears pushed up and got pointy before being covered in fur. A tearing sound split the air as his clothes ripped apart, unable to hold his new, furry form.

The monster-dog leapt toward him, snapping at his throat. Donavon was smaller and quicker though and managed to dodge the beast's teeth. It looked like Donavon had been aiming for the it's throat, but the monster-dog dropped its head just enough to force Donavon into a different strategy.

The werewolf pivoted on his back paws and lunged to sink his teeth into the thing's shoulder. The monster-dog let out a startled yelp and tried to shake off the werewolf.

Ramble stayed with me, his body pressing against my shins as if to keep me from running into the fight. No worries there. If a werewolf couldn't best this thing, then I didn't think I'd be much of a match. Not without the Artemis necklace anyways.

The cat suddenly ran back out of the woods and attacked me again, this time clawing its way up the back of my leg. What the hell? Was the cat working with the monster-dog? Weren't cats and dogs supposed to be enemies?

Ramble pulled away from me as I tried to dislodge the cat. The little bastard had wrapped its paws all the way around my leg and was trying to bite me through my jeans. I batted at it with my hands. It felt really wrong to try and hurt a cat, but the thing seemed possessed!

With a huff to get me to stop dancing around, Ramble opened his mouth, grabbed the cat by the ruff of its neck and peeled it slowly off my leg. It tried to twist around and get a claw in his eyes, but Ramble was too fast. The second the cat was free of my leg, Ramble whipped his head to the side and sent the cat flying off in the woods again.

I can't say I felt too bad for it. Cats always land on their feet, right?

A howl of pain brought my attention back to the fight between Donavon and the monster-dog. In the seconds it had taken to dislodge the stupid cat, the tide of battle had turned.

Donavon had broken away from the beast and was limping back and forth in front of it, keeping its attention on him while staying ready to dodge an attack. He was half-dragging his left leg as he moved. I didn't think he'd be able to hold out much longer against the beast by himself.

Apparently Ramble came to the same conclusion because he launched himself into the fray. He didn't roar or growl as he leapt to attack. Instead, he darted forward and smartly used his invisibility to gain the advantage of surprise. Unfortunately the beast heard Ramble's long claws click against the concrete as he ran, giving it a half-second of warning to turn toward the sound. It was just enough to keep Ramble from getting the throat hit I thought he'd been going for. Mid-leap, Ramble shifted his focus and twisted so that he landed half on the beast's back and quickly ripped into it's shoulder. It looked like the same spot Donavon had initially attacked.

The beast let out another roar of pain, then struggled to twist its giant neck. Donavon took advantage of the distraction and lunged forward to attack its left leg.

My mind was racing. What could I do to help? I had my knife, but if a werewolf and hellhound weren't having much luck against the beast, how would I fare against it with just a puny throwing knife?

Instead, I decided to find Donavon's keys so that we could retreat if needed. I ran forward and grabbed Donavon's shredded pants to fish in the pockets for his car keys. Nothing. Maybe they'd fallen out?

Keeping an eye on the fight, I turned most of my attention to the ground and shoved Donavon's torn shirt and jacket aside. Cold metal met my hand, jangling as I made contact. Aha!

Still kneeling, I grabbed the keys just as something black and furry shot out of the woods. The damn cat again! It ran straight for me and automatically swung the hand holding the keys at it as it leapt.

One of the keys stuck out between my knuckles and when the cat struck my fist, the key pierced its skin. It let out a hurt screech that sent my nerves on edge, dropped to the ground, and went racing into the woods once more.

The monster-dog let out a roar as if in answer to the cat's yowl and I looked up just in time to roll out of the charging beast's path.

I managed to keep my grip on the keys but wished I'd thought to get my knife out before this. If the thing stopped to attack me, I was screwed. But the monster didn't slow and instead picked up speed as it crashed into the woods and out of sight in the same direction the cat had gone.

I wasn't about to waste time staring after it. I hopped up and ran to check on Donavon and Ramble. Ramble snuffed at me as I approached. His dark fur was covered in streaks of blood. I hoped none of it was his. He seemed to be walking okay as he neared the werewolf.

Donavon had definitely come off the worst in the fight.

His back leg no longer worked at all and merely dragged limply behind him, leaving a dark streak of blood on the concrete. Like Ramble, Donavon's muzzle was smeared with blood, but I thought that was probably the beast's. When he started to limp toward the woods as if to go after the monster, I noticed that his front left paw was also injured and he could barely put any weight on it.

I put my hands up to stop him from chasing the monster. "Nope," I said and hit the unlock button on the key fob as I moved toward the werewolf. "Everyone in the car." I had a bad feeling that the monster might come back to finish us off.

It took both Ramble and I to convince Donavon not to chase

after the beast and then to support him over to his car and into the backseat. I spared half a second to lament that his fancy leather seats were going to be covered in blood, but clearly we had bigger problems. Ramble hopped into the passenger seat while I slammed both passenger doors and ran around to the other side of the car, heart pounding and feeling exposed.

Thankfully, nothing grabbed me in its jaws. I cranked the engine, backed up, then zoomed out of the parking lot. I kept glancing in the rearview mirror, expecting something to chase after us, but nothing loomed out of the dark.

"Shit," I breathed. Then, realizing I had no idea where to go, said in a different tone, "Shit."

I have a way with words.

"We need to get him to a hospital," I said to the hellhound.

Ramble gave me a withering look as if I were dumber than a box of rocks.

"What? If the Sheriff knows what he is, don't you think they'll know at the hospital and be able to help him?"

A moan of pain, half-animal, half-human, came from the backseat. I glanced back and almost drove us into a ditch at the nightmare sight.

Donavon was changing back to human, one body part at a time. I'd caught a glimpse of his face pasted onto the head of a dog. Yeah. I would not be getting romantically involved with *that* anytime soon no matter how hot a man he turned into.

"No...hospital." He managed to grind out between clenched teeth.

"Then we should call someone. Maybe someone in your Pack?" Though my brain had a sick sense of curiosity, I didn't dare glance back again for fear of what I might see this time.

"Motel..." The werewolf gasped.

165

"I'm not a doctor, Donavon. I won't be able to help you—

"Brother," he bit out against the pain.

Oh yeah. I remembered Donavon telling me that his brother owned the motel. I didn't know if his brother was a werewolf or not, but if Donavon thought he could help, I wasn't going to argue with him.

"Got it." I sped back to the motel, only second-guessing the route once or twice, and was careful to stay under the speed limit. I felt a definite sense of relief when I pulled into the parking lot and stopped the car in front of the motel's front office.

I left the car running and dashed inside. Though the front door was unlocked, the area behind the counter was empty. I could hear the sounds of a news program coming from somewhere in the back.

"Hello?" I waited but still got nothing. There was a little bell on the counter. I figured what the hell and started hammering away on the thing.

"I'm coming! Hold your damn horses!" A tall, pale, slightly lanky guy with brown hair who looked to be in his early twenties stepped around the corner. He looked like he needed a shower and a decent meal.

"What?" He demanded.

"Are you Donavon's brother?"

The only resemblance to Donavon was the man's bluish-gray eyes. If this was Donavon's brother, he must be more a werewolf brother than a brother by blood.

His eyes immediately narrowed. "Yes…?"

"He's hurt. I've got his car out front. He's in the backseat." My words tumbled out in such a rush that I thought he might not understand. I needn't have worried. His eyes flicked to the

166

front window and when he blinked, I saw they had become depthless black orbs. Fangs slipped down over his bottom lip. In one leap he was over the counter and through the front door.

I froze.

Shit! Donavon's brother is the vampire in town?!

I remembered that Ramble was still in the car and might also be hurt. I couldn't let the hellhound stand against this vampire alone, so I sprinted out the door before I could think too much about what I could actually do to help him against a vampire.

Chapter 13

Rushing outside, I opened my mouth to warn Ramble about the vampire before anything bad could happen. Too late.

The sound of breaking glass reached my ears as Ramble shattered the passenger side window to escape the vampire now leaning into the back of the car. Glass sprayed the blacktop all around him as Ramble landed between me and the car.

Quick as a flash, the vampire jerked his body from the car and turned to pursue the hellhound.

Ramble bared his teeth in a silent growl at the vampire who was baring his own pointy fangs. Both were crouched and ready to spring at each other. Though the vampire couldn't see Ramble, I could only assume that he'd followed the trajectory of the broken glass and had guessed where Ramble now stood.

Not today, vampire.

"Ramble!" I shouted and quickly pictured him standing next to me.

POP!

Ramble disappeared.

POP!

He reappeared standing next to me, looking slightly surprised.

Though the vampire couldn't see Ramble and so didn't know what had happened, he'd definitely heard me yell. He refocused his attention on me, stalking a few steps closer and completely ignoring the broken glass on the blacktop as it crunched under his shoes.

"Vânători! What has your beast done?"

My mouth dropped open. In my anger to defend Ramble, I forgot that I was shouting at a vampire. "Ramble didn't do shit! It was the murder dog-monster!" Okay. Not the best name for whatever the beast was, but it was the only thing I could think of right then.

The vampire stalked closer. Ramble moved to stand in front of me.

"We were...attacked," Donavon said. He leaned precariously on the open door.

His words froze the vampire in place where he gave me a long, hard stare. I remembered to avoid looking directly in his eyes. I didn't want to get mesmerized if he could do the vampire-hypnosis thing.

Instead of carrying out his assault on Ramble and I, he spun around and darted back to help Donavon. I heard him whispering with the werewolf but couldn't make out their words. Finally, the vampire twisted to look at me.

"We need to get him inside. Open the door to your room."

For a split second, I considered telling him to go fuck himself. I mean, he had just been planning to attack Ramble and I, yet I was supposed to just let him in my motel room now? Also, weren't there eight or nine other rooms here he could use?

I held my tongue when I remembered how Donavon had

fought the monster-dog. His distraction had kept the beast from attacking me. The least I could do was let him bleed all over my room.

Hands shaking with adrenaline, I headed for my room and fished out the key. It only took a few tries of nervous fumbling to open the door. I turned to tell the vampire it was open—and came face to face with him. He pushed past me, carrying a naked Donavon, to lay the werewolf gently on the bed.

"Shut the door," he ordered.

I glanced at Ramble to see if he wanted to stay outside. He limped past me but stayed near the window when I closed the door.

Turning on the overhead light gave me a better look at Donavon's injuries and I sort of wished I'd left them off. His skin was covered in blood, gore, and fur, not all of it his. I had to remind my stomach that I'd seen worse. His right forearm had a gash in it that was bleeding sluggishly but the vampire was ignoring this in favor of staunching the blood flowing freely from Donavon's left leg.

"Get me a towel," the vampire barked.

I let his bossy tone roll off me by reminding myself that I was helping Donavon. I slipped past the vampire and into the bathroom to grab a clean towel. I handed it to him, careful not to get too close. He immediately pressed it against Donavon's leg, making the werewolf gasp.

The vampire shook his head. "I don't understand why it's not healing more quickly. It should have stopped bleeding by now."

Donavon's eyes slit open and I was frozen to the floor. His pupils were completely white now. "Magic," he panted. "Needs to be sewn...to heal."

Tentatively I said, "I have a first aid kit in my bag. There's a needle in there you could stitch him up with." I crossed the room and dug the kit out of my backpack. It had one of those wicked looking curved needles. I honestly hadn't ever really expected to use it, but Jax had insisted I carry it.

Score another point for the absent hunter.

I moved closer to the vampire and tried to hand the kit to him. He didn't take it. I noticed he was breathing through his mouth. His fangs were still out, too.

"I can't." There was no inflection to his voice. "You'll have to do it."

"No way." I tried to shove the kit at him again. "I have no idea what I'm doing."

"There's too much blood." He wasn't looking directly at me, so I chanced another quick glance at his eyes which were still black.

That was probably bad, right?

"Okay," I said in my most soothing voice. "Why don't you wait outside and I'll take care of this." I had no idea how I'd accomplish that, but it would be much easier to do it if I didn't have a bloodthirsty vampire staring at the patient like he was a big juicy steak.

"Can't," the vampire said again. "It's not safe for you. Hurt werewolves are unstable."

I was thinking that I'd maybe take my chances with the unstable werewolf but Donavon suddenly let out a feral snarl. It was unnerving given that he was now in a human body.

Damn it. I should've stuck with Jax.

I took a deep breath and screwed up my courage. "Fine. You need to move then."

This got me a definite glare and I had to quickly drop my

eyes to keep from getting sucked into those black orbs. They fell on me like a weight and I went very still until I felt his attention shift away. Eventually, he moved to stand in the small space between the bed and the bathroom wall, one hand still holding Donavon down while his other one gripped a towel wrapped tightly around the werewolf's thigh like a tourniquet.

"I'll stop him if he attacks," the vampire said before falling silent.

I nodded, still not looking at him, and moved into the space he'd just vacated only to find myself staring at Donavon's very naked body. Focusing on his leg, I saw that there were two jagged tears on either side of his lower thigh.

I had to force my brain to shut up about the vampire in the room while I tried to thread the needle with shaking hands. "Um, shouldn't I sterilize the needle?"

"Unnecessary." The vampire's words were clipped. "He can't get an infection like a human would."

I finally managed to run the thread through the needle head. Now for the hard part.

Time to put on your big girl pants, Vi.

Sewing the wounds took longer than I expected. Turns out, skin is a lot thicker than cloth and is difficult to get a needle through. I also had to pause whenever Donavon moved so that I didn't jab the needle too far into his flesh.

The vampire, Ramble, and I were mostly silent throughout the process, leaving Donavon to fill the room with gasping and growling noises. At one point, when I dug the needle in too far, Donavon tried to lunge off the bed at me while gnashing his very human teeth like a wolf. The vampire intervened immediately, catching Donavon with one arm and slamming him back to the bed.

"Please continue," the vampire said in that same emotionless voice.

I took a deep, steadying breath and forced myself to return to leaning over Donavon's leg. Eventually I managed to stitch up both wounds, gently wiped them clean with a fresh towel, and wrapped them in bandages from the first aid kit.

"Done." I straightened, making my spine pop. A dull ache had settled into my back from being hunched over for too long. Still avoiding the vampire's eyes, I slowly fled to the relative safety of the bathroom to wash my hands and wonder what to do next. Luckily the vampire saved me from having to figure that out when I returned from washing my hands.

"You should pack your things."

"What?" I gestured toward the bed, ignoring the fact that my things were clearly already packed. "I just helped you keep him alive and you're going to kick me out?"

His eyes flicked over me. I noticed they were still black before remembering that I needed to look away.

I could still feel him looking at me as he said, "Donavon is staying in here tonight. I'm moving you to a different room."

Was that amusement in his voice or was I imagining it?

"Oh." All the anger drained out of me and was replaced by exhaustion. Being terrified for my life one minute and then fighting tension while giving a werewolf stitches under a vampire's watchful eye was definitely more than enough to kick my ass.

I returned to the bathroom and gathered my toiletries as well as the damp jeans I'd left to dry on the shower curtain rod. Back in the main room, I grabbed my backpack and shoved the items inside, too tired to care if the jeans got my other

BITE ME

clothes wet.

The vampire had moved to sit on the corner of the bed facing the door while I was in the bathroom. His eyes were no longer black, but I decided it would be smart to continue avoiding direct eye contact.

"Go to the front office and into the back room," he said. "There is a box on the wall with all the room keys." He pulled out a keyring and flipped through the keys until he found the one he wanted. "This will unlock the box."

Any other time, I would have objected at his bossy tone, but tonight I was too tired to bother. He held the keyring out by the key he'd selected. When I took them, my fingers brushed his cold skin.

"I'm Louis, by the way," he added when I'd taken the keys.

I didn't even have the energy to tell him that name was already taken by a more handsome, fictional vampire. Instead, I just nodded to him. "Vianne."

"...Thank you for helping Donavon, Vianne."

Exhausted and confused, I wasn't on my A-game so I just gave a second nod.

"What happened?" His tone was once again emotionless.

"We were at the park, checking out where the first victim was killed when a giant, dog-like beast attacked us." I paused, remembering that the monster-dog hadn't been working alone. "There was a black cat there too. It was like the cat was on the beast's side."

The vampire raised an eyebrow. "Cats and dogs working together?" Though the words were clearly meant to be funny, his voice was still toneless.

I wasn't sure how I felt that we'd thought of the same joke. His lack of emotion was starting to creep me out...and kind

174

of piss me off a little. Which is probably why I said, "Just like a vampire and werewolf being brothers?"

Apparently that was a taboo subject because he decided we were done talking. "Take room number five. It should be made up."

It would also be right next door to this room, giving him the ability to keep tabs on me. Whatever. It was better than staying in a room with a vampire and a werewolf.

"And, if you would, please turn off the vacancy sign and lock the office door."

"Sure," I mumbled and retreated from the room with Ramble at my heels. I successfully found the room with the box of keys and pulled one for room number five. It took me another minute to figure out how to turn the vacancy sign off, then I locked the door behind me.

Ramble and I had just settled into our new room when someone knocked at the door. My eyes immediately flew to Ramble. He stared at the door but wasn't growling. I took that as a good sign and peaked out the peephole.

It was the vampire—Louis.

"What now?" I asked as I opened the door.

He held out his right hand, palm up. "Keys."

Oh dang. I'd forgotten that he might want those back. I grabbed them from the table where I'd dropped them earlier and slapped them into his hand. It was maybe a little more forceful than I'd planned but whatever. I was tired.

"Thank you." He stared down at the keys for a moment. "We are not brothers by blood, Vânători, but by choice. When you are as old as I am, you must create your own family." Without waiting for a reply, he trudged back to the other room.

I stood in the open doorway for a moment. Not only had

175

he not tried to kill me—well, not after he realized Ramble and I hadn't been the cause of Donavon's injuries anyway—Louis the vampire had actually thanked me.

I wasn't sure what to make of that. I closed the door then ended up staring at it for another minute until an overdramatic huff rose from the hellhound. Only then did I remember that Ramble had been in the fight too.

"Did you get hurt, Ramble?"

Now that I was looking more closely, I could see a few scratches and bites here and there. I pointed at a gash on his right leg. "Will that heal by itself or do you think whatever magic keeping Donavon from healing will stop you from healing, too?

My concern only earned me an annoyed huff. Still…

"Maybe we should clean it, just in case." I wet a towel from the bathroom and, when Ramble didn't object, starting gently wiping the blood away from his wiry fur.

"Do you think we should leave town? You know, in case Rosalyn was wrong and Louis really does answer to Morvalden?"

The hellhound looked pointedly at the wall separating our room from where I assumed the vampire still watched over Donavon. When he saw I was watching, he gave an exaggerated eye-roll.

"Okay. So you don't think he's one of Morvalden's henchmen."

I thought about my conversation with Rosalyn. It seemed pretty convenient that a semi-friendly vampire lived in the same town that Jax had sent me to. Had the hunter guessed that I had to drink vampire blood in order to access the powers of the Artemis necklace? Is that why he'd sent me here, where

Louis was, to speak with the unknown Rosalyn rather than Myra, a witch I already knew? If so, why not just come right out and tell me about the need for vampire blood?

I mean, sure, I hadn't told him about *my* theory that I needed vampire blood, but I felt that I had some pretty good reasons for withholding that information. Namely, that I didn't want him to see me as a monster that he'd feel obligated to kill.

Maybe it really was just a coincidence that Louis happened to live in the town Jax had sent me to.

When it came down to it, it didn't really matter whether Jax had known about the need for vampire blood or not. The fact was, I needed vampire blood to make the Artemis necklace work and now I'd just met a potential donor. It was an opportunity I couldn't really afford to pass up. At least, not if I was going to keep putting myself in the path of this monster-dog and other supernatural creatures. Donavon and Ramble might not be there next time to keep the beast from attacking me. I needed to get the necklace working so I could defend myself from it.

"...and to defend myself from Morvalden and his minions when they inevitably find me," I mumbled, making Ramble look up. "Just thinking out loud," I said, waving away his questioning look. "I'm too tired to think about all this vampire stuff. Let's go to sleep."

Ramble snorted and moved to the other side of the bed to give me room before curling up to sleep.

I triple checked that the door was locked and added a chair under the handle just in case. I thought I'd have trouble falling asleep thinking about the monster-dog, black cats that attacked you, and vampires that didn't, but about two seconds after my head hit the pillow, I was out.

* * *

The dining table was so long now in my dream that it was almost cartoonish. There were even more details now. The walls were a rich red color and ancient looking tapestries gave the room a rather medieval feel. The dinner plates, glasses, and silverware sparkled from light given off by the ornate chandelier above.

This time however, when I looked down, I found I was no longer underdressed for the extravagant dinner.

I wore a red silk dress with a plunging neckline that hugged every curve. A quick touch of my hair told me that it had been made up by someone who knew how to do something outside my ability of a messy braid or ponytail. The dress revealed quite a bit of cleavage and the Artemis necklace warmed the spot at the base of my throat.

The last time I'd had this dream, Constancia had been sitting on my right. I whipped right to look for her, but found her seat empty. I was once again alone at this end of the table...but on the other end, far, far away, a shadowy figure moved.

"Vânători," a raspy voice called. "Ah, Vânători. Here at last. Let me get a CLOSER LOOK AT YOU!"

I gasped as the far-away shadow leapt onto the table and began stalking toward me. I tried to stand but found that my legs were suddenly bound to the chair.

"It's just a dream. It's just a dream." I squinched my eyes shut and willed the ropes to disappear. When I opened my eyes, the ropes were still there. This was my dream, damn it! Why couldn't I influence it?

The shadow man stalked closer, gleefully kicking plates and glasses off the table to shatter against the stone floor.

"Vânători!" Morvalden sing-songed. He was close enough now that I could see the two white orbs where his eyes should have been.

If I didn't free myself now, he would get me!

I grabbed a steak knife from the table and started sawing at the ropes around my legs with the dull blade. A quick glance told me Morvalden was more than halfway down the table. He was almost to me! I had to get away!

One rope burst apart. I immediately started sawing on the other rope. I took a chance to check the table top again, to gauge how close Morvalden was—and found he'd vanished.

I sucked in a panicked breath. Where had he gone?

"Vânători," he whispered in my left ear.

On instinct, I twisted left and thrust the knife at the source of his voice. The blade sank into one of his glowing white eyes.

He let out a high-pitched shriek—

I jerked up into a sitting position with a gasp. Heart pounding, I flailed around until I found the bedside lamp and flicked on the light. Ramble was huddled in the corner of the room, keeping a wary eye on me.

"I'm sorry buddy," I said breathlessly. "Are you okay?" I swung my legs over the side of the bed and something fell to the carpet.

I glanced down and froze. The steak knife from my dream lay on the floor. Somehow I'd managed to bring it into the real world with me. Dried blood stained the tip.

It took my brain another minute to jump start. Had Ramble been on the bed with me when I'd started dreaming? Had I lashed out at the hellhound when I'd stabbed Morvalden in the dream?

"Are you okay, Ramble? Did I…" I swallowed. "Did I cut you?"

The hellhound stared at me for another second, then lifted himself out of the corner and came around to my side of the bed. He gave a small huff. I hoped that meant all was forgiven. I did a quick visual inspection but didn't see any new cuts or gashes. In fact, the ones he'd gotten from his fight with the monster-dog had already healed most of the way. Thankfully the magic wasn't affecting his ability to heal.

There was no way I could go to sleep after that. I showered and dressed to give myself time to think. The hot water helped to wash away the lingering fear from the dream. I glanced at the knife for the millionth time where I'd left it on the bathroom sink.

Had I really stabbed Morvalden with it and then brought it from the dream into reality? I had no other explanation for how it had appeared in my room. If I could pull an object out my dream, did that mean Morvalden could pull *me* out of my dream?

I shivered even though the water was hot enough to steam up the bathroom. A wave of panic hit me. I really didn't want to drink vampire blood again, but I already knew from my dream-encounter with Constancia that if I was injured in my dreams, I carried that injury back into the real world. I was not going to give Morvalden another chance to kill me Freddy Kruger style.

If I had to drink vampire blood to keep his terrifying claws off me, then I'd do it.

There was a vampire next door who might be willing to donate his blood. Maybe, if I asked him extra, extra nice and reminded him that he owed me for saving his brother, and I tried not to piss him off again, he might be willing to help.

I finished showering, got dressed, and took my time blow drying my hair. Only after braiding it did I admit to myself that I was stalling. I blew out a breath and screwed up my courage to walk next door.

"You coming?" I asked Ramble. He'd gone back to sleep, apparently unconcerned about me trying to stab him again.

He made a great show of yawning and stretching as he stood.

"You don't have to go. I'll just go ask the vampire really nicely if I can have a little bit of his blood. Should be easy, right?"

The hellhound snorted at me.

So glad my loyal hellhound believed in this plan.

I threw on my jacket and immediately something jangled and vibrated. My nerves were wired so tight that I let out a little involuntary half-scream before realizing that it was just my phone.

The caller ID said it was an unknown number. It was two in the morning. Who would possibly be calling from an unknown number at that time? I had a quick flash of Morvalden, his eye-socket bleeding while holding a phone up to his ear. I quickly banished the vision, got my breathing under control, and hit the answer button.

"Hello?"

The voice on the other end was watery but familiar. "Vână-tori? I'm sorry for calling so late, er, early. I saw that you were awake and I needed to talk to you."

It was Cassandra.

"How did you see that I was awake?"

"It's my gift."

"To be able to tell when people are sleeping or awake?" What a piss poor gift. I think I'd have returned it if that had been my magic ability.

"Sort of. It's more technical than that. But I could tell you weren't sleeping anymore."

"Okay… is there something I can help you with? Did you remember something about Sadie?"

"Yes…sort of. I don't think I should talk about it over the phone though. Could you maybe meet me?"

I hesitated. I didn't think it likely that Cassandra had anything to do with these murders. Unless she was an award-winning actress, her grief over her girlfriend's death had been genuine. Still…

It had only been a few hours since we'd been attacked by the monster-dog and his cat sidekick. I wasn't so sure I wanted to go gallivanting around in the dark just yet.

"Please? I think it's important…but I'm not sure I should say it over the phone." Before I could ask why, she explained, "Someone might be listening."

Okay. So either Cassandra the witch was super paranoid or she suspected that someone—maybe the same someone who'd been murdering people—might be listening in.

I didn't think this was such a great idea, but I found myself wanting to help. Talking to Cassandra would also give me the opportunity to ask her about the black cat. Black cats were supposed to be associated with witches, right?

I had two options: I could face the vampire next door, ask him for some of his blood, and then meet Cassandra or I could take the chance that I wouldn't need the blood and simply go and meet the witch without going next door.

Option two meant I could put off a super awkward conversation.

Not really much of a choice there.

"Where do you want to meet?" I asked the witch and pocketed my car keys.

* * *

My slow driving to avoid random patches of ice on the road was severely annoying the hellhound in the passenger seat. Of course, Ramble was doubly annoyed because I wouldn't let him roll down the window to stick his head out. I didn't want to freeze my ass off just because he wanted to feel the wind in his spiky hair.

Cassandra's place was only a ten minute drive from town but the winding, mostly unlit back roads had me gritting my teeth and clutching the steering wheel in a death grip during the entire drive. There was one scary moment where the car fish-tailed on an invisible patch of ice as we rounded a particularly tight corner, but I was able to keep it from sliding off the road and into the woods.

How many cars have been lost in these woods after careening off the icy road? I wondered as I finally pulled into Cassandra's driveway.

The house was an old-school wood cabin complete with a little brick chimney protruding from the roof and a welcoming front porch that was wide enough for a small gathering. I would have considered it cozy, but even with the two porch lights on, the dark seemed to press in on all sides from the surrounding woods.

I killed the engine and turned to Ramble.

"You coming in this time?" I asked with some hope. Ramble wasn't a huge fan of the witches, but I kind of didn't want to walk around all alone in the dark after seeing the massive beast that was murdering people.

Ramble rolled his eyes but stood, letting me know that he would be joining me.

I stayed on high alert during the short walk from the car to the front door. I couldn't imagine living in a house so far away from neighbors. What if something happened? Would anyone even hear you scream for help?

Mainers were definitely made of sterner stuff than I was.

I knocked on the front door and waited. Nothing. I waited another second, then tried again, this time a little louder.

No one stirred in the house.

Ramble gave me a questioning look.

"Maybe she fell asleep?" I hedged, but my feeling of dread had only grown worse with every second we waited on the front porch. I didn't know Cassandra very well, but I thought it unlikely that she would call me, ask me to come over to talk about something important, and then fall asleep.

Leaving the safety of the porch, I braved the dark to move around to the side of the house thinking maybe I could peek through a window. The first one was completely blocked by a thick curtain. The one next to it, though, had a small gap between the side of the window and the curtain.

I peeked through and gasped.

The window looked in over the back of a couch with floral upholstery. Two chairs matching the couch faced the window. In the middle of the living room between the couch and the chairs was a low, wooden coffee table littered with magazines and books.

Everything in the living room was sprayed with blood.

The coffee table was the worst. There were two great big puddles of blood that had splashed on the magazines and soaked into their pages. I could just make out the shoulder of someone on the floor behind the coffee table.

I stood on tiptoe to get a better vantage point.

It was Cassandra. Murdered in her own living room.

Chapter 14

How could she be dead? I'd just spoken with her on the phone less than thirty minutes ago! I went up on tiptoes to get a better view of the body and make sure I was really seeing what I thought I saw.

The one eye I could see above the coffee table's edge was opened wide in surprise but staring vacantly past me. It was definitely Cassandra and she was most definitely dead. There was nothing I could do to help her now.

I pulled my phone from my purse and froze, panicking. Should I call the police? Donavon? Rosalyn? Shit!

Going inside would be a terrible plan since then my fingerprints would be all over everything. I could drive back to the motel and pretend like I hadn't seen anything. It wasn't like there were any witnesses out here to see me leave. But even with Cassandra already dead, leaving felt like I'd be abandoning her. It would be better to stay at the scene and phone in exactly what had happened.

I finally dialed 911 and, while the phone rang through, I sent Donavon and Rosalyn a quick text about Cassandra. This meant I could truthfully tell the cops I'd called them first. I felt pretty shitty texting Rosalyn that another one of her witches had been murdered. Getting a break-up text paled in comparison, but I figured Rosalyn would prefer to hear about it as soon as possible.

"Nine-one-one, please state your emergency," the operator patiently requested.

I had a half-a-second before deciding how to play this. In a breathless voice I said, "Oh my god! I came to meet a friend at her house but she didn't answer and I got worried so I peeked through the window and there's just blood everywhere!"

"Ma'am, please calm down. Can you give the address for the house?"

I rattled off the address then followed it with, "I think I can see her on the floor, but I haven't gone inside yet. I'm just looking through a window. Should I go inside? What if she's still alive?"

Now it was the dispatcher's turn to hesitate. "I'm not sure that it's safe to go inside, ma'am. Do you have a car you can go to?" I told her that I did. "Good. Get in your car, lock your door, and wait for the police. They should be there shortly."

"Okay." I followed her instructions and Ramble and I got into the car. Unfortunately, she wanted to wait on the line with me until the cops arrived.

Trying to make conversation with a 911 operator when you've just reported a murder is pretty damn awkward. I ended up just giving her the same details over and over again. I was on my fourth or fifth round of the story when a car I didn't recognize drove up and parked behind me, effectively blocking me in.

I reached for the ignition, wondering if I'd be brave enough to ram the strange car, but then Louis emerged from the driver's seat.

I wasn't sure if having the vampire here made things better

or worse. I didn't have much time to decide since he was heading straight for my car.

I might have checked to make sure the door was locked, though I did roll down the window a crack to talk to him. Hey, just because he hadn't killed me in the motel room earlier, didn't mean he wouldn't off me now. Especially since Donavon wasn't around this time.

I hit the mute button on my phone. "The police are on their way," I told the vampire. "I'm on the line with them now." I unmuted the phone. Louis nodded then leaned against my car to silently wait with his arms over his chest. He was wearing a white, long-sleeved, thin t-shirt with jeans but didn't look at all affected by the weather.

Wasn't he worried that not having a jacket yet clearly not being cold might be a bit of a dead giveaway that he was more than human?

Vampires.

Five minutes later, a car from the Sheriff's Department pulled in the driveway at an angle so as to keep both our cars from possibly leaving. I told the operator-of-many-questions that the cavalry had arrived and she finally let me hang up.

The sheriff climbed out of the driver's side. His young, over-excited companion hopped out, too, gun immediately drawn. I was suddenly glad that Louis was here to make sure Deputy Smith didn't accidentally unload his clip into me.

The sheriff threw a glance at us and let the deputy lead the way to the front door. We watched as the deputy vaulted the short staircase and knocked on the door while announcing, "This is the Sheriff's Department. Open up."

I was just thinking that maybe Deputy Smith could use a little training in tact when, barely having waited for a response, he stepped back and kicked the door in.

"Ken!" The sheriff chastised, but the younger officer had already stepped through, hands gripping his gun and pointing it every which way.

The sheriff followed him and they both disappeared from view.

"Some really great law enforcement you've got around here," I murmured.

Louis heard me and shrugged in answer.

There was a silent wait of about ten minutes before the two officers emerged. The sheriff was dragging the young deputy by the arm, forcibly removing him from the house.

"How many times have I told you, you damn dolt—don't touch anything!" They paraded past us to the sheriff's car. "Now, get in the damn car and call this in. It'd be the first useful thing you've done all night." He opened the passenger side door and roughly shoved the deputy through it.

Now a solo act, the sheriff took a deep breath, calming himself, before marching over to our side of the street.

"Louis." The sheriff dipped his head to the vampire and, though I saw him visibly notice that Louis was not dressed for the weather, he kept it to himself. "I got a call that there's a body in that house. Cassandra McDougall has been murdered and left in the living room. You the one who...found her?"

The sheriff's question had a different tone than when he'd spoken to Donavon. Then, it had been almost as if he were talking with an equal. With Louis it felt like he was having a hard time not accusing the vampire outright. I thought maybe the sheriff had considered asking Louis something else about the body. Did he suspect Louis had murdered Cassandra? Since the vampire had his back to me, I couldn't see his facial expression and didn't know what he thought of the sheriff's question.

"No," Louis jerked his head down toward me, "she did. I'm just here to make sure that whatever did this doesn't come back." He stepped away from the door so I could get out of the car.

"Miss Mason," the sheriff said in greeting. I was impressed that he'd remembered my name. When I was out of the car and standing next to Louis, he asked, "What brought you around to Cassandra's house so early?"

I started to answer but caught myself as Ramble climbed silently out of the car and bumped me a little. "She... she called me and asked me to come over." It was difficult not to stare as Ramble slowly sauntered toward the house, lithely avoiding the deputy as the young man strode back over to us with a purpose.

No one else, not even Louis, saw the hellhound slink up the porch steps and through the open front door.

I had to force my mind back to what I was saying. "Cassandra said she had some information about Sadie Greene's death that might be helpful."

The sheriff's eyebrows shot up.

"Oh?" Deputy Smith practically sneered. "And she wanted to tell *you* instead of the Sheriff's office, huh? Seems pretty unlikely."

The sheriff gave him a glare but didn't rebuke the deputy like I expected. Instead he asked, "Why didn't she just tell you over the phone?"

I shook my head. "I dunno. She said that she didn't want to be overheard. That someone might be listening."

What was Ramble doing in the house? Whatever it was, he

was taking a long time doing it.

The deputy stepped forward and jabbed a finger into my chest. "That's a pretty thin story, *girl*. Seems more likely that you killed the weirdo and called the cops in order to cover it up."

It was pretty rich that this deputy who looked like a twelve-year old was calling me "girl" but I was more annoyed that he'd just called a woman who'd been brutally murdered a "weirdo."

I opened my mouth to tell the deputy to go fuck himself, but Louis cut me off.

Though his eyes hadn't gone black yet, the vampire was staring daggers at the deputy. "Tell me, *deputy*, do you purposely bumble your way through a murder investigation, fumbling evidence and assaulting those who are trying to assist in capturing the murderer?"

The deputy's mouth dropped open and he spluttered, "I don't have to take shit from some *freak*—that's right, I know you're not human! I could arrest you right now and throw you in jail for…for… impeding a murder investigation!"

Louis gave the deputy a slow smile that would have chilled my blood had it been aimed in my direction. He kept his fangs in though. "Perhaps you should put a leash on your dog, sheriff."

Had Louis kept his mouth shut, the sheriff might have stayed on our side, but his last remark insulted the sheriff's ability to do his job and keep his subordinate in check.

"And perhaps you should keep your trap shut and let us do *our* job," the sheriff growled.

So glad we were all getting along.

I needed to calm things down or we wouldn't get anywhere tonight. "Look, I'm sorry sheriff. I did ask her why she didn't go to the police with her information but she didn't think anyone would believe her."

"Why on earth not? *Any* information would be good at this point. Something is running around my town and killing my citizens, dammit!" He dropped his voice as he added, "Even if they aren't entirely human, it's my job to protect them."

To be fair, he had a point. I tried to put myself in the sheriff's shoes. People in his town were being killed by something he didn't understand. Maybe he would be able to do more in finding the murderer if he had more information to work with.

"Well," I said, trying to figure out how to explain without sounding crazy, "I understand that there's a group of women in town who believe themselves to be witches. Cassandra and Sadie Greene were a part of that group."

Louis gave me a sharp look, making me think I was out of turn for speaking so openly about such things. But clearly the sheriff knew that Louis and Donavon weren't entirely human. I wasn't sure if he knew what they actually were, but that didn't really matter. I felt he deserved to have a better idea of what was going on in his town. Especially if he was willing to protect even those who weren't human.

The deputy scoffed at my explanation. "If you ask me, they were a bunch of freaks who needed to get laid more often."

My mouth dropped open. That was the second time this chauvinistic piece of shit had spoken ill of the murder victims.

"Nobody asked you, Ken." The sheriff said, throwing a glare at the deputy in an effort to make him shut up. "Please continue, Miss Mason."

I had to work to keep my anger under control. What I really wanted to do was ask Ramble to come back out and bite this asshat deputy.

I settled for ignoring the deputy completely and focusing on the sheriff.

"That was exactly the kind of reception she knew she'd get if she came to you, sheriff. I don't know what she actually wanted to tell me, but I think it might have had something to do with Sadie Greene's...ah... abilities as a witch."

I was purposely not looking at the deputy but could sense that he'd opened his mouth to spew more venom. I was more than happy when the sheriff shot him a dark look to shut him up.

"Explain what you mean by abilities," the sheriff said.

Shouldn't Rosalyn be the one talking about this? Was I giving out information that was taboo for non-witches to have? I had no idea. But I didn't want to get arrested so I quickly explained what I knew.

"I guess each witch has some sort of magical ability. Sadie Greene's was the ability to...um, know what others were feeling, I guess."

It sounded kind of lame when I put it that way, but I didn't know how else to describe it. Rosalyn could have done a much better job.

The sheriff took a moment to digest the new information. "Okay. How does Cassandra play into this, Miss Mason?"

"Cassandra and Sadie were in a relationship together."

It's ridiculous how many people still recoil at the idea of any relationship that is not solely between a man and a woman. I couldn't help glancing at the deputy which was why I saw a flicker of ugly excitement in his eyes before he opened his mouth to say something—and got elbowed hard by the sheriff before it could leave his mouth.

"Ken, get in the car."

The deputy's mouth dropped open and the flicker of excitement was replaced by outrage. "But I didn't even say anything!"

"Get in the fucking car and wait there!" The sheriff, livid now, pointed at the car with a shaking finger.

Without another word, the deputy slouched off.

After a moment, the sheriff seemed to get himself under control. "So, Cassandra had something to tell you. She called you and asked you to come over. She didn't want to come to us because she…didn't think we'd believe her. You think whatever Cassandra wanted to tell you had to do with Sadie Greene's murder, but you have no clue what it was and when you arrived at her house, she was dead." He paused giving me a minute to digest all that, then asked, "Is that about right? Am I missing anything?"

It was a pretty accurate summary. It also sounded like he was just about done with us and Ramble wasn't back yet.

"That's about it."

"I see." His neutral expression was suddenly replaced by a hard stare I thought might usually be reserved for an interrogation room. He took a step closer and lowered his voice while somehow strengthening his tone.

"Now, I don't know what you're doing in my town running around with the likes of this one," he jerked a thumb at Louis. "His brother has my respect but it's quickly running thin. If the *thing* committing these murders isn't caught and caught soon, there are gonna be a lot more questions for the people in this town who don't usually like to be questioned. Got me?"

I nodded slowly and tried not to perk up when Ramble finally came creeping out the front door. I missed the first few words of the sheriff's next tirade

"I don't know what you are, and if I thought you had something to do with Cassandra's murder, I'd arrest you on the spot." He paused and stared at me, waiting for me to blink or show some sign of guilt I guess. When I stared right back, simultaneously keeping tabs on Ramble as he padded down the porch stairs, the sheriff continued, "Right now, you're not a suspect. Now, get out of here and let us do our jobs. And if someone else wants to give you information about these murders, you bring your ass to me and tell me, got it?"

I nodded, unsure how I'd suddenly ended up on the receiving end of the sheriff's anger when it was Deputy Dipshit who'd really gotten the sheriff all riled up.

Clearly I'd made a mistake by being honest with him about Cassandra and Sadie being witches. He'd basically just ensured I wouldn't be trusting him with any further information.

Ramble calmly sank to his haunches next me as if he hadn't just gone traipsing through a murder scene.

"My office will be in touch when it comes time to make official statements about what you were doing here this morning." With that, he signaled for the deputy to move the sheriff's car, then strode back toward the house. Before he got halfway up the stairs, he paused and shouted over his shoulder, "And don't leave town!"

I glanced at the vampire who'd been standing silently beside me during the whole thing. He didn't look at me but must have felt my eyes on him because he shrugged and, without a word, walked back to his car.

I let Ramble hop up and over to the passenger side of our car before getting in myself.

195

"Well… I guess that went about as expected, huh?" I asked him once I'd closed the door. He was looking exceptionally pleased with himself. As much as I didn't want to feed the hellhound's ego, I couldn't help but ask, "Did you find anything interesting?"

He huffed a little. I was going to ask him another question, but Ramble lifted his head to look back toward the house.

The sheriff was staring at us from the front porch, hands on his hips. Clearly he was waiting for us to follow his orders and leave.

Floating behind him in the open doorway, Cassandra the witch also stared at us.

"I guess we'll be back later to get that information after all, huh?" I whispered to Ramble as I started the engine and backed out of the driveway.

* * *

Though Louis probably expected me to go back to the motel, I wasn't about to go sit in a room for hours while I waited for Donavon to recover. The only thing I could have done in the motel room was sleep and that was clearly out of the question unless I wanted to get another visit from Morvalden.

Instead I found my way back to Rosalyn's house and wasn't surprised to find there were lights on behind her curtains. I wouldn't be waking her and, though she hadn't texted or called me back, I felt like I should go and talk to her before the sheriff and his shitbag sidekick showed up to question her.

I was a little surprised when Louis parked behind me once again. I got out and opened the door for Ramble but he stayed in the passenger seat. "Not coming this time, huh?" He huffed once and looked at the house.

Hmm. I knew he wasn't nervous of Rosalyn so maybe he was limiting his exposure to Louis? I rolled down the driver's side window and explained to the hellhound, "Just in case you need to make a quick exit."

Louis got out of his car and intercepted me as I crossed the street.

"We should go back to the motel." Though his words made it sound like a suggestion, his tone was a direct order.

I ticked up an eyebrow. "I'm going to talk to Rosalyn and tell her what happened." I glanced at the horizon where light was just starting to seep back into the world, then looked back at vampire. "Cutting it a bit close aren't you?"

"I will not burst into flames or turn into a pile of dust from a little winter morning sunlight, Vânători."

Hmm. Not being afraid of getting crisped by the sun meant he was an older vampire. I stored that little nugget of information away to consider later.

"Great. Then you can come with me. I want to talk to Rosalyn before the sheriff does." I stepped around him and he let me pass. When I reached Rosalyn's front door, he was suddenly standing right beside me on the step though I hadn't heard him walking behind me.

Hello creepy.

The door opened before I even reached to knock.

"I knew you'd show up." It wasn't Rosalyn but a glowering Willomena who answered the door. This time, though, she also had tears in her eyes. It looked like she'd been a lot closer to Cassandra than she had been to Sadie Greene.

"Hi, Willomena. I'm really sorry. I know I should leave the coven to grieve, but I need to talk to Rosalyn."

She reached up and almost viciously wiped tears from her eyes. I could see the wheels turning in her mind. The glowering witch looked like she was thinking about what she could say that would give her a good excuse to slam the door in my face.

Fortunately, I heard Rosalyn's voice behind her. "Is that the Vânători? Let her in Willomena."

I made a move to step forward but Willomena blocked my way. Over her shoulder she said, "She brought the bloodsucker, Roz."

A collective gasp came from the living room. Apparently more than one witch had gathered at Rosalyn's house this morning. I guess that explained why Ramble had stayed in the car. I wondered if the witches had been here when I texted or if they'd gathered because of the news of Cassandra's death. I thought it might be the latter, otherwise Cassandra would have been with them instead of alone at her house, right?

The familiar face of the coven's leader appeared in the doorway. Her eyes were red and her skin blotchy from crying. She gave me a half-smile and caught sight of Louis behind me.

"You don't waste any time, do you?" She shook her head at me. "Managed to dig up the only vampire in town."

Curiosity crossed Louis's face before he wiped it clean of expression once more. I was caught by surprise when the vampire executed a sort of informal bow to Rosalyn.

"My apologies, Madam Rosalyn." If his tone hadn't been one of utmost respect, I might have thought he was mocking her. "I had not planned to call upon the House of Light on this morning, especially while you are dealing with the loss of two of your sisters."

Willomena still gripped the edge of the door, her knuckles

going white. "And how do we know that you weren't the cause of their deaths, bloodsucker? I bet witches blood is hard to resist—"

"That's quite enough, Willomena. I know you are grieving for our sisters, but we will not lash out at those who are not responsible for their deaths." She turned to a young girl in the corner who'd been nibbling a cookie and staring at us with wide-eyed interest. "Alexis, please get Willomena some water and help her find a quiet spot to grieve, would you?"

Alexis looked like she wanted to protest but seeing Rosalyn's no-nonsense look, the young girl nodded instead and held out a hand for Willomena to precede her into the kitchen. Willomena glared at Louis, turned her unblinking stare on me, then stomped off. Alexis followed, throwing one last look of longing over her shoulder at Louis and me.

Apparently someone was curious about the vampire and the Vânători.

Rosalyn beckoned us inside. I stepped over the threshold but Louis hesitated.

For an awkward second, I looked between the witch and the vampire.

As if fulfilling some sort of ancient ritual, Louis put his hand over his heart (did vampires have hearts?) and said, "I promise you, Leader of the House of Light, that neither you nor yours will come to harm at my hands."

Rosalyn nodded as if this was perfectly normal. "Then I invite you into my house, Louis Lawrence of the House of Red.

What the hell was all the House of Red and House of Light business? And I'd thought the whole needing-an-invitation thing had just been a myth propagated by vampires so people would feel safe in their homes. It was something I should have asked Jax about long ago.

Rosalyn snapped me out of my thoughts.

"Thank you for thinking to inform me of Cassandra's death—though I felt it the moment she died."

"You did?"

"There is a way to magically link the coven members to me so that I can tell when they are in need. Before Sadie's murder, we were not linked because the magical bond sometimes accidentally allows strong emotions or thoughts to be shared. But afterward, I linked to every member of the coven. When Cassandra was…killed," here she choked back a sob, "I felt it."

Producing a tissue from her pocket, she wiped at her eyes which had teared up. "But," she said, her voice becoming less watery, "how did *you* know Cassandra had been killed?"

My mouth went dry. Did she think I had something to do with Cassandra's murder?

"She called," I weakly explained, "and asked me to go over to her house because she had something important to tell me about Sadie's death." I suddenly wondered if Rosalyn was the person Cassandra hadn't wanted to overhear our conversation. Surely not?

"Oh? What information?"

"I don't know," I said somewhat lamely. "She was dead when I got to her house. I texted you and called the cops."

A voice came from behind Rosalyn. "Are you allowing simple human law enforcement to meddle with coven matters, Rosalyn?"

In the doorway of the dining room stood a woman with long, golden blond hair. It was she who had spoken. Her maroon satin dress with its high collar made her look like she'd dressed to try out for the role of evil villain in the next Disney movie. Even without the dress, she would have stood out in a crowd. She radiated a sort of beauty you only found on airbrushed magazine covers.

Beside me, Louis stiffened.

"Lady Gabriella," he inclined his head very slightly. "I did not know you would be gracing our town with your presence."

Gabriella smiled like a wolf who'd found the perfect prey. "I could not leave my sister-witches to face these terrible losses alone. Clearly they are in need of a steady hand." She looked at Rosalyn who, I noted, was now slightly flushed and looking less sad and more pissed.

So Gabriella and Rosalyn weren't exactly BFFs. Good to know.

I suddenly felt way out of my depth. On top of the werewolves, there were trolls, a vampire, witches, a giant scary beast, and one bastard of a black cat in this town. I'd definitely bitten off more than I could chew by agreeing to stay and help find the murderer.

"I'm really, really sorry, Rosalyn," I said interrupting the tense moment, "but I need to ask you about something." The coven leader turned to me, still looking a little too fiery for my peace of mind, but since she didn't blast me apart with a spell or whatever, I took it as a good sign and pressed on. "Earlier, before Cassandra called, Donavon and I were investigating the site of the first murder. We were attacked by the killer—it was a giant beast, like a dog—"

"I knew it was a werewolf!" Gabriella crowed, looking around at the other witches who had congregated around her. "I told you allowing them to live in your territory was dangerous, Rosalyn, and now you have two dead—"

201

—It wasn't a werewolf," I snapped glaring at the witch and cutting her off. "If you would let me finish, we might be able to figure out what it is before it kills again."

The witch dropped her piercing blue eyes on me. They flashed with power as she glared at me. "And who are you?"

"She is Vianne Vânǎtori and she is assisting my coven in capturing the murderer at my request."

The golden-haired witch looked like she'd just been slapped in the face. I couldn't say it wasn't gratifying. I hardly knew her, but it didn't take long to recognize she was a bitch.

"You invited a *Vânǎtori* to meddle in coven affairs?" She flashed those electric blue eyes at me and practically spat out my name.

I smiled. "Better me than someone who tries to dress like the wicked witch." It felt like the air was sucked from the room as my words landed, but I wasn't done yet. I leaned forward, swept my eyes over her ridiculous dress and mock-whispered, "I don't know if you know this, but it's not the 1700's anymore."

"Enough," Rosalyn chided, casting me a look. I could have sworn I saw a glint of amusement there though. "We have lost a sister tonight. This is not the time to spit and claw at one another."

"Yes," Gabriella snapped and raised her hand, closing her fingers into a fist with an over-dramatic flourish. "It is time to take our revenge!"

Was she serious?

I decided to ignore her and turned back to Rosalyn with a shake of my head.

"Can we talk privately for a second?"

Behind Rosalyn, Gabriella boomed, "Witches do not keep

202

secrets from each other!"

I was about to ask her then how come no one had told her that she looked ridiculous when Louis saved the day.

He swept over to the golden-haired witch with a half smile as if he'd just arrived at a ball and had spotted her from a distance.

"Lady Gabriella, it has been too long!" The rest of his greeting was lost to me as he lowered his voice and steered the annoying witch away.

Quickly, before we were interrupted again, I turned to Rosalyn. "I'm sorry to ask questions at a time like this, Rosalyn, but the beast wasn't alone. There's a black cat that seems to be working with it. If it's really the same cat I've been seeing around town, then it was outside your house yesterday when we talked to Cassandra and outside your store when you and I first met." I didn't mention that the cat had also been stalking me at the motel.

"A black cat?" Rosalyn said quietly, keeping our conversation as private as possible.

I nodded. "Donavon said it smelled like a witch. Is there anyone in town who can turn into a cat?" I specifically did not imply that it might be one of her witches.

She shook her head. "I could do it, but none of the other witches are powerful enough to change their form."

I lowered my voice even further. "What about her?" I jerked my head a tiny bit at the annoying Gabriella who seemed to be enjoying the vampire's attention.

"Yes…but it seems unlikely."

Unlikely was not the same as impossible.

"Would she have a reason to want to harm Cassandra or Sadie?"

"Well…" Rosalyn seemed to struggle internally with her answer. "Gabriella has aspirations to be the leader of the coven. If she can prove to the other witches that I'm not fit to lead, they might cast me out and adopt her as the coven leader. Cassandra and Sadie were my strongest supporters but… I just can't believe that a witch, even Gabriella, would do that to a sister…"

We both glanced over at the witch now leaning on the vampire's arm. If Louis hadn't been wearing the t-shirt and jeans, they might really have looked like they were at a ball.

"And," Rosalyn added with resolve, "it wouldn't explain the other murders."

"She could have done it to throw you off," I suggested.

"I don't know… it wouldn't explain who the beast is."

"True," I sighed. "You don't happen to have any idea what Cassandra wanted to tell me do you?"

Rosalyn's eyes clouded over with grief once more. "No."

Chapter 15

"Well, that was interesting," I said to Ramble as I dragged myself out of the car. During our short drive back to the motel, I'd explained to the hellhound everything that had taken place in the house. Now my lack of sleep was catching up to me. All I wanted to do was fall into bed and sleep for the next week, but I knew Morvalden would be waiting for me.

Looked like I would have to bite the bullet and drink more terrible motel coffee. Super. Maybe if I threw it back like a shot I wouldn't taste it.

The idea of a shot sounded really, really good right now.

Dammit. Great job bringing up alcohol, Vi.

I tamped down on the sudden need for a fifth of whiskey. Or vodka. Or anything really. I wasn't picky at this point.

Having beaten us back to the motel, Louis stood in the shade of the building though the sun still wasn't completely up yet and clouds covered the sky.

"You seemed to be on pretty good terms with that Gabriella witch, huh?" I asked the vampire. The comment made me sound like a jealous girlfriend, but whatever. Maybe it was none of my business but I was curious as to how they knew each other.

Louis's eyes darkened slightly but I didn't get the feeling like he was trying to use any vampire hoodoo on me. "She and I are acquaintances from long ago." He still used that emotionless, almost robotic tone which was odd when he paired it with a small smile and a shrug. "But I was a different person then."

"Oh, I see now. You're the tall, handsome loner with a dark tragic past but you've changed your ways now and are the model vampire every girl should swoon over, huh? You know they made a show about that, right? It's called, *Angel.*" Sometimes my brain doesn't filter everything before my mouth starts spitting out words. Especially when I haven't slept.

The smile slipped from his face. Apparently fang-face did not appreciate being made fun of. "*Angel* got it wrong—all vampires retain their souls."

I considered pointing out that I didn't think Morvalden had a soul but decided against it. I was only picking a fight with the vampire because I desperately wanted a drink. Also, I really didn't want to bring up asking him to donate his blood, so I steered the conversation to safer ground.

"You gonna tell Donavon about this morning or do you want me to fill him in?" My stomach chose that moment to give an audible grumble.

"I will fill him in while you get breakfast." As he spoke, he produced his set of keys and unlocked the front door to the main office, then disappeared inside. I followed him in as he unlocked the interior door to the back office. He pointed to a fridge in the corner. "Most of the free breakfast food is in there. Dry goods are in the cupboard beside the fridge. Help yourself."

"What about the other guests? Should I put some stuff out or something?"

He laughed. "You're the only guest, Vânători. Almost no one comes here this time of year. Just the newlyweds and nearly-dead but they're more interested in the Downeast part of the state." He turned to leave.

"My name is Vi, by the way."

"You've told me," he said over his shoulder. "After you've gotten breakfast, Vânători, let's talk with Donavon about the murdering cat-beast duo." With that he stepped outside and closed the outer office behind him.

Twenty minutes later, I sat sideways on a chair with my feet propped on the bed in my previous hotel room. Ramble sprawled at my side. The curtains were drawn to keep out the light and Louis stood on the other side of the room as far from the window as he could get. The room was littered with empty fast food take out bags. It appeared that werewolves needed a lot of food to heal. I wondered who had gotten him the food since Louis had been with me all morning.

Ramble and I listened as the werewolf and vampire discussed the situation. It was sort of like watching a tennis match since they couldn't seem to agree on anything and kept volleying theories back and forth.

"It's definitely *not* Rosalyn," Donavon growled from where he lay propped up in bed. He seemed to be growling at everything though. Maybe it was a werewolf mechanism for coping with pain.

Ramble and I flicked our eyes to Louis, waiting for the return volley.

"Calm down. I wasn't accusing Rosalyn. I said that the witches have a hand in this. It doesn't necessarily mean that

Rosalyn is involved." Louis said, leaning against the TV stand.

"You said she told the Vânători that only she and that other witch can change into a cat." They'd been deliberately avoiding saying Gabriella's name during his conversation, making me think that she could tell when someone was talking about her. It wouldn't have surprised me. Maybe that was her gift—the gift of being aware that people were talking about her behind her back. She struck me as the conceited type who would be just as happy receiving negative attention as positive attention. I bet she dominated on social media platforms.

"Exactly," The vampire replied."The simplest answer is usually the correct one and the simplest answer here is that Ga—the *other witch*— has, not only the ability to change into a cat, but also the motive to perpetrate these murders."

I raised my hand like a student in class. When Louis's eyes flicked to me, I dropped my hand and asked, "I get the ability part, but why do you think she has a motive?"

"Pay more attention, *Vânători*."

I jerked at the vampire's rebuke but he ignored it and continued talking, "Rosalyn said that Sadie Greene and Cassandra McDougall were her strongest supporters. I find it difficult to believe that the two witches who were murdered are also those who were most supportive of the coven's leader. Their deaths shift the coven's power structure and make it look like Rosalyn can't protect the members of her coven. Right now, her position could be easily challenged."

During my conversation with Rosalyn, Louis had been on the other side of the room talking animatedly to Gabriella, yet he seemed to have heard every word of the conversation between the witch and me. I filed away the fact that Louis had great hearing and could multitask, then refocused on what he'd just suggested.

"So you think Gab—the other witch—is trying to undermine Rosalyn before she challenges her? Is this challenge similar to how the werewolves Challenge each other?"

Louis's haughty voice was enough to set my teeth on edge. "No, Vânători. The witches are a bit more civilized than that."

Donavon lifted an offended eyebrow at the vampire's insult but let it pass. When Louis didn't explain how witches challenge each other, Donavon sighed and filled in the information gap for me. "This is pretty typical of how witches fight. Lots of backstabbing, undermining, and mind games before someone actually challenges the coven leader. Then the coven members vote on who their leader should be."

I shrugged. "Sounds like any other form of politics."

"Until you get a mysterious beast murdering people who are not members of the coven," Donavon pointed out.

"Good point. Except, if all of this is related to internal strife in the coven, why kill Kleinman and Duluth? Or Samuel Vance for that matter? He was a werewolf but he wouldn't have had any dealings with the witches, right?"

"No. The Pack and the witches don't usually mix," Donavon confirmed.

"You're mixing now," I said

"Only because we must in order to catch this beast."

There was another angle we were leaving out though.

"Could either of the other two victims—Kleinman or Duluth— could they have been part of the supernatural community?"

"The 'supernatural community?'" Donavon said, lifting an eyebrow and throwing a quick smirk at Louis. "Where do you get this stuff?"

"You know what I mean." I gave a dismissive gesture. "Were they something not human? Something...other?"

Out of the corner of his mouth, Louis murmured, "I feel as if we should take offense at that."

I took a page out of Ramble's book and gave the males a good eye roll before pressing on. "If Duluth and Kleinman weren't human, then it would mean that the killer is specifically targeting non-humans and might not have anything to do with the witch's power struggle."

They both considered this for a moment, then Donavon shook his head. "Other than the witches, my Pack, and Louis here, there aren't any other 'supernatural creatures' in Ricketts."

"Except for the beast," I added.

"And that, yes."

And at least one troll at the Flying Pie, I silently tacked on.

That explained why Rosalyn hadn't wanted me to tell Donavon about Mitchell's troll-tantrum at the Flying Pie. Apparently Louis, Donavon, and his werewolves had no idea that trolls lived in their neck of the woods. I wondered if the magic pin that Mitchell wore to keep him human was also spelled to keep his scent human. Otherwise it seemed like, with Donavon's werewolf sense of smell, he would have noticed a troll in town, right? I'd probably have to talk to Rosalyn again to find out if either of the other two men who had been murdered were something other than human.

I felt a moment of excitement that maybe we could figure out who the murderer was, but the feeling quickly faded as I considered how Kleinman and Duluth had died. Given the quickness of their deaths, they hadn't fought back much and hadn't turned into anything else to defend themselves. It seemed unlikely that they were anything other than human. I mean, that monster-dog had been big, but Mitchell the troll had been far bigger. He could have thrown one punch at the beast and knocked it out. TKO.

Then again, the two men could have been something supernatural that was just as vulnerable as a human. Like a Vânători unable to use her magical necklace…

"I have a question," Donavon's voice broke through my thoughts. I looked up to find he was staring at me. "Why is it that when we were attacked last night, only your hellhound joined the fight?"

Uh oh. I scrambled for an excuse and realized I sort of had one. "I was dealing with the cat!"

Louis crossed his arms over his chest in a gesture that looked forced like he was trying to appear more human. "During their entire fight with the beast, you were fighting the cat?"

"I mean, I wouldn't say I was *fighting* the cat. More like prying it off me and trying to get it to leave me alone without hurting it."

"You didn't want to hurt it," Louis's voice was dry and disbelieving.

"Well, no—"

"Are you keeping something from us, Vânători?" Donavon asked. Great. Now he'd stopped calling me by my first name, too.

"No, I—"

The werewolf cut me off before I could form another excuse. "Because if this is all that a Vânători can bring to the table, then all those legends about your people must have been vastly exaggerated."

Shocked that his wrath was suddenly aimed at me, my

mouth hung open stupidly. Ramble started to get up but I regained my senses enough to shake my head at him. He didn't need to defend my reputation. Hell, I didn't even really have a reputation. All this Vânători shit was for an ancestor I'd never even known about.

"Anything else?" I managed to say without spluttering.

"Yes," the werewolf said, clearly getting worked up by his own speech. He sat up straighter on the bed, which looked awkward given that his left leg was still splayed out straight in front of him. "You don't know anything about werewolves or witches and you let your hellhound do your fighting for you. The only thing you've done so far is see a few ghosts which hasn't helped a whole lot. I'm just wondering when we're going to see the great Vânători you're supposed to be.

As he spoke, I could feel my own anger bubbling to the surface. Not so much at Donavon, but at my whole situation. I waited until it was obvious he was finished before I pulled my feet from the bed and leaned toward him.

I wasn't sure if this was the right move or not but I was tired of pretending. And, when it came down to it, Donavon kind of had a point. It wasn't fair for him to expect me to have his back in a fight if I couldn't actually fight.

Reaching under the neckline of my t-shirt, I fished out the necklace and held it up. "This is the Artemis necklace." I paused for a beat, then explained, "I need it to have the full Vânători abilities. Unfortunately, it isn't working properly for me because I'm not a full Vânători."

"But... I thought that was a myth," Donavon said, glancing at Louis before turning back to me. "The Vânători... you really get your power from a necklace?"

I shrugged but I didn't like his tone. He made it sound like it was a dirty secret or something.

Louis hid behind his emotionless mask once again. "So," he prompted, "you said you're not a full Vânători? What does that mean?"

"Yeah," Donavon added. "You smell like a Vânători."

"Gee, thanks," I automatically responded, falling back on sarcasm. It bought me the few seconds I needed to collect my wits and figure out how to explain all this.

"So, I'm a descendant of the Vânători, but I'm not a direct female descendant—which means the necklace works for me, but not without a little help."

Okay. So far so good. They were both listening attentively and didn't seem to be wearing confused expressions yet.

"That's why you didn't help us attack the beast?" Donavon asked.

Though his tone was more curious than accusing, I couldn't help but wince. I really had been busy fending off the stupid cat, but compared to his and Ramble's fight with the monster-dog, it seemed like a pretty weak argument.

"Yes. I'm sorry. It's also why I needed to speak with Rosalyn. Right now, I'm really nothing more than human."

"A human with a tamed hellhound," Dovavon added.

I started to correct him about Ramble being tame, but Louis jumped back into the conversation and drove straight to the point. "You said it doesn't work 'without a little help.' What exactly does that mean?"

I licked my lips, suddenly nervous about explaining. I'd come this far though. I couldn't chicken out now. "It means that my blood is not…Vânători enough." I gave a very Ramble-like huff. "And it means that I need vampire blood to make the necklace work."

Chapter 16

"Absolutely not." Donavon's voice cut through the room like a knife as he levered himself off the bed to stand over me. It would have been a lot more menacing had he not been swaying slightly.

Ramble dodged out of the way to avoid the angry werewolf and bared his long teeth though he didn't growl yet.

Donavon stuck his finger in my face. "He's not giving you anything. He's been through enough and you'll have to go through me if you're going to try and take—"

"Don," Louis said so quietly I almost didn't hear him.

The werewolf tried to turn to the vampire, but the move was too swift for his healing body. He winced and staggered back to prop himself against the bed.

I should probably have been more afraid of the werewolf but I just couldn't muster up the energy needed. I slipped the necklace back under my shirt so that it once again fell into the hollow at my throat.

"Donavon, I just told you I'm little more than human. Do you really think I could take his blood without his consent?"

"Well he's not going to *give* any consent," Donavon mostly growled.

I was starting to get a little huffy myself. "It's not like I actually *want* to drink vampire blood and he's clearly not going to give it to me anyways. Forget I said anything."

"It's funny how both of you seem to assume you know my mind," the vampire said in that quiet, inflectionless tone of his while looking at the floor. Donavon opened his mouth to protest but Louis suddenly looked up and caught the werewolf with his eyes. It was enough to shut Donavon up.

He then turned those eyes on me.

They were jet black with not a bit of white reflected. Had he wanted to capture me in those bottomless depths right then, I had no illusions I would have been able to get away. He clearly allowed me to look away, which was the only reason I was still in charge of my body.

It turned out Louis was a pretty damn scary vampire. A little voice of self-preservation suggested it would be a really good idea to pretend all of this was a joke so I could haul ass to the car and floor it until we reached somewhere far, far away...like maybe Russia.

"Vânători," Louis's soft voice felt like a caress. It made me shiver...and not in a scared way. "Why is it that you need vampire blood?"

My mouth had gone dry at the sound of Louis's voice and I had to take a sip of coffee to rewet it. Something had changed about Louis when he vamped out this time. Before, he'd just been a semi-scary vampire. Now, he was...different. Alluring. Did he have some kind of sexy vampire switch that he'd just turned on?

Ramble shifted silently so that he could stand between the vampire and me.

"Like I said before," I explained, voice definitely not on the edge of trembling, "I don't have enough Vânători blood to make the necklace work because I'm not a direct female descendant."

Louis shook his head. "Yes, but why *vampire* blood?" He waved a hand at Donavon. "If all you needed was blood with magic, any supernatural being should do."

"Oh," I said, feeling stupid. "I guess you're right. I just assumed that it had to be vampire blood since that's what has worked so far."

Anger flickered across his face and I realized I'd just implied that I'd bled other vampires. Shit.

"Uh, I was jumped by a vampire who forced me to drink his blood." I quickly explained, "And then again by a vampire named Constancia."

Silence filled the room. I'd thought it was tense before, but now I felt like I could barely draw a breath.

"Constancia," Louis finally said. "*The* Constancia?" Another moment of shocked silence passed. "She gave you her blood? Just like that?"

I shrugged. It had been more like she'd ripped her wrist open and forced her blood into my mouth, but I didn't figure they needed those kinds of details. Instead I said, "And after she did, I was able to use the necklace. But the ability kind of faded over time."

"Because you didn't have any more vampire blood after that." The vampire's soft voice still sounded dangerous.

"Exactly. At least, that's what I think." No point in sharing that Rosalyn thought the same thing. I didn't want to drag the witch into this in case Louis was about to lose his shit.

There was another long moment of silence while Louis stared at me. Nothing like being stared at by a scary, suddenly sexy vampire.

"I see," Louis finally said and broke eye contact with me.

I suddenly felt less trembly. I also didn't feel as attracted to the vampire as I had been for the last few minutes. He just seemed tall and lanky again. Was this another form of vampire hypnosis or something?

"I am not inclined to think that anything other than vampire blood will work for you, Vânători, though you may try other supernatural beings if you want to test the theory."

Now I was confused.

"Why? You just said it could be any kind of blood."

"Call it a hunch." Though there was no emotion to his tone, his small smile made me feel like he knew a whole lot more about the Vânători line and why he thought only vampire blood would work.

Before I could ask him any more questions, we were interrupted by loud hammering on the door that made us all jump except for Ramble.

"Open the door! I know he's in there!" A booming voice sounded through the door.

Louis turned to Donavon and said, "I guess they found you, brother."

"What? Who?" I asked looking from the vampire to the werewolf.

Donavon sighed but began limping over to the door. "My Pack. Some of them will want to Challenge me while I'm injured." Before he could explain more, he yanked the door open.

A large man about the same build as Donavon but slightly taller stood outside. He wore a black winter jacket over a t-shirt that probably cost more than I made in a month at the pawnshop. His fist was raised like he'd been about to pound on the door again.

"Patrick," Donavon said, quickly scanning behind the were-wolf to make sure no one else was about to jump out. I thought maybe Donavon would say more, but apparently the one word greeting was enough.

"We felt a disturbance in the Pack last night and you didn't go home," Patrick said though I didn't hear any warmth or worry reflected in his voice. As he spoke, I saw him quickly assess Donavon and realized he was looking for injuries. Would his own Pack really take advantage of Donavon's temporary weakness and try to Challenge him for the Alpha position? If that was the way Packs worked, I didn't think I wanted anything to do with them.

"I've been working," Donavon retorted. "What do you want?"

"We thought you might have been hurt." Patrick didn't sound like that would be a terrible thing. His eyes flicked past Donavon, breezed over Louis as if he was beneath his notice and then landed on me. "Who's she?"

Donavon crossed his arms over his chest. "A friend. You can see now that I'm not hurt. Is there anything else?"

I could see Patrick weighing his options. While standing in one spot, Donavon didn't look hurt. It was only when he walked that you noticed a bit of a limp. Patrick might have a hunch that Donavon was hurt, but now he was second-guessing himself. I got the feeling that Patrick was unlikely to beat Donavon in a fair fight.

Apparently the other werewolf felt the same way because suddenly it felt like he was backing down.

"Actually, yes. There is something else," Patrick's voice was crisp now. All business. His eyes flicked to me then back to

Donavon. "But it's Pack business."

It looked like I'd just been granted a reprieve from having to deal with the angry werewolf and scary vampire. I leapt at my chance to escape.

Smiling at Patrick, I stood and headed toward the door. "Not to worry, boys. I was just leaving." Ramble followed me, but when we went to walk through the door, the new werewolf stepped forward, effectively blocking my path.

"Vânători," the werewolf sneered, nostrils flaring.

I really needed to figure out this whole smelling like a Vânători thing. I fixed Patrick with a stare and ratcheted up my smile though the emotion didn't reach my eyes. "That's right. With my hellhound partner. Is there a problem?"

Ramble obliged me by letting out a rumbly growl. I made a mental note to thank him later for playing along.

Patrick took a staggering step back, his nostrils flaring wildly as he took in the hellhound's scent. I didn't wait for him to answer my question, brushing past him to walk toward my car. Let the boys have their private discussion. I'd rather not know any more information that might complicate working with the werewolves.

Ramble hopped through the driver's door when I opened it and landed in the passenger's seat, giving me a questioning look when I slid into the driver's seat and pulled the door closed.

"We're gonna go visit our good friend Mitchell the troll."

Ramble's eyebrows rose in comical doggy surprise.

I started the car and pointed us in the direction of the Flying Pie. "I have a hunch and I want to talk to him about it. I'm guessing you didn't smell anything or get any ideas about who the beast is when you were in Cassandra's house, huh?"

The hellhound gave a very slight shake of his head.

"I'd guessed as much. You would think there would be some sort of scent, right? But you haven't smelled anything at any of the crime scenes and I bet you couldn't smell anything at the park when the beast attacked, right?"

Ramble cocked his head to the side, clearly thinking about his fight with the monster-dog, before nodding that he hadn't smelled the beast.

"That's what I thought."

Rambled whuffed at me, demanding more of an explanation.

"I think the beast is using a pin like the one Mitchell has."

It didn't take long to get to the restaurant. I pulled into a fairly empty parking lot. I wasn't sure if that was a good thing or not. More people might mean Mitchell would be less likely to pull me apart like a kid dissecting an insect. On the other hand, I wanted to have a private conversation with Mitchell about his magical pin and how it worked. I wasn't sure how I'd do that if the place was hopping and he was too busy to talk.

I killed the engine and stared at the restaurant.

Before I could chicken out, I forced myself to open the door and strode across the parking lot, Ramble at my side.

As I walked, I thought hard about all I'd learned in the past few days. "Rosalyn created the pin for Mitchell. She's definitely not a suspect, so the question is, can any of her witches make a pin like that?" I mused to Ramble.

The first witch that leapt to mind was Gabriella with her pretty, sneering face. She wasn't a part of Rosalyn's coven and she was clearly trying to undermine Rosalyn's position as coven leader. And Rosalyn had told us that Gabriella could turn into a cat.

I also considered Willomena but dismissed the idea. She's been genuinely upset about Sadie and Cassandra's deaths. She didn't like me very much, but that didn't mean she was the killer.

"Okay, Ramble," I said just before we approached the door. "We're not going in to fight him. We just need to talk to him. But if anything happens, we run. No fighting. Just running. Agreed?"

The hellhound stared at me with a look of disappointment. Finally he huffed, rolled his eyes and lifted a paw. I shook it. I guess I'd just entered into another agreement with the hellhound. Not sure if that was a good thing or not.

"Oh," I added, "see if you can smell him or if the magic pin thingy keeps you from being able to tell if he's a troll by smell as well as sight."

I opened the door and we stepped inside the warm, deserted foyer. The skin on my face was cold and raw just from walking across the parking lot. Maine was definitely not my go-to state for a winter getaway.

The front area was now decorated with plastic orange pumpkins and other halloween decor. A four-foot tall electronic witch had been placed next to the host's podium. As soon we stood in front of it, a sensor made the thing leap out at me with a cackle.

I might have jumped a little, earning an amused look from Ramble.

Footsteps approached and a second later, Mitchell rounded the corner, smiling and opening his mouth to greet us. His Flying Pie pin was firmly in place on his chest.

"Welcome to—" The moment he saw it was us, the smile fell

from his face. "You." His eyes flicked back to the dining room and kept his voice low. "You're not welcome here."

I couldn't say I hadn't been expecting the cold reception.

"Nice to see you too, Mitchell." I smiled but kept my voice down as well. "I wondered if I could ask you some questions—

"No." He took up a stance behind the podium and pointed to the door. "Leave. Now."

I sighed. "Look Mitchell, I think we might have gotten off on the wrong foot." I left out that this had clearly not been my fault. After all, he was the one who'd gone berserk and tried to flatten me with his giant troll fist.

"Paying customers only," he snapped.

"Fine," I snapped right back, crossing my arms over my chest. "I'll be having lunch then."

Mitchell stared me down. I thought I saw a brief flash of green in his eyes, but it was gone before I could be sure.

"Fine." He jerked a menu off the stack, snatched up a roll of silverware, and stomped away. "Follow me."

We wound through the dining room where a few people glanced my way before returning to conversation with their lunch partners. Mitchell stopped at a table set against a window at the back of the room. Without another word, he dropped the roll of silverware and menu to the table before turning on a heel and returning to the foyer. So much for talking to him.

After pulling off my oversized jacket, I draped it on the extra chair and sat so that I could face most of the room. I'd only had a second to glance over the menu when a woman's voice sent a jolt through me.

"Back again, I see."

It was Mitchell's wife and she didn't look thrilled to see

me. Though, to give her credit, at least she was smiling and putting on a better customer service show than Mitchell had. Her name tag said Delores.

"Yes." I smiled back. "I've been helping Rosalyn figure out what's going on around town and I wondered if I might ask you some questions."

Delores drew herself up and threw a look around the room before answering in a low voice, "We have nothing to do with those deaths, Vânători."

"I know," I reassured her, "I've seen the killer but I think he's using a magic doohickey sort of like what you use." I jerked my head toward the pin on her chest. It was identical to the one Mitchell wore and was even worn in the same spot. I could only assume that she must also be a troll.

"You'll have to talk to Rosalyn about that kind of thing."

I grimaced. "I plan to, but she's a little busy at the moment. I thought I'd try here first."

The woman stared at me for a second, then looked pointedly at my menu. "Are you going to order?"

I mentally reviewed how much cash I had left and decided to keep lunch light. I hadn't paid for the extra days at the motel yet and assumed Louis would want me to settle up soon. I ordered the cheapest thing off the menu—a bowl of soup with a glass of free water. The minute I'd finished ordering, Delores took the menu and strode away.

This wasn't going very well. Then again, I wasn't being chased by a giant troll yet, so I guess I wasn't doing too badly, either.

Ramble sat up and scented the air.

"Can you smell that they're trolls?" I whispered.

He gave a quiet snort—a no, I thought—and continued to

smell the air as he walked quietly away from the table.

Maybe he smelled something else supernatural?

"Don't go far, Ramble. Witches, remember?" I didn't think he'd enjoy being a witch's familiar. Though, to be fair, I had no real idea what a witch's familiar did.

Apparently the hellhound agreed with me because he stopped at the doorway to another dining area then turned around to rejoin me at the table.

Delores brought me my food without another word then disappeared through a door to the kitchen. I didn't realize how hungry I was until the moment the broccoli soup was before me. I needed a reason to stay and talk to Delores or Mitchell about their pins, though, so I slowed down my eating to buy more time in the restaurant. I wished I had enough money to order more food. Or to get a slice of pie.

Mmm. Pie.

Throughout the meal, Ramble lay quietly underneath the table. I couldn't exactly sneak him soup and I vowed to stop somewhere on the way back for some fast food for him. While still eating, I kept my voice low and asked, "Can you smell the trolls at all, Ramble?"

He gave a quiet snuff, which seemed like a definite no.

Ha! Maybe I was right about the beast having a magical pin!

I had another thought and whispered down to Ramble, "Do they have a human smell at all?"

I got another negative snuff. Huh. So Mitchell and Delores's pins didn't just keep them in human form and keep them from smelling like trolls. It also kept them from leaving *any* scent.

"Well, well," a familiar voice trilled, jolting me and making me splash soup over the rim of the bowl with my spoon.

I might have had an angry expression on my face as I looked

up at the perfect Gabriella. She'd had the brains to change out of her ridiculous dress from earlier and now wore a blindingly white sweater over crisp gray dress pants. "If it isn't the Vânători." She glanced behind her to where Willomena stood. The other witch looked a little surprised and—was that guilt?

Knowing it would irk her, I kept my seat. "Hello, Gabriella." I ate a spoonful of soup while keeping my eyes on the witches. Rosalyn was nowhere in sight. I suddenly realized why Willomena looked guilty.

"Planning a coup already?"

Even though a few more diners had arrived for lunch, the room was still fairly empty. A few of the other patrons threw glances at the lovely Gabriella, but they didn't seem to be paying attention to our conversation. I couldn't blame them for looking at her. She was one of those people who commanded attention when she entered a room.

From the corner of my eye, I saw a very concerned Delores frozen in the kitchen doorway. I wondered if she was worried she'd have another mess to clean up after my second visit.

At my comment, Gabriella's cheeks developed red circles as she flushed. Even when angry, she still managed to look gorgeous. I bet she was even a beautiful crier. I always got all blotchy and red when I cried. Ah well. I guess we can't all be supermodels.

"My affairs are none of your business, hunter," Gabriella all but hissed, causing more faces to turn away from their food to look at her. She must have realized she was drawing too much negative attention because she smiled—and it was like a little ray of sunshine penetrated a cloudy sky. Though her power was nothing compared to Lady Moyra, it was quite evident that Gabriella could definitely pack a punch when she

225

wanted.

The moment she smiled, the other patrons automatically smiled back before returning to their meals.

I glanced around at them and then back to Gabriella.

"Impressive," I said. "Of course, they probably wouldn't be too happy knowing you'd just influenced them."

One of her perfectly sculpted eyebrows arched gracefully. In a pleasant, conversational tone, she replied, "And what difference to me are the emotions of sheep?" She sneered down at my half-eaten meal. "Enjoy your slop, Vânători." To Willomena she said, "Let's go. This place is going to the pigs."

I caught Willomena cast an apologetic look at Delores as she left, but she stayed quiet and right on Gabriella's heels.

"Well, that was interesting," I muttered to Ramble.

It looked like Rosalyn was right and that Gabriella was already working to get the coven's witches over to her side. It shouldn't have mattered to me, but I liked Rosalyn. And more importantly, I really disliked Gabriella. It might have been petty, but anything that Gabriella wanted, I was strictly against.

That and I had a sinking feeling she was either the cat or the monster-dog.

I finished my lunch in silence and paid the bill, leaving a decent tip that I knew I'd regret later. The food had been good, though, and I thought leaving a hefty tip might let Delores know that the restaurant did not serve slop.

I hadn't gotten to ask them about their pins, but at least I'd learned something. I'd take that as a win.

I was pleasantly surprised when Delores caught up to me in the foyer.

"Vânători." She held out a clear plastic to-go box through

which I could clearly see a perfect slice of pumpkin pie with a dollop of whipped cream. My mouth watered at the sight of it. Beside me I heard Ramble lick his lips.

I really wanted that pie.

With a pang of regret, I shook my head. "I'm sorry. I've already spent my lunch budget."

Ignoring my protest, she pressed the box into my hands and with a small, tight smile, said, "It's on the house, but only if you give me your impression of the witch."

My eyebrows shot up involuntarily. "Gabriella?"

Delores nodded.

"To be honest, this is only the second time I've met her... but I can't say she's made a good impression."

This got another nod from Delores and she waved me to follow her through a small side door. She flicked on a light and revealed what looked like a coat closet. She stepped inside and after giving Ramble a moment to step in, I followed. It was a tight fit but we had enough room that we weren't touching.

"Gabriella says she'll be taking over the coven soon. She knows about Mitchell and me."

I nodded to show her that I understood she meant Gabriella knew that they were trolls.

"We settled here because the coven was friendly to our kind. But if she takes over..."

I hesitated. "My last encounter with Mitchell gave me the impression that you weren't a big fan of my family...but now you're asking for help?"

"There's some bad blood between the trolls and the Vânători, but both sides were at fault. I—we—can't keep living in the past and holding onto old grudges. It's time to move on." She took a deep breath. "Mitchell and I have made a good life here.

227

We're peaceful. We're a part of this community. But I don't know what will happen if that...*witch* is allowed to take over.

Slowly, I cautioned, "I don't plan to interfere in coven business, but I agree that someone like Gabriella would not be a..." I searched for the right term before finally settling on, "...peaceful leader. I get the feeling she's power hungry. She might not be too keen on letting others live in her territory."

Delores wore a pinched expression. "This is our livelihood and we need the witches' continued assistance to help us maintain it." She tapped the Flying Pie pin.

"So each pin's magic only lasts so long?"

Delores nodded. "Every month the spell has to be renewed. Without their magic, we'd have to close down the restaurant and go back into hiding."

"What does Rosalyn's crew get in return for helping you?" I wasn't sure if I was just curious or if this might be useful information.

"Physical protection when they want it." It was a funny statement coming from a small woman—but remove the pin from her blouse and she would explode into a very large, very destructive troll. "Plus a discount on the food here," she added.

I blew out a breath. "Look, I can't guarantee anything. I don't want to get any more involved in their business than I have to, but if she seems like a danger to you or others, then I'll step in."

Here I was making promises again to help people when I had exactly zero ability to back up my promises without the Artemis necklace. I really needed to have a private conversation with Louis and talk him into the whole blood-donation thing.

"That's all we can ask." Delores gave me a weak smile. "You

said you wanted to ask us something?"

"Actually, yeah." Most of my questions had already been answered, but I still had one more. "Can anyone use a pin like that?"

"Yes and no. Anyone could have a pin made for them, but these pins are set to only work for us. I can't even borrow Mitchell's since the pins are made to work for us individually."

"Do you think a human could have a pin made that turns them into something else?"

"I don't have magic like the witches, so I'm not sure," Delores answered, "but I don't see why they couldn't."

I nodded. I couldn't think of any other questions right then, so I reassured her that I'd keep an eye on the witches and let myself out of the closet.

I'd gotten the information I needed but somehow I'd managed to take on yet another task.

Gah.

The hunting business was not what I'd been expecting.

I looked down at the box in my hand. At least I'd gotten some pie.

Chapter 17

There were a few moments during the drive back to the motel when Ramble had to nudge me awake. A quick stop to pick up some fast food for Ramble helped me wake up, but not for very long. It wasn't like I'd gotten a lot of sleep between running around the park last night and then getting the call from Cassandra. The third time Ramble had to wake me up behind the steering wheel, I decided I needed to at least try to get some sleep. If I didn't, I was going to end up causing an accident the next time I drove. That and I'd be even more useless to this investigation.

By the time I pulled back into the motel parking lot, I was exhausted. Still, I was awake enough to notice that Donavon's car had been moved to a parking space near the office and the broken glass was gone.

Could Louis walk around in broad daylight? The cloud cover had finally cleared off and, though it was still cold, it was a bright, blue sky day. Maybe the vampire had simply gotten one of the other motel staff to sweep up. Otherwise, it seemed that Louis was a lot older and maybe more powerful than I thought.

I hadn't had a chance to eat the pie yet. I was thinking I'd save it for a snack but found that the container had already been opened and licked clean.

"Not cool, Ramble," I said, deflated. "You didn't even save me any."

Not even bothering to look guilty, Ramble dragged himself out of the car and stalked beside me to the motel room. Apparently I wasn't the only one who needed some sleep. There was a moment where I forgot that I'd switched rooms and Ramble had to nudge me in the right direction toward the correct door. Whoops. I glanced at the closed door of our previous room. Was Donavon still in there recuperating or had his good buddy Patrick whisked him away?

Not my problem, I reminded myself.

I forced my mind to focus on opening the room door, shuffled inside then made sure to lock the door behind me. I did my best to get the stupid curtains to block the room from the daylight then propped one of the wooden chairs against the door handle. Just in case.

Finally, I collapsed into bed.

"If you hear me having a nightmare, wake me up before Morvalden murders me in my sleep, will you?"

Ramble curled up on the bed beside me and gave me a huff. I hoped it was a yes.

I fell asleep with a faint sense of foreboding, hoping that maybe Morvalden was too busy sleeping in a coffin or something to bother attacking me in my dreams.

* * *

I stood in a long, dark hallway lined with detailed oil paintings. A partially open door at the end of the hallway emitted fingers of bright white light into the darkness. I could hear voices on the other side of the door.

Ha! I almost pumped my fist in the air before remembering that, like the dream with the fancy dinner, this dream usually also ended with Morvalden finding me. Great.

Then again, when I'd had this dream before, I'd always been curious about what was on the other side of that open door and that had been what led to Morvalden finding me. What if I just stayed right here and didn't do anything?

That lasted for about five minutes before I was bored to death. Plus, the longer I stood there doing nothing, the more I felt compelled to walk down the hallway and open the door.

Apparently you weren't just supposed to stand around doing nothing in your dreams. Who knew?

Fine, I thought *and turned to survey the paintings instead.*

I expected to see the same ones from the last time I'd had this dream, but the painting was of me doctoring Donavon's leg. The only difference was that rather than seeing Louis holding the werewolf back from attacking me, there was only a translucent figure where the vampire had been.

I'd never seen anything like that in one of these paintings.

I stepped away and ventured down the hall to the next painting. It brought me closer to the open door, but I felt compelled to keep moving.

This one was of Cassandra's house after she'd been murdered. Her body lay on the floor in the same position I remembered from real life. Only the moment captured in this painting must have been right after her death because the shadow of her killer fell over her body.

The shadow was in the shape of a person, not a monster-dog or a cat.

The paintings I'd seen before in these kinds of dreams always seemed to be true. If the events in the paintings hadn't happened yet, they usually occurred but the details could be changed.

This painting seemed to confirm that the monster-dog was a person who was using some sort of magical ability or device like the trolls' pins to turn into the beast or to remain human.

The voices on the other side of the door got louder.

Crap. That was never good.

I hurried to the next painting, unable to restrain my curiosity now—and drew in a sharp breath. The voices on the other side of the door abruptly went silent. They'd clearly heard me. I knew they were coming, but I couldn't tear myself from the scene before me.

In the painting, I stood in front of the monster-dog, one foot forward, as if ready to attack it. Hands crackling with green light reached into the scene from the side of the canvas and seemingly from just behind me in the painting. I couldn't tell who the hands belonged to, but it looked like they were about to ambush me with some kind of green colored magic.

"Vânători," a slithery voice sounded in my ear.

I ripped my attention from the canvas and caught a flash of Morvalden grinning wildly, fangs bared, just before he lunged.

Backpedaling, I tripped over my own feet and landed hard on my ass. The accidental move helped me dodge Morvalden's initial attack, but it didn't buy me much time. Morvalden loomed over me, bleeding from the eye I'd stabbed in my last dream and salivating at the idea of sinking his fangs into my neck.

Behind him, the door at the end of the hall was wide open. Through it, I could see the fancy dinner table I'd more recently been dreaming about.

In my mind, I heard the very faint voice of the Artemis necklace say, I cannot protect you anymore, Vânători. You are truly on

233

your own now.

A presence I hadn't realized was with me, suddenly vanished.

"Shit," I said and Morvalden's grin only widened. His good eye blazed white like a searchlight and I did my best not to look directly into it.

So much for him being distracted by sleep during the day.

"I imagined I'd have such a fight on my hands with the new Vânători, but you are not a real Vânători, are you little mouse?" Spit dripped down his chin as he spoke. He stepped toward me and crouched to be on my level. Cocking his head to the side, still grinning, he added in a low whisper, "And you're all alone."

But wait...I was almost never alone. I had Ramble.

I imagined the hellhound beside me and hoped this would work—

Pop!

Suddenly Ramble stood beside me on the same level as the vampire. Only this was a new version of the hellhound I'd never seen before. Instead of spiky black fur, his body was covered by curling black flames that didn't seem to affect him. I could feel the heat radiating off him.

Morvalden jerked to a standing position and fell back a step just as Ramble opened his mouth and let out a great gout of red, searing hot flames.

The vampire shrieked—

—and I woke up in bed, hands clapped over my ears. I frantically looked around the room. No Ramble.

"Ramble!" I shouted and pictured him standing in the motel room.

Pop!

He was back—and back to normal, I was happy to see.

I shoved off the bed and rushed over to throw my arms around him. He wasn't a huge fan of that kind of thing, but I couldn't help it.

"Thank you for coming to get me, Ramble," I mumbled into his spiky fur. His body was warm and I could see wisps of smoke rising from him.

He snorted but gave me a second to compose myself before pulling away from me.

I wiped the tears away on the back of my arm and only then did I notice that the hair there had been singed off. My brain caught up to what my nose had been trying to tell me about the smell of burning hair in the room. I guess I'd been too close to Ramble in the dream when he'd breathed fire at Morvalden.

I didn't think Ramble had killed the vampire, but hopefully he'd put the bloodsucker out of commission for a few days.

Looking at the hellhound, I realized something else I'd seen in the dream.

"Did you... did you have two other heads that weren't there in the dream?"

Okay, I promise that question made sense when applied to what I'd seen. In the dream, beneath the black flames, Ramble had definitely had two other necks that ended in stumps. It looked like someone had lopped off two extra heads that had been on either side of Ramble's normal head.

The hellhound just stared at me.

One of the things I'd read in the myths about hellhounds was that they were supposed to have three heads. I'd assumed that maybe the myths and legends had just been wrong since Ramble clearly only had one head. Now I wondered if maybe Ramble had once had two other heads.

But someone had cut them off.

"Did the vampires cut off your other heads?" I asked,

wondering if the vampires who'd held him captive in their basement had been the ones to do this.

Ramble snorted derisively at my question and turned his back on me to look at the door. I took that to mean that it hadn't been the vampires who'd done this to him and that his turning his back meant he didn't want to talk about it anymore.

"Vânători?" Louis called from the other side of the front door.

Louis's voice shook me from my thoughts. Apparently imminent company was the real reason Ramble had looked at the door. I opened it to find it was almost dark out. Somehow I'd managed to sleep through the day.

Louis held a paper takeout bag that smelled like greasy burger—Ramble's favorite. The vampire's nostrils immediately flared when I opened the door and his eyes shifted to black before he dropped the bag to the ground and shifted his weight into a defensive stance.

"Morvalden." His voice held a clear note of fear as he took in the room behind me. "Where is he?"

"Relax," I told the vampire, though I'm sure he could tell I was still trying to calm my own frantically beating heart. "He's not here. He was…"

What, in a dream? Would a vampire buy that?

"He's been coming after me in my dreams," I explained.

Louis looked around the room once more as if to confirm my explanation before he nodded—like a vampire attacking someone in their dreams was an everyday occurrence. What a weird world I lived in now.

Louis slowly came out of his defensive stance and retrieved the takeout bag. "Why does it smell like burned hair in here?"

He asked.

I really didn't want to rehash the dream right now. And I was pretty sure Ramble would rather I didn't, too. Instead, I changed the subject.

"What's up? Did you want something?"

"Yes," Louis's voice was back to neutral again. "I thought you might want to go back to Cassandra's house. And dinner." He held out the paper bag.

I absently took the bag while my mind flashed to the painting in my dream. If Cassandra's ghost was still there, she might be able to tell us who killed her since the shadow in the painting had been human.

I started to say yes to Louis, then caught a whiff of myself. Beneath the burnt hair odor, I smelled the sour scent of fear-sweat. I needed a shower in a bad way.

"Give me twenty minutes and I'll be out." I shut the door then opened the bag to find three cheesy bacon burgers. Ramble licked his lips.

"Looks like he's trying to butter you up for something, buddy." I unwrapped two of the burgers, set them on the floor, and told the hellhound, "Leave that last one for me, will ya?" I retreated to the bathroom for a quick rinse.

In the shower, I thought about how Artemis had said I was on my own now. Was she the reason I hadn't started the dream at the fancy dinner table and had been in the hall of paintings again? It was impossible to tell without speaking to her and now it seemed she was truly gone. I kept the necklace on though.

There was really no way around it: I needed to suck it up and ask Louis for his blood today. I couldn't stay awake forever and the minute I fell asleep, I knew Morvalden would be waiting for me. I could hold out hope that Ramble had wounded him, but something told me it wouldn't keep the vampire from coming after me again.

As much as I didn't want to ask Louis for his blood, I'd have to if I wanted to ever be able to go to sleep again without getting murdered in my dreams.

The lamprey bite looked a little better today, so I decided not to bandage it. I threw on some clothes and hustled to the front door. I'd just have to wait for the right opportunity and ask Louis today. And if the right opportunity didn't manifest on its own, I'd ask anyways.

Chapter 18

Louis stood waiting with his car door open. He'd parked his car next to mine. I started to ask if he wanted to drive separately but he nodded to the passenger door, answering my unspoken question.

Why do guys always have this need to be the driver? Whatever. I wasn't going to argue since I had to ask him for a pretty big favor later.

Before leaving the room, I'd topped off my outfit by tucking my throwing knife into a boot. After a moment's hesitation, I had also dug a purse out of my backpack for the specific purpose of carrying my gun.

Now the purse felt heavy on my lap as we drove in the awkward silence. Even Ramble was quiet in the backseat, not bothering to ask the vampire to roll the back windows down. I thought about making small talk, but what kind of small talk do you make with a vampire?

"No Donavon?" I finally asked.

"No. He's with his Pack, showing how not hurt he is." Though the vampire's words suggested annoyance, his voice remained toneless.

After that, I couldn't think of anything else to say so we sat in awkward silence during the rest of the drive through the Maine backwoods. Cassandra's house was dark when we pulled into her driveway. The temperature had fallen with the dark and I wrapped my coat more tightly around my shivering body as we got out and headed up her porch steps. I was suddenly glad I hadn't washed my hair. If I didn't get killed by Morvalden stalking my dreams, I didn't want to catch my death from a cold because I'd gone outside with wet hair.

Louis strode straight up to the front door with purpose. I had half a second to wonder if the door would be locked when he reached out and, with a quiet show of vampire strength, twisted the doorknob and shoved. There was a metallic snapping noise as the lock broke.

I suddenly felt a little less safe about locked doors. Awesome.

"Trick or treat," he quietly dead-panned. His words sent a chill down my spine as I realized it was Halloween. Wasn't that the night that all the ghosts and ghouls were supposed to come out and play? And here I was actively seeking out a ghost in an old cabin surrounded by the dark woods where anything could be hiding.

Louis ushered me in and closed the door when I nodded that Ramble was inside.

Cassandra's tiny foyer acted as a mudroom with two jackets neatly hung on wooden pegs. Scarves, winter hats, and gloves were neatly stowed in a pink plastic bin and a pair of lonely boots stood sentinel at the doorway, waiting for an owner who would never wear them again. For some reason, that drove home the fact that Cassandra had been murdered. Anger burned in my chest.

I'd hardly known the witch but she'd seemed so nice. My mind flashed to her blood-splattered living room. It wasn't fair that she'd been murdered in her cozy little home where she should have felt safe. It wasn't fair that the woman she'd loved had been murdered only the day before. Just like it wasn't fair that I was being hunted by vampires just because of who my family was.

I suddenly wanted nothing more than to catch this killer and make them pay.

With that in mind, I screwed up my courage to follow Louis through the doorway that led to the living room. I wasn't sure what I'd expected. Maybe that someone would have come and cleaned the room already. Or maybe that's what I was hoping for.

The vampire ghosted over to the window and pulled the curtains shut.

"The light switch is behind you," he said quietly.

I flipped the switch and light immediately flooded the room from two tall floor lamps set on either side of the couch against the window. The switch also lit the lamp on the table sitting between the two chairs. All the cream lampshades were spattered with blood.

They weren't the only things.

Just as I remembered, there was blood on the low wooden coffee table between the couch and chairs. It had congealed in some places and dried in other spots like on the magazines, leaving the first few pages brittle and slightly lifted.

Though Cassandra's body had been removed, it was evident where she had fallen since that's where the largest and darkest stain of blood was on the beige carpet. The fibers had been crushed and dried that way, leaving almost a perfect impression of a body. It was all too easy to imagine where her shoulder, head, and hips had come to rest against the carpet.

Ramble nimbly picked his way over to the spot, careful to avoid the dried red splotches on the carpet. He sniffed around a bit, then gave me a negative huff. I wasn't surprised. He hadn't smelled anything out of the ordinary before. Why would he now?

"You came," Cassandra's voice was as ethereal as the wind.

I spun to face where she stood—floated, actually—behind the two chairs. Louis jerked his head up from where he'd been leaning over the coffee table to follow my gaze. A look of confusion crossed his face and I realized he couldn't see her. I briefly hoped he hadn't been trying to get a little contact high from the congealed blood he'd been smelling.

"It's Cassandra," I quietly said to the vampire but kept my eyes on the ghost.

She stared down at the spot on the carpet where she'd died. "It was…horrible."

"I'm sorry, Cassandra. If I'd have gotten here sooner—"

Cassandra's gaze lifted to meet mine. "You'd have been ripped apart, too." There was a fire in her eyes, making her seem more alive than any of the other ghosts I'd encountered. Her tone brooked no argument as her brows drew down and her mouth became a thin, angry line.

I waited, hoping she wouldn't become what Jax called an angry ghost—basically a poltergeist that got lost in its own anger. They tended to destroy anything or anyone that got too near them.

No whirlwind hit the room though. Instead, Cassandra appeared to take in a deep breath (though I'm pretty sure she no longer needed oxygen) and as she exhaled, all her anger seemed to leave her body. This time when her eyes met mine, they emitted a strong sense of peace tinged with sadness.

"It is a difficult and steep path, Vânători." Cassandra let the sentence hang in the air.

My brow wrinkled. "You mean finding the monster who killed you?"

Instead of answering, she merely stared at me, her eyes growing a little more sorrowful. It reminded me a little of Rocker Ghost, a depressingly sad ghost who had wanted to show me his death so I would agree to find and kill his vampire ex-girlfriend.

It was complicated.

But Rocker Ghost hadn't been able to really communicate with me. Perhaps being a witch allowed Cassandra greater ability to communicate as a ghost.

When she didn't answer my question, I nudged her along. "Cassandra, did you see who killed you? Did you see them in human form?

"YES."

I jumped. Her voice was like a gong, reverberating through the living room. A glance at Louis told me that the vampire couldn't hear it. Ramble, however, was looking directly at the ghost.

Apparently thinking of her murder knocked her out of that peaceful state. I had a feeling we were back on the edge of angry ghost here, but I needed to know who the killer was when they were in human form.

Her eyes bore into mine. If she'd been a vampire, I would have been sucked in and mesmerized immediately.

"Can you tell me who it was?" I asked.

Her eyes flashed. Something fell off the bookshelf in the corner, making Louis jerk. The moment he turned, she flicked her eyes at the lamp on the table. It skidded across the table top and smacked into his knees. Like a cat suddenly startled, he literally jumped straight up into the air, landing awkwardly on the coffee table.

I raised an eyebrow as he gingerly stepped back to the carpet. Jumpy much? Then again, he couldn't see the ghost in the room. It was bound to be a bit creepy when inanimate objects started zipping around with no warning.

She was staring at me again when I turned back.

"It's important that you tell us, Cassandra."

Her eyes began to turn red. Probably not a good sign, but there was nothing I could do but press on. It was time for a guilt trip.

"We have to stop whatever it is from killing again. You don't want anyone else to die, do you?"

"Murderers." Her voice had lost its ringing echo and dropped to a low, barking whisper. "They're murderers."

"Who are the murderers, Cassandra? Do you know?

The entire bookshelf tipped over and crashed onto the end of the coffee table. Louis leapt backward, putting himself so close to me that his shoulder brushed mine.

Was Cassandra going after the vampire on purpose? Did he or other vampires have something to do with her murder? Surely Louis didn't. It seemed unlikely that he would attack his own brother...but then again Donavon had lived.

"Cassandra. Was your killer someone from the supernatural community?"

Her anger faltered and her tone shifted to that of amusement."Supernatural community?"

Why did everyone find that so funny? I tried not to get annoyed that a freakin' ghost was making fun of me now.

"You know what I mean. Was it a vampire or maybe a

witch?"

At the mention of vampires, Louis jerked his head at me. I guess he didn't like the implication. Whatever. We needed information here.

"Witch!" The ghost screamed, all amusement now gone. Her outline feathered and became less substantial before reaching an unseen zenith then flowing back the other way to be more solid.

A wind picked up, playing with the tendrils of my hair that had escaped my ponytail. It seemed we'd reached the whirlwind stage of the angry ghost. The wind grew stronger with every passing second. The bloody magazine pages flipped violently until they tore themselves out and were tossed into the air, quickly followed by each whole magazine. Small objects from the overturned bookshelf rose up from the floor and began to whirl around the room.

We now stood in the middle of a spinning maelstrom with the winds getting stronger and stronger. Larger objects like the coffee table began to jitter and shake as if itching to join the fray. We lost most of our light when first the table lamp and then one of the free standing lamps took to the air. The table lamp was jerked to a stop by its cord still plugged into the wall before it finally ripped free, too.

One of the free standing lamps was spared. It must have been just beyond Cassandra's influence. At least we had some light by which to see and therefore avoid the flying debris.

"Now what?" I could barely hear myself over the wind. Louis turned to say something but was smacked in the face by a heavy, cat-shaped bookend. Ouch.

A magazine slapped my shoulder and stuck there for a moment, its pages fluttering violently before it finally rejoined the other objects in flight.

I hadn't had this kind of trouble with Rocker Ghost. He'd just floated around looking sad all the time. Well, until he'd done something that allowed me to see his death when he touched me.

I thought back to that moment. If Rocker Ghost could do that with me, could I make that work for me with Cassandra? Could I make her show me her death? Or at least compel her to calm down enough to tell us what had happened?

It was worth a try.

Going against my instinct to run away from the scary ghost, I took several steps forward until I could reach a hand into her translucent body. Nothing immediately happened, though I did get smacked in the arm by a little glass figurine.

Closing my eyes, I thought about how it had felt when Rocker Ghost had pulled me into his memories. I tried to recapture that feeling with Cassandra.

Instead of seeing a replay of her death, I heard everything in the room go silent. I opened my eyes. The whirlwind had frozen, leaving everything hovering in the air. It was as if we'd hit a pause button.

Okay. This was good I guess. "Tell me what you know, Cassandra. Who did this to you?"

Cassandra's outline gained some substance again. I felt her struggle against our tenuous bond—and the moment I thought of it as a bond, it seemed to become stronger. I redoubled my concentration, focusing on holding her still. Her struggle weakened but when her eyes met mine, they were bright with defiance.

I decided to try another tact.

"Cassandra, you were going to tell me something before you

died, remember? You called me and said you had something important to tell me. Do you remember what that was?"

"Murderers!" She screeched. "Backstabbers!"

"Who stabbed you in the back, Cassandra?" I had to redouble my efforts to hold the bond between us and put more force into my voice as I demanded, "Tell me."

"She said she wanted to join!" Cassandra screamed. "But she had no magic! She wasn't a witch! *He* had a little magic, but he was a liar! Backstabber!" Spittle flew from her mouth but disappeared when it got too far from her body.

My mind raced to process the new information. I assumed she meant someone had wanted to join the coven. I'd thought Gabriella was the murderer, but she clearly had power, so maybe I was wrong about her. And she'd said it was a male who had magic. Who could that be? I needed more information.

"Who wanted to join, Cassandra?"

I instinctively cringed when she let out a long, piercing scream. The bond between us slipped a little and she started to wriggle free. If I let her loose now, I didn't think we'd get anything else coherent from her. She'd just tear her house apart in a rage.

Until that moment, I hadn't known one could mentally perspire. I gathered my resolve and imagined wrapping the bond around my hand like a dog leash. I still had my hand outstretched into her body and it actually helped me maintain the mental image of holding onto her.

The effort made it feel like I'd just finished hiking up a mountain. Holding onto Cassandra was quickly draining all the energy I'd gotten back from sleeping through the day. We needed the information though.

"Tell me who wanted to join the coven, Cassandra," I panted.

Her eyes bulged and her mouth opened. For a brief moment I thought she was going to spew ghost-vomit all over us—if there was such a thing—instead she screamed, "The whore! The waitress! She wanted to be a witch! Murderer!"

"Okay. We got it, the whore waitress," I yelled above her scream though I could barely hear myself. I had a feeling I knew who she was talking about. "But what about the other person? The person with magic?"

"Whore! Backstabber! She brought death to the coven!" She raved, ignoring my question.

"Cassandra! Who was the man with magic?"

The ghost merely shrieked and began thrashing around, straining the mental leash I had on her. I glanced at Louis for help but he didn't seem interested in joining the conversation. Hell, he couldn't even *hear* half of it.

Out of the corner of my eye, I saw Ramble edging toward the door. Maybe he had the right idea. How was I going to escape this room without getting pummeled to death by all the stuff still floating in the air?

"Cassandra, I'm going to catch the people who did this to you." I hoped some part of her heard me but I had a feeling I'd pushed her too far over the edge. To Louis and Ramble I said, "I'm going to count to three and then drop my hold on her. I'll wait until you're outside though. I'll make a run for it when she's free."

Louis shook his head. "I'll stay and try to deflect the bigger objects from you."

"You can't even see her. How will you do that?" I asked. My voice strained against the effort of maintaining the bond. It was like holding back a large dog who wanted to run after a

248

squirrel.

Louis looked pointedly at the objects in the air. "I can see the things that she'll try to hit you with."

Fair enough. I wasn't going to argue if he wanted to keep me from getting beaten to death by flying objects.

"Okay," I said. Ramble stepped into the foyer but watched us through the doorway. "One, two…" I took a deep breath and prepared to run, "THREE!"

I let go of the bond and made a beeline for the door. The objects already floating in the air rose up by another foot and then every other object in the room rose into the air to become deadly projectiles—all pointing at me. Our only source of light, the free standing lamp, finally gave up its fight. When its cord snapped, it threw the room into darkness.

"Shit." My words were lost to the sound of the maelstrom. Now the room was filled not just with the sound of the wind, but also with a cacophony of breaking glass, pieces of furniture ramming into each other or against the walls, and fabric tearing.

Before I took two steps in the dark, I was smacked hard in the knee by something that sent me tumbling to the floor. True to his word, Louis yanked me up with a cold, strong hand under my arm, then led me toward the doorway.

I cried out when something whipped across my face, slicing my cheek. Whatever it was spun away again. Beside me, Louis let out an "Oof" sound that made me think something had rammed into his stomach. His guiding hand fell away, leaving me in the dark. I had an idea of where the door was, but I didn't want to leave the vampire to be staked by pieces of wooden furniture. How much would that suck?

My eyes were slowly adjusting to the dark but it was still

difficult to make out what was happening. I turned toward where Louis last stood and stuck out a hand only to find the couch now beside me. It was slowly being pulled away by the wind. I crouched down in the hopes that it would help me avoid any other objects and started to move back along the couch's length.

"Louis!" I screamed into the maelstrom. The couch was suddenly shoved forward and the vampire grasped my outstretched hand. I had a moment to think how odd it was that his presence made me feel a little better in this dark, mini-tornado, and then he yanked me forward and we ran for the door.

This time we made it to the safety of the foyer where Ramble waited. Light trickled into this room from the window set high up on the front door. I leaned against the wall for a moment, relieved that we'd escaped the room but also close to exhaustion. Holding Cassandra had taken a lot out of me. I felt drained, like I'd just spent a day swimming under the hot sun.

You know what helps after a long day in the sun? An ice cold beer.

Ugh. Not helpful. I told my subconscious to pipe down and took stock of what we'd learned.

I wiped blood off my face and pointedly ignored the way that Louis's eyes had gone black. Had they been black when we'd first exited the tornado room or had that happened just now when he saw my blood? Probably better not to think about it.

"I bet I know who the whore waitress is that Cassandra was talking about," I said to Ramble. His look of concern shifted to a fierce, toothy grin. *"And* she knew at least one of the victims.

Intimately."

Seeing where my suspicions lay, Louis said, "I've known Cheri her whole life. She's not a murderer." His voice had a tiny hint of disbelief. Wow. For him, it was like an explosion of emotion. "Perhaps she wished to be more than she was, but that does not make her a murderer.

"No, it doesn't," I neutrally replied, "and she might not be the one murdering people, but she definitely has *something* to do with it."

"You're jumping to conclusions."

"I'm just following the clues," I countered. "Look, she was married to Samuel Vance who, incidentally, was a werewolf who was murdered and she doesn't seem too shaken up about that. Also, if she's the waitress Cassandra was talking about, then she apparently wanted to be a witch." I shook my head. "She might not be a murderer, but somehow she's tied up in all this. Maybe the murderer is the second person that Cassandra was talking about."

This got me a look from the vampire and I remembered that he hadn't been able to hear both sides of the conversation with the ghost.

"Cassandra suggested that there was another person involved," I explained. "A male, I think. She said he had some magic and the waitress didn't."

Louis shook his head. "I cannot believe that Cheri is involved in these murders. More importantly, I know what a killer looks like," he glanced at me, "and she is not a killer."

Okay. He might have me there. I wasn't exactly sure of Louis's age, but he'd probably witnessed quite a few murders in his time… and had probably committed some, too. I had to acknowledge that he would be better at judging the qualities of a killer.

That and I'd only met Cheri once.

"She's the only real lead we have so far," I pointed out. I wondered whether I should mention that I suspected the murderer had a magical talisman that let them become something else without leaving even a trace of a scent for who or what they were. I was withholding information, but I'd promised Rosalyn that I wouldn't tell the wolves about the trolls living under their noses. I had a feeling that telling Louis would be like telling Donavon.

Then again, sharing the information might suddenly open his mind to other possible suspects like Cheri. After all, she might not have innate magic or whatever, but she'd clearly wanted to if she'd been interested in joining the witches, right? And what if whatever talisman was being used made her lose her humanity or something weird like that? Could she murder someone then?

I decided to keep the information to myself when a new thought hit me.

"You know… Sadie Greene was a recruiter for her coven. Cassandra told us Sadie could sense when someone had magic abilities. Maybe she tried to recruit someone the night she was killed—the man who Cassandra mentioned—and he didn't take it very well?"

"Which could be why her murder was different," the vampire said slowly. "Unplanned."

"Okay, so Cheri *might* be involved and there is definitely someone else who has a little magic," I recapped. "I wonder if Rosalyn knows all the people in this town who are magic?"

"Perhaps. But if one of her witches is involved, she will undoubtedly not be of much help."

Shit. I hadn't even considered that. Plus I still wasn't sure how the cat played into this. I'd been convinced that the cat was Gabriella, but now I wasn't so sure. "Do you really think it's someone in her coven?"

He gave the barest of shrugs—which seemed unnatural for him. Sometimes his gestures made it seem like he was playing at being human again. Maybe older vampires had trouble remembering how to be human.

"It would explain why Cassandra called the killer a back-stabber."

"True enough," Louis said, "but if the killer is a witch whose sole goal is to usurp Rosalyn as a leader, then why kill Samuel and the other human victims?"

I ignored that he'd just used the word "usurp." I mean, who says that?

"I think that's where Cheri comes in." I pushed off the wall, feeling a little better. "Maybe we should visit Samuel Vance's apartment next. His ghost might come out now that it's dark out."

"Maybe. You appear to be... on a roll with ghosts."

Ramble snorted and my eyebrows shot up. "Was that sarcasm? I thought you didn't do emotions."

Louis ignored my comment and instead let out a little sigh. "I think we should visit Cheri, next instead, Vânători. Speaking with her might help clear her name. At the very least, it will give us more insight into how she might be involved with these murders."

I was surprised by his sudden willingness to speak with Cheri, but his reasoning made sense. I noted that his eyes had flipped back to being blueish-gray again. Good. I'd feel a lot more comfortable getting into the car with him if he wasn't all vamped out.

"Okay." I glanced back into the tornado room. Things weren't quite as loud in there anymore, but I wouldn't be going back in anytime soon. I jerked my head toward it. "What do we do about that?"

Louis tried for another shrug that looked just as weird as the first one had been. "We'll deal with the ghost later. Right now we need to figure out who the killer is so we don't end up with more bodies on our hands."

Chapter 19

We drove back into town and over to a duplex which was basically just a large house that had been split right down the middle, separating it into two units. The front porch had two doors and Louis led us to the left door...then just stood there looking at me.

I guess this was my show.

I knocked and waited.

When Cheri answered the door, I knew we were at the right place but maybe for the wrong reasons. She had a black eye that was partially swollen shut and her lip had been split. Her good eye narrowed when she realized who was at her door.

"I know you. What do you want?" There wasn't much steel in her voice and the tough attitude was somewhat diminished as her eyes flicked up and down the street behind us.

"Cheri, right?" I tried on a smile. "I'm Vi— we just wanted to talk to you."

"We?"

Only then did I realize that Louis had stepped out of her immediate view. And, of course, she couldn't see the invisible hellhound on my other side.

Why was Louis hiding?

"Um," I tried to smoothly slip past her question. "I'm

working to help solve the recent attacks and I understand that your ex-husband was one of the victims?"

She stared at me for a beat before finally saying, "He wasn't really my ex."

"He wasn't?"

"Sam and I weren't divorced, just separated. He didn't want to get a divorce," she said.

"But you did?"

"You've never been married have you? It's not all sunshine and roses."

"That and he wouldn't make you into a werewolf," I said, deciding to move things along.

Her good eye opened wide, then narrowed as she asked. "Who are you, again? And why are you *investigating* the attacks instead of the cops? "

Louis's voice made us both jump. "Perhaps we should talk inside, Cheri."

"Louis—what are you doing here?" She unconsciously tried to smooth her hair into place.

"I'm helping the Va—Vi with the investigation." He gave Cheri a toothy, rakish smile and his eyes darkened slightly, suggesting deliciously naughty things might happen if she let us in. I almost got caught in the crossfire of that smile. "Would it be alright if we came in?" He asked, still smiling.

"Sure…okay." She stepped back and ushered us inside and took one last glance outside before shutting the door.

She led us to a small living room furnished with a couch and a recliner both facing a wall-mounted, flat screen TV. Cheri gestured for us to sit on the couch while she perched on the edge of the recliner.

After sitting, there was a moment of awkward silence while

I tried to come up with what to ask. Thankfully Cheri saved me by ignoring me and addressing Louis.

"I haven't seen you in a while."

He shrugged. "You stopped working nights."

"Oh..oh yeah." She smiled a little then winced as the movement tugged at her split lip.

I guess that meant she knew he was a vampire.

"What happened, Cheri?" Louis's voice was soft. Almost caressing. "How did you get hurt?"

Her hand flitted self-consciously to her face. "Oh..I fell. Clumsy me, you know?"

Before Louis could confront her on the obvious lie and get us both kicked out, I said, "Cheri, I wanted to ask you about Samuel. Is that okay?"

Cheri's gaze flickered a little at her husband's name and she pulled her attention off the vampire to fix it on me.

"What do you want to know?" Her tone suggested she wouldn't be telling me anything useful. Maybe I should have let Louis carry the conversation after all.

I restrained myself from making a smartass comment or blowing out an irritated sigh. This woman might have answers, so I needed to play nice.

"I'm sure you already talked to the sheriff—

"Yeah, like five times," She interrupted. She looked nervous now though.

I pushed forward. "But I'm thinking that you might have kept a few things to yourself so you wouldn't, you know, accidentally let slip that Samuel was a werewolf."

"I already talked to Donavon, too. I didn't keep anything from him."

I fixed her with a stare. "You sure?"

"You calling me a liar?" Her voice rose.

Well, this was going well.

"Cheri," there was that caress in Louis's voice again. "Are you sure you didn't leave anything out?"

"Louis, I wouldn't keep something from Donavon." Cheri didn't give Louis the attitude she gave me, but she definitely wasn't going to continue falling for the charm thing, either.

"What really happened to your face, Cheri?" The vampire's voice was like silk and his eyes had shifted all the way black. I'm not sure that I could have kept anything from a voice that sounded like that.

Cheri's hand moved to her face again, but instead of defiance, she blinked back tears. "I told you..."

"Cheri..." His tone held just the right equation of sympathy and admonishment.

"It's...it's nothing. Really Louis. It's just this new guy I'm dating..."

"Who is he?" Louis asked, his voice was intense now. Almost protective.

All the sympathy I'd held for Cheri went right out the window when I saw a hint of satisfaction at the care she'd heard in Louis's voice. Apparently she was one of those women who liked to have men fight over her. Ugh. I'd never understood the need to cause fights among men just so I could feel loved.

"It's fine, Louis." But now I could tell she was enjoying the conversation. Shit. She could probably play this out forever without ever telling us anything.

Except that it turned out Louis wasn't interested in playing that game either. He leaned forward and, touching the back of Cheri's hand where it rested on her leg, he poured on the vampire compulsion.

"Who are you dating, Cheri?" He asked in a quiet, emotion-less voice. "Who hit you?"

She sucked in a breath and her good eye widened. "It was—"

A howl cut her off. It wasn't the howl of a dog or a wolf. This was the throaty, feral howl of the beast. And it had come from just outside the closed living room window.

My head automatically whipped right to find one great big amber eye staring back at me through the glass. The hair on the back of my neck stood up and adrenaline shot through my body. I leapt to my feet and then stopped—I had no idea where to go from there. I couldn't exactly run outside since that's where the beast was. I fumbled for my purse to retrieve the gun.

Ramble was not as affected as I was. His spiky hair bristled as he shot to all fours, glowing eyes on the window.

Louis must have released Cheri from her hypnotic state because she let out a moan. "Oh god. He's here!" She looked at Louis and me. "What did you do? He'll kill us all now!"

"Who, Cheri? Who turns into this beast?

"Noooo!" She moaned, wrapping her arms around herself. "I didn't tell them anything! I swear!" Her eyes were wild with fear as she shouted at the beast out the window.

A cat streaked into the living room from the hallway, bypassed Cheri and leapt straight at Louis. It wouldn't have been a match for the vampire, except at the same time, the beast crashed through the window, taking most of the wall along with it.

Shards of glass and pieces of sheetrock flew everywhere. I abandoned fumbling for the gun and threw my arms over my face to protect it from debris while backpedaling. I tripped over the coffee table and went sprawling with my ass on the floor and my legs on the low table.

The beast darted at me but before he could reach me, Ramble leapt in front of me and whipped his claws across the beast's face.

This bought me about thirty seconds to scramble to my feet. I turned to Louis—and instead faced Gabriella.

I had a split second to see that Louis was facedown and crumpled half-way off the couch while Cheri watched in horror with her hands over her mouth. Gabriella reached out with a little black pouch and smacked me in the forehead with it.

Everything went dark.

* * *

Two sharp slaps to either side of my face woke me.

"Come on, witch."

I opened my eyes. A familiar face swam into focus only inches from mine. It was Deputy Asshole. His eyes were full of an emotion that I couldn't quite place. He hooked a hand under my arm and dragged me up. My hands were, I realized, cuffed behind me. I was having trouble remembering exactly why I'd been arrested. My immediate thought was drunk and disorderly conduct, but I didn't remember drinking alcohol…

An image of a monster-dog crashing through a living room wall sprang to mind but my brain felt foggy, making it difficult to remember what had happened.

The deputy levered me from the back of a car that was parked in front of a brick building. He half-dragged me toward the entrance though I tried to get my legs to stop moving.

My brain and body felt sluggish. My legs felt like I was trying to walk through quicksand and several times I almost fell as the deputy pulled me up the sidewalk to the building. I had to stare hard at the words on the sign over the door before they made any kind of impression.

"The Sheriff's Department?" I slurred.

The deputy grunted and, opening the door one-handed, pulled me through the doorway, past an empty front desk, and through the booking area.

It's a sad statement of my life that I actually recognized each section of the Sheriff's Department building. I can't say that gave me the warm and fuzzies, but at least it was familiar.

"I get a phone call," I managed to say without mangling the words too much. As much as I hated to admit it, the first person I thought of to call was Jax.

The deputy let out a bark of laughter. "Non-humans don't get protected by our laws, freak." He led me past the fingerprinting station and straight to the back where all the cells were. "My job is to protect citizens from monsters like you."

Only then did my brain really start to catch up to the situation.

I suddenly remembered getting knocked unconscious by Gabriella when the monster-dog attacked. Now I was being dragged directly to the back of the Sheriff's Department by the deputy…

…was the deputy the monster-dog?

I found it hard to believe that this pissant could turn into a giant beast, but all evidence seemed to suggest otherwise.

Unfortunately the realization came too late. I tried to dig

my heels in and stop the deputy from dragging me any further, but he just slid his grip from my arm down to where my wrists were cuffed behind my back and yanked upwards. I cried out and stumbled to a knee.

With almost no pause, the deputy got a grip higher up on my arm and jerked me to stand again then pulled me forward through an open door and into a room with two large holding cells on one side. The other side of the room held several desks.

As he marched me across the room, the deputy paused at a desk and dropped my purse onto its surface with a loud thud. The noise caused someone in the far holding cell to move. It was Louis, struggling from the floor of the cell to his feet. I opened my mouth to say something to him—

—and the deputy's fist connected with my cheek. My face exploded in pain just as I heard Louis shout a protest. I let out a bleat of surprise and stumbled backward into one of the desks.

"No one said you could talk." The deputy caught my arm again and dragged me to the door of the cell next to Louis's. "You witches think you're so high and mighty. That you can just do whatever you want, huh? Well, not in my town. You're *nothing* here." He shook me roughly, "Nothing!"

I suddenly placed the emotions I'd seen in his eyes earlier: madness and rage.

His scream sent spittle into my face but with my arms still cuffed behind my back, there was nothing I could do to wipe it off.

Instead of shutting me in the cell, he shoved me against the bars beside the door. The back of my head smacked into one of the bars and for a second I saw stars. I tried to blink them away.

The deputy turned his rage on Louis. "I know just what to do with your kind, bloodsucker."

I'd thought it was a secret that Louis was a vampire. My expression must have shown it because suddenly the deputy's attention flew back to me.

"Oh yes, witch. I know that your little fuck buddy is a vampire." The deputy had one hand on my shoulder, holding me against the bars while his other hand pulled a pocket knife from his belt. "I know all about how you witches like to sleep around with all the other freaks like him." He snicked open the knife and pressed it against my cheek, sending a pang of fear through me.

Wait, I thought, trying to wrangle my fear, *I have a knife, too.* I could still feel it in my boot, pressing against my ankle. Apparently the deputy wasn't very good at frisking someone for weapons. Too bad I couldn't reach it with my hands cuffed behind my back.

"Deputy Smith," Louis's booming voice filled the police station. "Look at me." The vampire's voice was an iron demand not to be denied. He hadn't even been focusing on me, yet I felt compelled to look. His voice promised safety and protection for obeying but denial of that voice promised swift punishment. I had to look, which meant turning my cheek into the very sharp knife. The blade bit into my flesh and, even against the sudden pain, I still had to look at the vampire.

The deputy laughed. He pulled his other hand from my shoulder, keeping the knife at my cheek.

I struggled mentally to get a hold of myself. It was like walking in a river against a strong current, but I finally managed, panting, to drag my eyes away from the vampire and back to the deputy. I needed to call Ramble. The hellhound could pop into the station and take out this sick bastard. Then I could take the deputy's keys and free us both.

I stopped when I remembered I wasn't just dealing with the deputy.

If I called Ramble now, could the deputy morph into the beast fast enough to kill Ramble? I wasn't sure. Ramble hadn't been able to kill the beast even with the help of Donavon in his werewolf form. I couldn't risk that the deputy wouldn't be able to turn into the beast before Ramble could kill him. If he was faster than Ramble, he would tear the hellhound apart.

Plus, I wasn't sure where Ramble was. Was he even alive? Before Gabriella had knocked me out, Ramble had distracted the beast from attacking me by making himself a target. I hoped that protecting me hadn't cost Ramble his life.

I couldn't think like that though. I needed to focus on the here and now. Figure out a way out of this.

When the deputy twisted to look at Louis, I noticed something hanging from his left hip. It looked like an animal pelt. Was that the magical talisman that allowed him to turn into the beast? It had to be, right? I mean, why else would someone wear a random piece of fur on their belt?

If I could get it away from him and then call Ramble...

"I'm immune to you, *vampire*," he spat the word at Louis, "but I bet," he went on, turning his attention back to me again, "that she won't be immune to you."

"Deputy Smith, whatever you're planning on doing—don't." Louis's words were lost on the crazed deputy.

The knife suddenly left my face and the deputy's other hand pulled my giant coat open. He grabbed the neckline of my shirt and used the knife to cut it open. He managed to cut it and the tank top beneath right down the front, leaving my bra exposed. When he got to the bottom of the shirt, he nicked me with the knife.

I cried out and automatically raised a knee to slam him in the groin but missed when he took a step to the side. Instead of getting him to double over and give me an opening to run, he reared back and stabbed me in the stomach.

It slid in like I was hot butter.

I let out a cry of disbelief.

"NO!" Louis yelled in that same booming voice.

Shocked, my mouth dropped open as I sucked in air. Slowly, like blood dispersing in water, the pain lit up my synapses. I screamed at the same moment that the deputy wrenched the knife from me, causing more pain and cutting my scream off at a higher pitch.

"You stupid bitch. Now look what you made me do." All the color had drained from the deputy's face. He seemed a little less sure of himself now.

My knees crumpled and he caught me as I fell. He paused for a moment as if deciding what to do with me, then dragged me into the cell next to Louis's. He dropped me to the concrete floor without ceremony and I landed on my side. My brain screamed at my body to *do something* while the deputy dragged me into the cell, but my body had shut down, focusing everything on the knife wound in my stomach. I couldn't even stop the blood flow because my hands were still tied behind my back.

The vampire, nostril's flaring, had followed the deputy to where the bars separated his cell from this one. He dropped down so he was closer to me and the deputy.

"It's not too late, Deputy Smith. You can call an ambulance. You didn't hit any organs. She could live if you call them right now. We'll tell them she fought you with the knife and it was an accident."

For a brief second I thought the deputy might go for it. He seemed so shaken, standing over me and staring down, his face whiter than the vampire's. Then it was like he suddenly came back to himself. A sneer made his feature's ugly as he looked at the vampire.

"Do you think I'm stupid? No. This… this was the plan all along. She'll just…die a little faster this way." He forced himself to shrug as he looked down at the blood pooling on the concrete.

I wanted to look, too. Maybe I could figure out how to staunch the blood? The moment I tried to sit up, pain ripped through my stomach. It was nothing compared to the fresh explosion of pain that the deputy caused as he shoved me back to the floor.

I sucked in air and tried not to scream again.

Louis tried another strategy. "You hate the witches, but why kill Kleinman and Duluth?" The vampire asked. "Were they part of the plan too?"

Seriously? Was he really trying to get information right now? Who cared why he'd killed the two humans! He was in the process of killing a third: me! Stalling wouldn't help us in this situation. I tried to convey this to the vampire with a dark look, but he ignored me.

"Duluth was helping the werewolves. He deserved what he got. I could have done so much more to him," the deputy fingered the fur talisman as if it comforted him while longing tinged his voice, "but then I was interrupted by that idiot,

Kleinman."

The deputy was staring down at me as he spoke, but I got the feeling he wasn't really seeing me.

"It wasn't my fault that the running nut saw me kill the wolf-lover." He shrugged. "He wouldn't have recognized me in my purer form, but I couldn't chance it that he might have seen my car in the lot."

His "purer" form? Give me a break!

"Was Sadie Green's death not your fault either?" The vampire asked in that toneless voice of his.

The deputy laughed. "Can you believe that bitch tried to recruit me into the coven? Me! Who did that witch think she was?"

He shook his head and knelt down in front of me, keeping me between him and the vampire. His gaze pointedly ignored where he'd stabbed me and instead roved over my chest. I still had on my bra but it was clear that he was still enjoying the view. When he reached out the hand with the knife in it, I flinched back.

His answering smile made me want to crawl away somewhere and hide from all the scary things in the world.

"Witches lie," he said and lightly ran the point of the knife from my stomach, up my sternum and across my breasts before moving it to the pulse at my throat. "Everyone knows it. You pray to Satan, don't you witch? And he's the father of lies," he said, getting in my face for a second.

I got the feeling that he wanted to do a lot more than call me a liar and run a blade over my skin. Fucking shitbag.

"Too bad witches aren't really my thing." He grabbed my cheek with the other hand and forced me to look into his face. "Suffer not a witch to live."

I had two choices here: die in fear, or die fighting.

Though it made my stomach scream in agony, I laughed at him. Hey, if I was going to die, I did not want the creep who killed me to think I was terrified of him.

"Seriously? Scripture? You do know that you're part-witch right?" I had to pause for a wave of pain. "Why do you think Sadie Greene tried to recruit you? And if you're working for that bitch Gabriella, then you're working for a witch, dumbass."

I knew I'd hit the nail on the head when he pressed the blade harder against my throat. I could feel it start to slice into my skin.

"Shut up, bitch. You don't know anything. You're *nothing*."

I thought of a dozen retorts but decided it would be better to let him rave. I really didn't want to get stabbed again.

He stayed frozen like that for a few moments before suddenly saying, "Stick to the plan, Ken." Then he withdrew the knife from my neck and put his hands under me to roll me over. I ended up on my side, facing Louis's cell.

Suddenly the deputy jerked back away from me and I immediately saw why: Louis had stuck his arm through the bars up to the shoulder in an attempt to grab the deputy.

The deputy scurried from the cell, slamming the door and brandishing the knife at the vampire. "How long do you think you can hold off, huh? Ten minutes? Fifteen?" He wiped an arm across his sweaty face. "She told me all about you, vampire. You haven't had a real drink in *years*. Well, now. Here's your chance."

I shifted my focus to the vampire in the cell next door.

Louis moved so quickly to the other side of the cell that he was a blur. He turned his back on me and wrapped his hands around the bars before sinking to his knees.

Oh shit. That couldn't be good. Someone was a little more like *Angel* than he'd let on.

Would the bars keep him from me? I judged the distance between where I lay and the bars separating me from the hungry vampire. I was way too close for comfort. With a lot of effort and waves of pain that didn't seem to abate, I used my legs to slowly spin myself around. For a moment, my feet were actually pressed against the very bars I was trying to get away from. I kept my eyes on the vampire's back but he didn't move.

"Can't you smell her blood, vampire? I bet it smells amazing to you, huh? Just a taste, yeah? Just a little taste. You might even be able to put her out of her misery. Just listen to her."

Only then did I realize that I was making low gasps of pain. I sounded like a wounded animal. I clamped my mouth shut and forced myself not to make any noise. Slowly and with ever-increasing pain, I shuffled backward, pushing myself across the dirty floor with my feet and leaving smears of blood in my wake. When I was as far as I could get, I propped my head against the leg of a metal bed I'd backed into.

I still couldn't get to my knife. Even if I could, what good would it do me against Louis? Maybe I could call Ramble now. If I had him appear in the same cell as me, would he be safe from the monster? Maybe. But once he popped into my cell, then what? He couldn't get me out, so what good would calling him do?

My brain was starting to feel a little fuzzy. *Blood loss*, I thought. It was only going to get more difficult to think through my limited options. My eyes started to slip closed and my fear quotient tripled when I forced my eyes open and

269

saw Louis.

The back of his shirt was drenched with sweat. He was shaking and letting out gasping breaths that rocked his whole body. His hands, still wrapped around the cell's bars, were gripping so hard that I could almost see the bones standing out underneath.

Also, the bars were starting to bend under his hands.

Oh shit. I was going to get pounced on and sucked dry by my vampire ally.

Fuck. That.

Ramble! I pictured the cell I was in. Specifically focusing on the bed behind my head.

There was an immediate POP! The vampire whirled around at the noise. The deputy's head snapped in my direction, too.

"What was that?" He barked.

Oh my god. I'm so stupid. I'd forgotten that the deputy wouldn't be able to see Ramble. I should have called him before the bastard had stabbed me!

A familiar snout looked down from the bed. Ramble had popped into the exact right spot. His lips began to rise in a snarl, but I took in a gasping breath and as quietly as I could said, "Shh." He stopped and blinked at me, waiting.

"The deputy is the beast. Find Donavon," I gasped, "and bring him here." I had no idea how my invisible hellhound would accomplish this. But I knew he couldn't stay here. Scary, vamped-out Louis was striding toward the bars separating our cells. "Hurry, please," I said.

There was another POP! and I was left alone to face a terrifying vampire and a potentially scarier beast.

Chapter 20

I'd been around vampires who had lost themselves to hunger, but with the exception of Morvalden—who was a whole different level of scary since he was the uber vampire—I'd never seen a vampire as heart-stopping as the thing in the cell next door.

Though I could still discern the features that made him Louis, his face had morphed into something that made me think of scary, slippery things that lived in the depths of murky water. His high brows had disappeared and it was as if his whole face had been tugged downward somehow. His empty, black eyes begged me to look into them. Instead I fastened my gaze on those pearly white pointy teeth.

All the better to rip out your neck with, my dear.

I wasn't sure why he looked so much different than other vampires I'd seen lose their mind to bloodlust. It was like he was more feral.

"That's right bloodsucker. Go get her." The deputy sounded like he was getting excited in more ways than one.

"Shut up…Deputy Dumbass." Why was I having trouble breathing all of a sudden? Was it because my neck was canted at such an odd angle? Or was it just because I was panicking? I forced myself to take long, deep breaths as the vampire slammed himself against the bars that separated us.

I flinched, sending another wave of pain through my body—but the bars held.

"You thought you were so smart, huh? Finding that dumb witch Cassandra? We had our eyes on you though. The minute she called, we went over and took care of her. Basically signed her own death warrant by calling you."

I wanted to tell him to shut up again but all my attention was focused on the vampire now struggling to push the metal bars apart. Faint creaking sounds suggested they wouldn't last long against his supernatural strength.

When I didn't respond, the genius deputy just kept talking. "We're gonna clean out all the witches, you know. Then Cheri and I can finally be together."

Bleeding, losing breath, and noticing that my vision was starting to go dark around the edges, I still found room for curiosity. Would he really spit out his whole diabolical plan?

"Why can't you…be together now?" I managed to wheeze.

"Cheri's confused. Wants to be a part of their dark world. But if there aren't any witches or werewolves to join, then she'll stay with me."

"Got news…for you. Too many vampires, werewolves…and witches… to kill. She's…never gonna love you." I haltingly pointed out, then jerked, wincing and gasping as one of the bars began to bend under Louis's strength.

"Cheri loves me! She's just confused!" He shouted, but I could see I'd planted a tiny seed of doubt.

Something dinged and the deputy pulled his phone out. Suddenly the whole scene seemed somehow startling with it's normalcy against what was happening in the cells.

"Damn. Looks like I won't be able to stay to watch the grand finale." He tucked the phone away with a little grin. "I have a coven Halloween party to get to and I'm pretty sure I'll have the best costume." He patted the fur talisman on his hip.

Shit the coven was having a Halloween party? Seriously? After two of their members had just been murdered? Seemed like a pretty horrible time to host a party.

The deputy strolled over to the door, glancing back one last time before he left. "Have fun with your boyfriend!"

The door closed and I heard a terrifying sound issue from the bar Louis was working on. It let out a squealing groan and bent a little to the side.

Shit!

I looked around. Was there a way to get out of here? I could shuffle back over to the door and try to pick the lock—but that would put me in grabbing distance from the vampire. Not to mention my hands were still cuffed behind my back. How the hell could I pick a lock like that?

The bar bent a little more and it was just enough to let the vampire's thin frame pass through.

"Louis—stop!" I cried.

Before I'd even finished my plea, he'd flown across the cell and dropped his weight onto me. In one swift move, he yanked my head to the left and bit deep into my neck.

I screamed and tried to get him off but nothing worked. There was a burning sensation in my neck, which only got hotter as he drew in my blood.

"Stop! Louis! Louis..." I couldn't keep my eyes open anymore. The pain seemed to lessen. I couldn't even feel the stab wound in my side now. "Louis," I croaked but then I couldn't really remember why I was protesting. The pleasant scent of vanilla seemed to surround me and I drifted...

273

Something jerked on top of me. Pain lanced hotly through my neck. It seemed too distant to really worry about. I could hear growling in my ear. Ramble? I thought I'd told him to get away. I didn't want Louis to attack the hellhound.

I tried to rouse myself enough to demand that the hellhound get out of here. The room seemed too bright now. My eyes didn't want to adjust. I considered letting myself drift again but another growl from somewhere nearby helped me refocus.

Ramble. I needed to tell him to get out. I couldn't let Louis hurt him.

I managed to open my eyes, squinting against the harsh overhead lights. Everything was blurry and out of focus. It made me think of all the times I had been so drunk that I'd had to block out all the other stimuli that my brain couldn't handle and just focus on one thing. I let my eyes fall on a blurry shape near the cell door and willed my brain to take in its details.

It took a moment, but eventually I saw that the thing crumpled near the cell door was the vampire. Was it—he—dead? I stared at it a little longer and saw it move. Something penetrated my brain and I realized that there was a sound coming from it. A weird, high-pitched keening sound.

Louis the terrifying vampire was crying.

He turned his face towards me and I saw tears of blood glistening on his cheeks.

Had I died and gone to some weird-ass alternate universe?

"I'm sorry. I'm sorry." The vampire was saying over and over. He made as if to move toward me but Ramble stepped into his path, shielding me with his body. A menacing growl ripped from the hellhound's throat. The vampire jerked back again. Apparently, I'd underestimated my hellhound's chance of survival against the vampire. I'd have to think about that another time though. Right now I was mostly concerned about not dying on the floor of the local drunk tank. I mean, how ironically shitty would that be?

"Ramble," I tried and utterly failed to say. I took a shallow breath and ignored the pain in my stomach and neck to try again. "Ramble."

This time he heard me. His head jerked down and he stepped to the left so that he could keep both the vampire and my face in his view.

"Blood." I fought to keep my eyes open so I could look meaningfully in the vampire's direction, then back to the hellhound. Ramble's ears twitched and he glanced at the vampire. I hoped that meant he understood because I was pretty much done.

My eyelids had grown too heavy to keep open so I let them slide shut. I was starting to drift again. I had a feeling if I let myself float away, I wouldn't be able to come back.

I heard Ramble's nails clicking on the concrete, then growling, followed by a loud SNAP of something—bone?—breaking. A short keen of pain hit my ears before something was dragged across the floor.

"No, don't take me near her. Hellhound! I'll kill her! No—" His voice became strangled before cutting off entirely, as if someone had closed their hands around his windpipe.

I felt something fall against my mouth, struggle, then lay still. Cool liquid flowed over my lips, chin, and throat. Some dripped into my mouth, tasting salty and metallic.

Yes, I heard Artemis sigh in the back of my mind. *Almost there, Vânători!* As she spoke, her voice grew in strength and volume. *Just a little more...*

275

The world was coming back now. For a brief, agonizing moment, the pain was no longer at the back of my mind but rather front and center. My wounds screamed to be healed—and then, as if a switch had been flipped, the pain stopped.

I opened my eyes. My full range of vision was back and clearer than ever. I could even read the fine print on the posters all the way across the room. Sounds were more intense, too. Though no heartbeat came from the vampire leaning over me, I could hear the thump of Ramble's powerful heart in his chest.

The hellhound stood over me, gripping Louis's throat in his jaws. I guess that explained the vampire's inability to talk. The thing that had fallen over my mouth was the vampire's wrist. Something had broken the skin and it was the vampire's blood I was drinking.

I wanted more.

Without a second thought, I jerked my hands apart behind me, effectively snapping the cuffs, and brought them around to grasp the vampire's wrist more closely to my mouth. I knew some part of me should be revolted as my tongue darted out to lick his wrist, but the need for his blood—ten times more demanding than any need I'd ever felt for alcohol—overrode my disgust. I sealed my lips against his skin and sucked directly from his veins. My eyelids fluttered in ecstasy. Why had I put this off?

As I drank, I felt a glow of power building within me. I felt strong and fast. It felt like I could conquer the world.

The vampire moaned. My eyes flicked unwillingly open. Above the hellhound's grip, I saw the vampire's eyes, still black, beginning to sag closed.

Could this kill Louis? Could I actually drain him to the brink of real death?

Some cold, calculating part of me wanted to know if I could, but this wasn't just some vampire I didn't know. It was Louis. Then again, that other part of me drawled, I really hardly knew this vampire. And hadn't he just tried to kill me?

I took another pull on Louis's wrist, relishing the fresh mouthful of power coursing down my throat, through my veins, and lighting my body with an internal glow. The vampire slid slowly to the floor though I kept a tight hold on his wrist.

The image of Louis standing in the motel doorway, holding a bag of takeout he'd brought for Ramble and me flashed through my mind.

Louis wasn't a bad guy. He'd been trying to help me. He'd only attacked me when he'd been stuck in a cage and I'd been bleeding out. He'd lost his control. I'd done that before, right? Hell, I'd done it over and over—losing control and spiraling into a drinking binge. I could hardly point a finger at Louis for falling off the wagon when I'd done the exact same thing.

Wait... was I falling off the wagon right now? Was I just substituting vampire blood for alcohol?

Though the thought of killing Louis made me hesitate, it was the idea that I was succumbing to my addiction that had me yanking Louis's limp wrist from my mouth.

I gasped for air and sat up. A quick look confirmed that the stab wound in my stomach was gone, leaving only a light pink mark as any indication of trauma. I felt my neck and found there, too, that the place that Louis had sunk his fangs was little more than two small indents. Even the lamprey bite was completely gone.

Ramble released the vampire's throat and stepped away, looking at me with question.

"Good job, Ramble." I said and jerked at the change in my voice. I sounded *powerful*.

You are *powerful, Vânători,* Artemis said in my mind.

Carefully, I moved to the vampire and rolled him over.

Yes. We must finish off the vampire.

"What?" I said. "No. He's our ally. We're not finishing him off."

Louis's eyes had narrowed to mere slits but I could still see that they were all black.

"Louis?" I said, not sure he could hear me.

"Sorry," he mouthed more than said.

"It's okay. Not your fault. Are you okay? Did I...take too much?" Okay, slightly awkward to ask if I'd drank too much of his blood.

He shook his head slightly. "I'm okay. Need to...sleep."

I had a feeling what he actually needed was more blood, but I wasn't too keen on offering him any more right now. I felt like I needed to be somewhere and the power surging through my veins was a little heady. It was sort of like getting really drunk and knowing that you needed to do something but getting distracted in your drunkenness.

A surge of guilt at the possibility of being drunk on vampire blood washed over me. The blood hadn't even been freely given. Ramble had helped me take it by force. Jeeze. Had I just blood-raped Louis? Was that even a term?

You did what you had to do, Vânători. Now you have me once more and we must Hunt those who have wronged you.

"Yes," I said, remembering the Halloween party the deputy had mentioned.

278

Ramble growled at the outer door just before it slammed open, splintering the wood frame. Donavon raced inside as a blur in his human form, Patrick close on his heels. There was another person with him, a woman I didn't recognize. Like Donavon and Patrick, she moved with a powerful grace. I could only assume that she was part of his Pack.

Yes! A fight. We will slay the werewolves first, Vânători, then Hunt those who left you to die, Artemis said with a scary, bloodthirsty glee that I had some trouble resisting. *Just let me take over and—*

"No!" I shouted at the necklace. More quietly, I said, "The werewolves are also our allies."

The werewolves slammed to a halt.

"Louis," Donavon saw his brother lying prone on the floor. He glared over at me and bared his semi-human teeth in a growl. "What did you do?"

I stood with a grace I didn't usually possess. "The deputy cut me and left me here so Louis would drain me." I waved in the direction of the bars that Louis had bent in his blood-lust state to get at me. "He almost killed me, but I took his blood and was able to heal."

Donavon raised his head and roared at the ceiling.

Perhaps "took" was too strong a word?

"Gave her...my blood." Louis managed to say when Donavon had finished with his tantrum.

Donavon stared at the vampire.

Artemis spoke in the back of my mind again, this time sounding confused, *You have aligned yourself with these... wolves?*

"Yes, we're on the same side."

There was a moment in which I got a flash of her stunned

disbelief before she rallied once more. *Then command them to release you from this cage and we will slay our other enemies.*

Shit. That's what I was supposed to be doing. Getting to the Halloween party.

I ignored Artemis's suggestion to "command" the werewolves and instead said to Donavon, "The deputy is the beast," I explained. "He's going to kill all the witches at their Halloween party tonight. We have to stop him."

"Deputy Smith? He's just a human…"

"Actually he's part witch. Can you break open this door? We need to move. I'll explain on the way." I walked to the cell door, planning to rattle it to reinforce the need to get out. Instead, when I pulled the door back, the metal lock snapped and the door, protesting on its hinges, swung backwards—the opposite direction it was supposed to go.

I was just as stunned as the werewolves who gave me reassessing looks.

"Nevermind. Can someone stay with him?" I glanced at Louis, still laying on the floor.

Donavon stared at me as he asked the vampire, "Are you okay, Louis?"

"Nothing a little rest won't fix," the vampire quietly said without moving.

Donavon still looked like he wanted to rip my limbs from their sockets. Oddly enough, I was kind of itching for him to try it. Part of me wanted to test my strength against him.

I guess vampire blood is just as bad as alcohol for impairing one's judgment.

"Fine," Donavon finally bit out. "Chrissy, take Louis to his place."

Chrissy nodded and immediately moved into the cell. I

watched as she easily lifted the dead weight of the vampire's body as if he were a sack of flour.

Damn. Werewolves were strong.

But on vampire blood, I felt stronger.

"Patrick, you're with me and the Vânători," Donavon continued. At a growl from Ramble he added, "And the hellhound."

"Where would they have a Halloween party?" I asked, suddenly realizing I had no idea where I was even racing off to.

"The graveyard. Where else?"

Chapter 21

Though I had the odd urge to go running off into the cold, snowy night, Artemis cautioned me to reserve my strength for the beast. I decided this was a good idea, which was how I ended up in the backseat of Donavon's car with Ramble. I was doubly glad to be riding to the cemetery when the storm that the meteorologists had been promising finally arrived and started dumping snow on us.

There hadn't been any spare shirts lying around the Sheriff's Department to replace the one the deputy had cut open, so I simply wore my coat over the ripped clothes. I'd just have to leave my jacket on or risk flashing everyone.

I'd also snagged my purse from the desk where the deputy had dropped it before we left. It might not be the best weapon, but at least having the gun was something.

"You said the deputy is the beast? How?" Donavon asked from the driver's seat, glancing at me in the rearview mirror. Patrick sat in the passenger seat, occasionally throwing quick looks at me like he wasn't sure I was real.

I wondered briefly if I was glowing with the power I could feel inside. It certainly *felt* like I was glowing.

"Oh, yes." I'd forgotten I was supposed to be filling him in. The power of the necklace was quite heady. Was this what people felt like when they did cocaine?

"The deputy has a magical talisman on his belt that lets him turn into the beast. It looks like a little pelt of fur."

Gosh, that didn't sound at all crazy.

"Gabriella—a witch who's trying to steal the coven from Rosalyn—gave him the talisman. But Cheri's a part of this, too."

"Cheri?" Donavon glanced in the mirror at me. "No way. She's not part of our world."

"No. But I think she wants to be." My mind started plugging all the clues in. "She seems to know about most of the people in this town who are more than just human. I think she wanted to be part of the werewolf Pack, which is why she married Samuel, but that didn't get her into the Pack, so their marriage fell apart."

"Enter Deputy Dumbass who has a magical talisman that lets him turn into a monster-dog."

"Monster-dog?" Patrick said from the front passenger seat. I realized it was the first time I'd said it out loud.

"The beast that's been killing people," I explained, then clarified. "The deputy. I think he and Cheri started dating, then the deputy got jealous of Samuel and decided to kill him so that Cheri could never go back to him."

"But why kill the witches then?" Donavon asked.

"I think you're asking the wrong question," I said. "The right question is: Where did the deputy get the magical talisman? And I think the answer is from Gabriella. She wanted to take over the coven here. Rather than fighting her own battles she recruited the deputy and gave him the talisman knowing he would eventually go after the witches." I paused. "He really has a thing against witches. Maybe it's because deep down, he knew that he was part witch himself."

This got me another glance from Donavon in the mirror. I shrugged at him, "Some of this is just guesswork, but I know for sure that Gabriella and the deputy are behind the murders. She's the cat and he's the beast."

"Monster-dog." Donavon corrected with no hint of irony.

I unzipped my purse, pulled the gun out and tucked it into my jacket pocket so it would be easier to reach once we arrived at the party.

Are you finished talking now? It is bad enough that you have made allies out of so many creatures, the necklace said, *but now we also have to rehash the enemy's plans with these creatures before meting out justice to those who have wronged us?*

"You're kind of blood-thirsty, aren't you?" I asked Artemis out loud, earning a look from Ramble and the two werewolves in the front. I pointed to the necklace and rolled my eyes, "She wants me to stop talking and start killing."

"So Louis's blood worked, huh?" Though Donavon's tone was neutral, I heard the steering wheel pop and his knuckles turned white as he clenched his hands.

It appears that I am not the only blood-thirsty one, Vânători.

I felt a brief flash of guilt coupled with self-disgust for taking Louis's blood. It was only made worse by the fact that Ramble had helped force the vampire into the act. It had been wrong, but it had also been my only option to live.

I ignored the necklace and tried for a neutral tone when answering Donavon. "Yes, it did work." I waited until his eyes flicked to mine again in the rearview mirror before adding, "Which is good because he had almost bled me dry."

Anger replaced my feelings of guilt. Good. Anger would help me focus on stopping the deputy and Gabriella from taking over the coven. I had a feeling if the members of the coven didn't accept her as their new leader, they would be massacred.

Donavon's eyes were still cool toward me, but he didn't respond.

Good choice, wolf, the necklace added though it wasn't like he could hear her.

Apparently the necklace had quite the attitude and *really* didn't like anything that wasn't human. Great. I'd somehow tied myself to a magical necklace that had the same attitude as Jax. Wonderful.

The car stopped and I realized we'd arrived at the graveyard. Other cars were parked along the outskirts of the gated cemetery. A lone, square building sat in the middle of the graveyard. A mausoleum. It was snowing in earnest now and the flickering lights from within the mausoleum turned it into what seemed like a warm sanctuary.

Too bad it was really more of a slaughterhouse. Or it would be if the deputy got his way.

The moment the car stopped, I opened the door and let Ramble out with me.

Time to play. I could feel Artemis's glee at the back of my mind.

I started to head toward the building but Donavon caught my shoulder. I felt strong enough to break his hold and keep moving, but out of curiosity I stopped.

"Cheri wouldn't do this," he whispered, glancing toward the building and back to me. I could see worry in his eyes. "She wouldn't have gotten someone to kill Samuel."

I was annoyed at the hold up, but Donavon had said Cheri was like a little sister to him, so I reigned in my emotions and said, "Maybe she didn't know that the deputy would kill him, but she certainly kept dating him after Samuel had been murdered." I kept my voice low but didn't whisper.

"Maybe… maybe she didn't know that the deputy was the one who did it."

I highly doubted that. The fear on Cheri's face when the deputy had shown up at her house in his beast form hadn't been just because the beast was terrifying. Her fear had come from the idea that the deputy would turn on her for thinking she'd told someone about his being the beast.

"Could be," I said anyways but made sure Donavon heard the doubt in my voice, "but if she's in there," I waved to the mausoleum, "then I recommend treating her like a suspect and not like an ally."

The whole time I'd been talking, it felt like I'd been holding onto the reins of an excited horse. The necklace was jonesing for the fight and the power of the vampire blood coursing through me agreed with the necklace. When I finished my warning to Donavon, I let go of the reins a little

I started toward the building, passing through the open gate of the cemetery with Ramble beside me. As we crossed into the graveyard, I felt a zing of magic wash over us. It was coming from the graveyard itself. Interesting. Apparently with the necklace fully working, I could sense magic. That could come in useful.

A scream from inside the mausoleum made me pause and listen. Another echoed it. I glanced back at the two werewolves who were following behind Ramble and I.

"If you get a chance at the talisman on the beast, rip it from him." I said, remembering the way that Mitchell had gone from normal human waiter to towering troll the moment he'd ripped off his magic pin. "It will make him turn back into a human."

Donavon gave a brief nod and finally I was able to give in to the urge to run toward the screams. I had a brief moment to note that, without this power surging through me, I'd have wanted to run away from the screams issuing from the building.

Instead, the moment I opened myself up completely to the power within, I felt swept away. The gun bumped against my side in the jacket pocket as I ran, but I didn't want to use that. Instead, I followed the instincts brought out by the vampire blood and pulled the knife that was still in my boot.

It glinted in the light from the mausoleum. I suddenly wanted to laugh out loud. I felt so alive! I was surging with power! I was going to run into that building and rip apart whatever was making those people scream.

Easy, Vânători. You are blood-drunk.

"Am I?" I asked out loud, exhilarated and not at all worried about sounding crazy for talking to myself. Ramble shot me a worried look but easily kept up with my run through the graveyard, dodging headstones as we headed toward the mausoleum.

Being blood-drunk felt *great.* I vaguely wondered what the hangover would be like, but it was a fleeting thought.

Let me guide you in the fight, Vânători. I felt a feathery light touch at the back of my mind. It almost felt like someone knocking lightly on the door and requesting permission to enter.

My automatic response was to put up a wall against that request. With the vampire blood singing in my veins, I could take on the world. I didn't need Artemis taking over my body.

I felt Artemis' reaction as a sting of rejection, then suddenly we passed through the doorway of the mausoleum. There was another tug of magic, but this time it felt like I'd run through many different layers of magic before I tore a hole in them.

The witches' magic is layered as a ward against intruders. Though she sounded a little hurt at my rejection, Artemis was still helping at least. Her tone became smug as she added, *Their magic is not strong enough to keep out a Vânători.*

A roar echoed through the stone building. I guess the magic wasn't enough to keep Deputy Dog-Monster out, either.

Nameplates of the deceased bearing their date of birth and death lined the walls. Somehow, like a weird, horror-movie TARDIS, the mausoleum was bigger on the inside. Without knowing how I did it, I mentally probed the magic around me and found that a streak of purple magic covered the whole building. I had a feeling that's what had enabled the building to become so much bigger.

Another color, a radiant green magic, also surrounded the building but at the doorway I'd just entered, that color was absent. All the other colors representing the witches layered magics were still there, though they were torn where I'd pushed through them. The green magic, however, had left a perfect, rectangular opening at the door.

Interesting. I had a feeling I knew exactly who that green magic belonged to. I was pretty sure I'd seen it in one of the paintings within my dreams. Of course, the painting had also shown me that whoever wielded that green magic was going to ambush me when I attacked the monster-dog.

Another scream brought me back to the present.

Hurry Vânători. Be ready.

The two wolves were suddenly at my side. They must have

stopped to shift to their wolf form in the graveyard. I waved them on and jogged down the tomb-lined hall, heading toward the source of the screaming.

We turned a corner and headed for a door with a flickering candle set on either side of it. A pentagram was drawn in chalk on the floor before the door. Another ward. This one I was ready for. Without hesitating, I jogged toward it, found a corner of the layered magics with my hand and ripped them downward diagonally to create a doorway.

Here, too, that green magic had failed to cover the entryway. We'd definitely found the party room.

The high ceilings soaring above could only have been created by magic. Orange and black candles dotted the walls and here and there were carved pumpkins lit from within by more candles. Cocktail tables draped with heavy purple velvet and set with still more candles were evenly distributed around the room. This was a very elaborate and tasteful set up. Or, it had been before the monster arrived. The beast now towered over an altar at the front of the room having knocked tables aside and mauled several party guests already.

Two women were trying to help a third to stand, but she howled in pain and they had to forcibly lift her from the floor. They turned in my direction, ready to flee to safety—and froze at the sight of me.

Could they see the power of the blood at work in me just as I could see their individual magic glowing on their skin? Was their magic like their aura? Did non-magical people have auras?

Vânători, Artemis snapped, pulling me out of my thoughts. *Either kill them or let them pass.*

Like surfacing from deep water, I brought my focus back

to the present and realized I recognized one of the witches. Alexis, the young witch I'd seen at Cassandra's house, was helping to support the injured witch. She stared at me with wide eyes, clearly convinced that I was here to aid in exterminating the witches.

Her stark fear made a wave of shame wash over me. The only people I wanted to cower in fear were the deputy and Cheri.

I quickly stepped aside so the witches could carry their injured sister to safety, but they didn't move. Confused, I looked at the doorway and found the two wolves blocking it.

"They're the good guys," I said to the wolves. They finally moved aside and the witches didn't waste any time scurrying away to safety. Only after they'd left did I wonder if they really were the good guys. It was possible that some of these witches were on Gabriella's side.

I shook my head. I was here to stop the monster-dog and Gabriella, not pass judgement on Cassandra's witches.

Turning back to the beast, I realized he was clawing and biting at something on the floor, but a brilliant purple magic and a darker blue magic were impeding his efforts. I looked more closely and saw that the beast was trying to attack Rosalyn. She was on her back, staring up with defiance and fear at the beast as purple light streamed from her fingers and formed a solid purple shield around her.

The dark blue magic was coming from someone else. Visually following the tendril backward revealed a fierce Willomena trying to protect her coven leader.

"You said you would make us a stronger coven!" Willomena screamed, and though her attention seemed focused on Rosalyn, it was a different witch who answered.

"I *am* making it a stronger coven—you two just won't be in it." Somehow the voice sounded laced with green magic. I whipped to the left. There, in the corner at the back of the dais stood the beautiful Gabriella with a wide-eyed Cheri beside her.

So much for Cheri not being involved.

I wanted to go after the smiling witch, but we needed to deal with the beast first and free Rosalyn from beneath its claws. Knife in hand, I started toward the beast. Ramble, unseen, circled the other way around the dais.

"Deputy Dumbass!" My voice rang out with a clear, strong note.

Surprised, the beast jerked his head toward me. In the light of Rosalyn's purple magic, I saw the talisman as a slightly different colored patch of fur at the base of his throat. The beast lifted his lip in a snarl to reveal razor sharp shark-teeth.

Three sets of growls responded and suddenly the wolves and Ramble bounded forward, racing to attack the beast from the rear. I ran forward too, focused on the getting the talisman, but Gabriella's magic laced voice stopped me.

"You again."

A wall of green magic shot up in front of me, blocking me from the beast. I tried to find a way around it, but I was effectively cut off. I had a feeling that, unlike the other magical barriers I'd crashed through, if I tried to go through this wall, very bad things would happen to me.

Instead, I spun and stared at the witch who had caused all of this.

Gabriella wore a long dress with capped shoulders that was straight from a Shakespearian play. Her shining hair fell perfectly around her shoulders, not a strand out of place.

Green magic hovered around her like a fine mist and she glared at me with those electric blue eyes like she could shoot lightning bolts from them.

Can she do that? I mentally asked the necklace.

Not this witch. She is a sad remnant of the powerful witches who came before her.

Good to know.

Moving around an overturned table, I inched closer to the witch and her, what? What exactly was Cheri? I still wasn't completely clear in her role in all this. She'd wanted to be part of the supernatural world...but had she known that the deputy was killing all those people and still continued to date him? Or had he forced her to continue the relationship by threatening to kill her too?

"Just can't keep your nose out of coven business, can you Vânători?" Gabriella smiled, projecting her voice over the din of snarls coming from the dais. "You know, I hear the king of vampires is looking for you. I bet he'd give me quite the reward for bringing you in."

If she told Morvalden where I was, he would most certainly catch me and kill me. Or worse. I couldn't let that happen.

She's trying to distract you, Vânători. Look! She's weaving a spell around you.

I looked down at myself. Sure enough, green tendrils of magic encircled me, slowly tightening around my body. Could I influence them or break them like I had the magic over the doorways?

You can do more than that, Vânători. Let me show you.

I didn't want to give the necklace full control, but I didn't want to be trapped by Gabriella's magic either.

Just tell me what to do, I mentally replied.

Artemis huffed but complied. *Imagine the magic breaking apart,* she said. I followed her instructions and the tendrils stopped tightening around me. They lost their definition and instead became more fog-like.

Now, picture yourself absorbing them.

"What?" I said out loud, making Gabriella raise her perfectly curved eyebrows at me.

You are going to absorb her magic so you can use it against her.

I really didn't have time to argue. I could hear the ongoing fight with the beast and I wanted to get in there and help Ramble. That and the idea of using the witch's magic against her sounded sort of poetic.

Also… a part of me reveled in the idea of having more power.

I opened my mouth and inhaled, imagining the magic flowing into me. It fought me, but only for a second, before swirling up and into my mouth. Her magic became mine and it felt…really good. Somehow, the new power also helped me focus better than the vampire blood had.

That's one way to do it… The Artemis necklace remarked, clearly not happy with me swallowing the magic. How else was I supposed to do it?

Gabriella's mouth dropped open when I absorbed her magic.

"What's wrong, witch?" I asked, sauntering closer. I don't think I'd ever sauntered in my life. Was her magic affecting my actions? "Afraid of a little ol' Vânători?" I smiled, showing my teeth much like I'd seen Ramble do.

The witch grabbed Cheri and dragged her through a back door I hadn't noticed. I started to follow but a shout from Willomena stopped me.

"Gabriella! Stop this beast!"

I whipped back around. The green wall was gone. Apparently Gabriella had dropped it when she fled. Willomena, looking terrified, had broken her focus and her blue magic had disappeared, leaving Rosalyn to fend for herself against the beast.

For a second I thought her magic would hold, especially with the two wolves and Ramble harrying the beast and keeping it from completely focusing on the witch. But then the beast easily shook off the wolves and slammed a clawed paw into—and through— the purple shield.

CRACK!

Rosalyn screamed. The thing had stepped on her leg and broken it.

One wolf recovered enough to leap at the beast and latch onto its shoulder. As I watched, the other werewolf leapt from a tabletop and onto the beast's back, biting down and making the beast cry out. While the two wolves distracted the beast, Ramble darted forward in a bid for the talisman.

The moment the hellhound touched the beast, it jerked its chin down and snapped at him.

"No!" I shouted as the beast managed to grab Ramble by his shoulder, shook him roughly, and threw him at the marble wall. He hit with a sickening thud and fell to the floor in a motionless heap.

Rage boiled in my veins. I wanted to rip open the beast's skin, yank out his insides, and show them to him while he still breathed.

Easy, Vânători.

I ignored the necklace's caution and instead ran at the beast brandishing my knife. It snapped at me and, with lightning quick reflexes, I jerked to the right while simultaneously shoving the knife into the side of the monster's head. I felt a little resistance when the knife was halfway in and tried to put my shoulder into it, but was suddenly yanked off my feet. The monster had lifted its massive head in an attempt to get away, but I clung to the knife half-buried in its head.

When it realized I was still attached to the knife, the monster shook its whole body as if shaking off water. I lost my grip and immediately slammed into the ground.

The fall should have broken bones or at least left me winded, but I barely felt it. I leapt back to my feet, noting as I did that the wolves had also been shaken off the beast's back and were now lying at opposite ends of the room.

Apparently even in his beast form, the deputy wasn't too keen on such a fair fight, it let out an ear-splitting howl and bounded forward, knocking Willomena to the ground, and ran toward the door Gabriella had dragged Cheri through. Its body was way too big to fit through the normal-sized door and just when I thought it would smash into the marble, it somehow shrank just enough to slip through the door.

I jerked as something touched my hand. Looking down I found Ramble back at my side. A quick assessment of the room told me that the other wolves were coming around. Rosalyn stared at me from the floor, her face white from pain as she bent over her broken leg.

With an eerie detachment, I noted that bone poked through the skin of her leg.

You can do nothing for her, Artemis said, confirming my own thoughts. *Your quarry is getting away.*

She was right. I needed to go after the beast, Gabriella, and Cheri. A small part of me unaffected by the vampire blood was screaming through the curtain of power coursing through me, demanding that I make sure Rosalyn was okay. I also wasn't sure I should kill Cheri. Though Gabriella and the deputy were obviously guilty, I wasn't so sure about the waitress. Or Willomena for that matter.

Before I could go after the trio who'd escaped, I needed to make sure I wasn't leaving an accomplice in this room.

"Willomena," I boomed, stomping over to the witch. She'd been knocked on her ass by the beast and was curled around her left arm. Was it broken? I didn't really care.

I easily yanked her into a standing position by her right arm. She cried out, but I felt that I was being easy on her by not grabbing the possibly broken arm.

"I saw you having lunch with Gabriella, Willomena. You've obviously been working with her—did you help her and the deputy kill those men and your sister witches?"

Willomena flinched as one of the wolves behind me snarled, but it was Rosalyn—her coven leader— that she looked at when she answered.

"No! I swear I didn't know she was the one killing people!"

Part of me wondered if she'd have a different story if I squeezed that broken arm. If this conversation had occurred at the beginning of this fight, I definitely would have been a lot more brutal. However, I was starting to come down from the major vampire-blood high. I still felt powerful, but I was better able to think through my actions.

When I didn't show any sympathy for the witch, Willomena pleaded with Rosalyn for understanding. "I...I didn't think you were doing enough to stop the killer. I only started talking to Gabriella after Sadie was killed. She promised she could catch the murderer...and I believed her. I'm so sorry! I loved Sadie and Cassandra—I just wanted to catch their murderer."

Tears streamed down the witch's face and clogged her voice.

I let go of her. It sounded like the only thing she was guilty of was being a traitor to her coven leader. That was definitely not my business. Let Rosalyn deal with that mess.

"What about Cheri? What's her role in all of this?"

"Cheri?" She sniffed, "I don't really know. I didn't know she had any part in this before tonight."

Damn. Not helpful. And the longer we stood around gabbing, the further away the real culprits got. I spun to the wolves.

"Donavon, I'm going after them, but these witches need medical attention." I left it up to the werewolf to decide how to deal with getting help for the witches. With Ramble back at my side, I ran through the back door the others had taken.

I hoped we wouldn't be too late to catch them. With the beast having shrunk to fit through the doorway, I thought we had a better chance of beating him and getting the talisman off. Once off, the deputy would be just another human—well, part human since he was also half witch. I didn't think he'd be much of an obstacle once he was back in human form though.

Though Ramble kept up, I noticed he was limping slightly. It was something I'd have to take into account when we met up with the beast again. After all, Ramble hadn't bested the beast before he was injured. He'd have an even harder time fighting him now.

We ran through a dark hall and turned a corner to find an open door that led outside. Cool air hit my face as we exited the mausoleum. It was still snowing. I looked down and saw clear prints left by the monster-dog. It was the first time I was actually thankful for the snow.

We followed the prints, running full out through the heavy

snow. My jacket slapped my side and I remembered the gun. Why hadn't I used it to shoot through Gabriella's shield earlier?

I do not think it would have worked, Artemis said echoing my own thoughts.

I drew on the strength of the vampire blood to run faster. Ramble started to fall behind a little, but I didn't want to slow down and risk losing our quarry altogether.

Through the wind blown snow, I suddenly caught a glimpse of the beast running in front of us. As we drew closer, I pulled the gun from my pocket (with only a second of fumbling). I probably wouldn't be able to hit anything while running, but if I were being honest, I probably wouldn't hit anything if I stopped and took careful aim either.

Let me help you Vânători. You are wasting precious energy. I can focus your efforts and finish this if you'll just let me in.

Again, I felt that feathery touch at the back of my mind, probing for an opening. It didn't feel right though. I didn't want her to just take over my body. What if she decided not to give it back? I ignored her mental invitation.

Still running, I snicked off the gun's safety, pulled the slide back to chamber a round like Jax had taught me, and fired two rounds at the beast.

I missed him, surprise, surprise, but I heard a scream of pain from a human mouth. We were on the outskirts of the graveyard, and I hoped I hadn't hit an innocent bystander.

I didn't have much time to worry though. The beast slammed to a halt, turned, and leapt back at me. It closed the distance between us in just that one leap. I didn't even have time to be impressed since suddenly there were snapping teeth and tearing claws bearing down on me.

It knocked the gun from my hands and snagged my shoulder in a claw. I barely felt the pain. I was too focused on keeping its ginormous teeth from sinking into my face. My hand found the hilt of my knife still buried halfway in the beast's head. I grabbed onto it for leverage and used it to angle the beast's mouth away from my body.

Taking advantage of the distraction, Ramble darted between the beast and me. He had to claw at the beast's mass of hair before he found the talisman. Taking it in his teeth, Ramble yanked backward.

The change was immediate.

The beast disappeared and suddenly I was holding a knife sunk halfway into the deputy's skull. His eyes rolled back and he fell, lifeless, to the ground, while Ramble scrambled out of the way.

I stared at the body for another second. Revulsion creeping into my throat. I'd just killed a man. Okay, he'd been a beast when I'd shoved the knife in his head, but still...

Worry about your humanity later, Vânători. We have a wicked witch to catch!

Was she joking or had she used that term in all seriousness? Either way, it helped me tear my eyes from the deputy's lifeless body.

The witch and Cheri were hobbling away. Cheri had her shoulder under Gabriella's arm and was half carrying her. One of the shots I'd fired must have hit the witch because she hadn't been injured earlier.

"Hurry!" Gabriella shouted at the other woman. She turned to see how the deputy fared. I saw the panic hit her the moment she realized the deputy was dead.

In an instant, Gabriella yanked Cheri around like a shield,

drew a small knife, and pressed it to the other woman's throat while facing me.

"What are you doing!" Cheri cried. Her wide eyes, full of fear, found mine.

I had a hard time feeling any pity for her, though. And that wasn't from the vampire blood. In fact, I wasn't feeling as all-powerful as I had before. I knew I still had super strength, but I didn't feel the innate need to tear and rend something limb from limb just for the fun of it. Thinking about that previous urge sort of made me sick.

You've burned through some of the power the blood gave you, Artemis explained.

I felt the same kind of disappointment I got when coming down from a drunken binge. Old memories from drunk Vianne rose up and self-disgust began to overwhelm me. I thought I'd gotten past all that—that I was a better person now, but hadn't I just left Rosalyn to die? Hadn't I put Ramble in harm's way by calling him into the cell with Louis the vampire? I'd also thought about causing Willomena pain just to get information from her.

I felt worthless. Worse than dirt. How could I possibly win against this beautiful witch? I'd certainly never best Morvalden.

I might as well just lay down right here and let Gabriella finish me off.

Footsteps and a growl made me look down. A wolf—Donavon, I thought—stood next to Ramble. Only when I looked down did I notice a flash of green.

My eyes followed the flash. There was Gabriella's magic again. It was wrapped even more tightly around me this time. With a growl of my own, I reached down and yanked the green tendrils away. I couldn't believe it when they broke apart immediately and wriggled in my hands like they were alive.

In disgust, I threw the tendrils at the witch. She shoved Cheri out in front of her. The green magic immediately wrapped around the waitress.

"No!" She screamed. The magic engulfed her and she fell to her knees. "I just wanted you to notice me!" She wasn't looking at me as she spoke, but at Donavon. "I thought if I could be different, like you, then you'd notice me! I married that numbskull, but you still wouldn't Turn me! And then the witches refused me! Ken didn't though! He loved me! He would do anything for me!"

She seemed to be raving now, almost foaming at the mouth. Was that what the green tendrils were supposed to do to me?

Words spilled from Cheri's lips. "I helped kill the one that told me I couldn't join their little club! I made sure Ken would run into her at the gas station." Her eyes took on a mad glint now. "Am I monster enough for you now, Donavon?" Though the mad glint was still there, somehow she also managed to plead with her eyes. "I just wanted you to notice me!"

I thought maybe I understood Gabriella's green magic now, but Artemis put words to my theory.

Her magic makes one feel all the horribleness of their existence.

Made sense. It was why I'd felt so terrible when it was wrapped around me. I wondered why it hadn't done that when I'd absorbed it.

The tendrils tightened to a certain point, then smoothed out across Cheri's body, no longer snake-like but more like a bodysuit.

"No!" Cheri screamed. She opened her mouth to scream

again but it looked like she couldn't draw air. Her mouth opened and closed like a fish, her eyes rolled back in her head. When her body started to jerk and spasm, Gabriella stepped away from her. Cheri dropped completely to the cold ground, facedown, and continued to spasm for another second before she suddenly stopped.

I tried to ignore the feeling of relief that I wouldn't have to kill the waitress now. I might not have minded when I was in the throes of the vampire blood, but now that I could reason again, I didn't want her blood on my hands. Then again, I had been the one who'd thrown the green magic at her. So maybe I *was* at fault.

Now is not the time to ponder your morality.

Point taken. There was still a powerful witch before us. I stepped forward, Donavon on one side and Ramble on the other, to square off with the witch but was stopped short by another green wall shooting up from the ground. Several gravestones in its way were vaporized into thin air.

Shit. Good thing I hadn't tried to walk through that green wall earlier in the mausoleum.

Donavon took a step forward, a growl tearing from his throat.

"Stop!" I pointed at the gravestones that were no longer there. "You'll just get vaporized." The wolf stared hard at me as if pissed that I was bossing him around. "Fine. Run through it, then. Your funeral."

The green wall of magic seemed to go on forever on both sides. If we tried to run its length to get around it, Gabriella would be long gone. The shimmering green was just transparent enough that I could see the blond witch smirk at us before she turned her back and began hobbling away.

Damn it! We'd managed to stop the beast but unless we caught Gabriella, she was likely to just find another gullible moron to do her dirty work like the deputy had. And now that she knew that we were onto her, I had a feeling she'd be a lot more difficult to find.

"Step back, Vânători."

Rosalyn's voice startled me. I'd been so focused on staring daggers through the shimmery green wall at the retreating witch that I didn't notice when Patrick, now back in human form, walked up behind us. He was naked and his feet were bare, but none of that stopped him from carrying Rosalyn across the frozen graveyard. He stopped beside me, getting Rosalyn as close to the shimmering wall as he dared.

"That witch is my responsibility," Rosalyn said. Her face was drained of all color and her broken leg was bound by strips from one of the velvet tablecloths.

"Step back." She said again. When I met her eyes, I noticed that they were crackling with purple magic.

Ooookay. That was different.

I took a few steps back. Ramble followed suit and after a moment's growly hesitation, Donavon did too.

Rosalyn raised a hand. Purple light streaked from her fingers and flew at the green wall. As she slowly moved her hand, the purple light followed. I was suddenly reminded of a welder using a blowtorch to cut through metal. Where the purple magic met green, I expected the colors to grow muddy, like mixed paint. Instead, when they touched, the purple grew brighter in intensity. I had to look away from the bright magic or risk blinding myself.

"Follow her," Rosalyn commanded. When the wolf let out a slight growl, I risked getting blinded by the bright light to chance a look at the werewolf holding the witch. The sound was odd coming from a human throat.

Apparently wolves did not like to be bossed around.

Rosalyn's blowtorch act had created an opening in the wall, not unlike a doorway, though not as perfectly cut.

"*Please* follow her," Rosalyn said, switching her order to a request. Patrick complied, ducking to avoid touching the top of the opening, he stepped through.

Donavon immediately followed and Ramble and I were only seconds behind.

In the distance, I saw Gabriella's back. The fleeing witch had been slowed down by the wrought-iron fence surrounding the cemetery. I had a moment to wonder how she could do so many things with magic, yet a normal fence was thwarting her before I caught a familiar faint blue magic shimmering along the length of the fence.

Though I couldn't see the other witch, apparently Willomena was still in this fight.

"Damn it, Willomena! Let me out!" Gabriella screamed at the fence. "You know I'm the better leader for the coven. Look what this weak "witch of the light" has let happen! Two of your sisters are dead because of her!"

Patrick, still carrying Rosalyn, was a few paces in front of us, getting the coven leader closer to the fleeing witch. I saw him falter as another figure materialized from air that shimmered blue.

The shimmer faded, leaving Willomena standing a pace in front of the witch and werewolf. Blue, shimmering magic outlined her body. It was so thick it fairly dripped to the ground.

"My two sisters are dead because of you, Gabriella." Willomena's cold voice was just loud enough to carry. "You orchestrated their deaths so that your hands would seem clean."

The beautiful Gabriella managed to make herself look pitiful, clutching the gunshot wound in her leg and cowering before the other witch. She ruined the act though when she saw Rosalyn approaching.

"This is your fault!" She screamed, her face ugly with anger. "You're trying to pin the acts of hate-filled humans on me! I told you that you should have wiped this town clean of the human and dog filth—

Both Donavon and Patrick growled.

"—but you thought our kind could live in harmony with inferior creatures! Wake up, Rosalyn! Other creatures will always be jealous of our power. They will *never* be as great as us! It would be a mercy to put them down."

Though I couldn't see Rosalyn's face, I did have a perfect view of the hate-spewing witch. She truly believed what she said. In her view, any person or creature that wasn't a witch, didn't deserve to live.

"The light is weak, Rosalyn. Blood and darkness will always be stronger."

Rosalyn sighed. When she spoke again, she sounded tired and resolved. "You forget, Gabriella: The light will always burn away the darkness."

Before Gabriella could respond, the space around the witch exploded in white light. I jerked back and had to throw my hands up to protect my face and eyes from the sudden light and searing heat.

A scream tore through the graveyard and then grew softer as it was carried away by the wind.

When I risked lowering my hands, Gabriella had disappeared. In the spot where she'd stood was a perfect circle of melted snow. The metal fence directly behind that spot sagged forward as if it had been hit by a superheated wind.

Well, that was one way to make for less clean up.

Patrick turned so that he and Rosalyn could face us and, though the coven leader's eyes seemed tired, her voice rang with authority.

"I apologize that my sister caused so much strife and death in our town, Alpha. I cannot bring back your wolf or the members of my coven," Rosalyn paused and took a deep breath, clearly fighting off a wave of pain from her broken leg, "but I can promise that we will continue to fight witches and other creatures like her who wish to tear apart the peace we have built between our kind and the humans here."

Donavon stared at the witch. I wondered what was running through his predator mind. Would he accept Rosalyn's apology or would he want to try and run the witches out of town?

After a quiet, tense second, Donavon's nose bobbed ever so slightly.

The coven leader's piercing eyes suddenly landed on me. "And you, Vânători, will you join us in our struggle to keep the peace?"

How could I not say yes to those demanding eyes? And seriously, could I really say no to a witch who could clearly vaporize me?

"Uh, yes?"

The witch jerked her head down in a nod as if sealing our agreement.

Your duty is to remove these creatures from the earth, Vânători. Not protect them! Artemis almost shouted in my head.

My duty is to stay alive, I mentally replied. *Besides, it's good to have allies.*

Rosalyn looked at the gathering in the field—she even raked her gaze over where Ramble stood—and said, "Then let this be the beginning of something new."

Chapter 22

Now that I'd come down from the vampire high, I could feel the cold again. I wrapped the oversized jacket around my shivering body, wishing I could just get in the car instead of standing beside it and waiting for Donavon to open the damn thing.

The witches had insisted that the wolves wait to take them to the hospital so that they could clean up the graveyard. I hadn't stuck around to watch, but I had a feeling that the cops would be hard-pressed to find any bodies.

Time to move on, Vânători. It is likely that Morvalden will figure out where you are soon. Though she didn't sound mad that I'd gone against her wishes earlier, she'd taken on a more formal, almost robotic tone. Was this her version of the cold shoulder?

I don't think we can leave just yet, I carefully answered. Something felt like it had been left incomplete but I couldn't quite put my finger on it. We'd managed to discover everyone who had been directly involved in the murders and with all of them now dead, there wasn't much left to do. I had a feeling Rosalyn would dole out a suitable punishment to Willomena, so I didn't view her as a loose end that I needed to take responsibility for.

I still felt like I was forgetting something.

Maybe it was nothing more than that empty feeling left in the pit of my stomach from coming down off a drunken binge. I didn't think so though.

I heard tires crunching up the drive and turned to see a Sheriff's car pull up beside me. Well, shit. The sheriff was driving. This might get interesting.

Luckily I could see the bedraggled group of witches and werewolves returning from the graveyard. Not fast enough though. The Sheriff got out of his car, looked at the group approaching in the distance, then came around his car to me.

"Care to explain why I got a call from Donavon telling me to meet him here?" He looked me over. "And why you look like you just lost a fight?"

"Didn't lose," I mumbled.

"Come again?" He had his cop face on now.

"Nothing." I looked him in the eye as a new idea popped into my tired brain. Surely the sheriff hadn't been a part of Gabriella's scheme? It seemed unlikely, but how could he possibly have overlooked his deputy's clear hatred for anything nonhuman?

"You seem to be in the know about the, ah, unique residents in this town. Did you also know that your newest deputy was bent on cleansing the town of anyone not human?" I quirked an eyebrow at the sheriff and waited for his reaction.

"Deputy Smith gets a little carried away at times, but he's still a man of the law."

"Well, the deputy didn't think the 'serve and protect' schtick applied to nonhumans. He was the one behind all the murders, sheriff." I watched surprise and disbelief steal over his face. They looked like genuine emotions. Hmm. I guess the sheriff wasn't in on it. That was good. I was too drained to do anything about it if he had been.

I jerked my head at the approaching group before the sheriff could splutter anything else about his deputy. "I recommend you get ready to talk to the two non-human groups who were most affected by your deputy's killing spree."

The sheriff shifted his attention to the approaching group. Patrick, now clothed, still carried Rosalyn while Willomena walked beside them, holding her broken arm. Donavon, now back in his human form, led the small group our way.

He'd managed to find his shirt and pants and I was a little disappointed that he'd put them back on. Ah well. The pants were only slightly ripped. Apparently his shoes hadn't survived when he'd shift to werewolf. I winced in sympathy as his bare feet crunched across the fresh snow.

"Donavon, care to explain what the hell is going on?" The sheriff's eyes flicked to me for a few seconds. I was very glad I'd thought to put my gun back in my purse. "And why this girl is telling me one of my deputies is accused of murder?"

Authority filled Donavon's voice as he rumbled, "Bart, your man, Deputy Ken Smith, has been tried and punished for the murders of Joseph Kleinman, Tony Duluth, Samuel Vance, Sadie Green, and Cassandra McDougall." I could hear the anger still in that wolfy voice. It didn't seem fair to take it out on the sheriff.

"He wasn't the only one, though." I shot a glare at Donavon then returned my attention to the sheriff. "Cheri, the waitress from the diner, was part of it, too."

"Cheri Demlin?" The sheriff asked. It was a struggle not to roll my eyes at the disbelief in his voice. Cheri had really pulled the wool over a lot of people's eyes. Namely those eyes that belonged to males with some authority.

"Yes. That Cheri." I had no idea if that was actually her last name, but I'd take his word for it.

"Where is she? And just what do you mean that my deputy has already been tried?"

"Cheri's dead," Donavon answered before I could, "and so is your deputy." Donavon came to a stop a few feet away from the sheriff with Patrick beside him.

Rosalyn wore a pain filled grimace, "Sheriff, we need to talk, but I'm afraid Willomena and I are in need of medical attention first. Donavon has agreed to fill you in on tonight's events. The coven trusts that you will make good judgment of how to move forward from there." The witch nodded at the sheriff. It must have been some sort of signal because Patrick and Willomena immediately moved off toward a white SUV.

The sheriff's attention flicked from Donavon, to the werewolf and witches as they walked away, then over to me before landing back on the Alpha. I did not entirely appreciate being included in that look.

"What the fuck is going on, Donavon?"

"When you became sheriff," the werewolf explained, "I informed you of my people and," he glanced at me, "of the supernatural community that lived peaceably in this town."

I managed to hold back a snort as he used my phrase.

Though the sheriff looked like he wanted to interrupt the werewolf, he smartly kept his silence while Donavon continued, "I told you that you were the law of the town unless something affected my wolves."

The sheriff nodded, "And I've been working with you, giving you all the information I had, to bring the murderer to justice."

"Yes. But what you don't understand is that when my wolves

are killed, human justice is not enough." Donavon's eyes began to glow white. "The wolves and witches have meted out justice to those who had a hand in murdering our people."

"Donavon, that's not how things are done. There are laws—"

"We have our own laws, sheriff," Donavon bit off.

The sheriff stared at him for a moment. I couldn't blame him. Finally, he said, "So, you killed my deputy and Cheri Demlin without a trial?"

"They were guilty, sheriff," I couldn't keep my mouth shut.

"And what exactly," the sheriff rounded on me, "do you have to do with all of this? Who are you?"

I opened my mouth but Donavon beat me to it.

"She is the lawman of our kind."

What?

"She is judge, jury, and executioner."

WHAT?

Once upon a time, that was true, Vânători . We tracked down those who broke our laws, weighed their crimes, and executed those we found guilty. Is that not what you did here, in this town?

I started to argue, but dammit if she wasn't right. That's exactly what I'd done, though if I were being honest, killing Cheri hadn't been the plan. I just hadn't realized that Gabriella's magic would kill her when I'd flung it at the woman.

The sheriff and the werewolf were both staring, though with different expressions. The sheriff's of utter disbelief and the werewolf with resignation.

Finally the sheriff opened his mouth but Donavon cut him off. "You can't arrest her, Bart. Well, you could, but you won't find any bodies so you won't be able to charge her with murder."

This instantly took the sheriff's attention off me, which was good because I had no idea what the hell to say.

"Let's talk." Donavon pulled the sheriff aside while the white SUV pulled out of the lot and headed presumably to the hospital. I hoped Rosalyn would be okay but I still couldn't drum up any sympathy for Willomena.

I waited again next to the car, freezing my ass off while the sheriff and Donavon talked about who had the biggest balls or whatever. As long as I didn't get arrested and got to get somewhere warm in the next few minutes, I would be happy.

Finally, the sheriff returned to his car but not before throwing me a dark look. Whatever. I'd taken care of his town's "wild animal" problem and almost gotten killed by his sleazy deputy in the process. If he didn't want to thank me, that was his problem.

Donavon made his way over to me. He placed himself squarely between me and the sheriff, and held out my knife as he got closer. "I pulled this from the deputy," he said quietly. "Best not to leave it lying around."

I took the knife, silently glad that someone, probably Donavon, had cleaned it of any blood.

"I'm going with Bart to meet Rosalyn at the hospital," He said, then leaned across me, opened the driver's side door and jerked his head toward the car keys that lay on the driver's seat.

Damn. I could have been sitting in a warm car this whole time!

"You are welcome to take this car back to the motel. It's Patrick's and he'll pick it up later." His voice was strained and I realized he was struggling not to give me orders. Was he being more polite now because I had helped bring down the murders or because he'd seen what I was and what I could do as a Vânători?

Perhaps a little of both. He sees you exactly as he said earlier: you are a lawman.

Lawwoman, I inwardly grumbled.

Artemis ignored my correction. *You are a formidable predator to him now.*

Hmm. Interesting…but I had no intention of throwing down and Challenging him. Instead, I pushed the door open a little wider, allowing Ramble to jump into the passenger seat before I leaned down and grabbed the keys.

"Thanks." I sank into the driver's seat.

Before I could close the door, he said, "You're welcome to stay in town as long as you need." With that, he turned and headed for the sheriff's patrol car. They pulled out of the lot a moment later, leaving just me and my hellhound hanging out at the graveyard.

The engine easily rumbled to life when I turned the key. It didn't need to warm up before we went anywhere, but I needed to think, so Ramble and I just sat there, staring at the snowflakes as they hit the windshield and melted. The past few hours were like a blur in my mind.

I turned toward Ramble. "Are you okay? You were limping. Is your leg okay?"

He sighed and lay down across the front seat, propping his head on the center console. Though he couldn't verbalize his thoughts, his eyes were enough to get his message across: *I'm okay—are you okay?*

I let out my own sigh and looked back out the windshield. The little building in the distance was now completely dark. Had I really just fought the beast in there? Stuck a knife into its—his, the deputy's—head and killed him? Had I really been able to see magic as colors and absorbed it?

Had I really drank vampire blood?

That thought brought to mind Louis's pitiful form, crumpled against the cell door before Ramble had dragged him over to me. Me grasping his wrist and forcing him to give me his blood…

The last image sent a shiver of anticipation through me, back-washed with an overwhelming sense of shame. Vampire blood had been the highest high I'd ever experienced. I closed my eyes and tipped my head back against the leather headrest. Louis's blood had filled a need I hadn't really known I'd had.

I thought about alcohol—and the cool way it slid down my throat and left me light-headed and eventually numb after enough drinks—but didn't feel that craving anymore.

Before I could really feel any sense of relief, my brain shocked me with the image of looking into Louis's glossy eyes as I pulled more of his blood into my mouth, down my throat and into my very being.

That was what I craved now. I'd replaced alcohol with a substance much more addictive and much more vile.

Do not be ashamed of who you are, Vânători .

"No other Vânători had to drink vampire blood to hear you or have your powers, did they?" I demanded. "How could I not feel ashamed?"

You are right. Your blood is not as pure as those who came before you—

Her attitude reminded me of the deputy when he'd raged against the witches.

—but that is through no fault of your own. You are destined to take up the Vânători *mantle and do good in this world, and if that*

means imbibing the blood of vampires, then so be it.

She didn't understand. I opened my eyes but the image of Louis stayed in the back of my mind. I turned to Ramble.

"What do you think? Should we stay on here a little while longer? Your call."

The hellhound shrugged and gave a small whuff.

I took that as a yes.

I sighed. It only made sense to stay in town. It was the only place where there was a vampire who might be willing to donate his blood to me. Plus, I'd agreed with Rosalyn to help protect the supernatural community. After seeing what she was capable of when angry, I wasn't about to piss her off by skipping town.

I put the car in drive and pointed us toward the motel. Tonight we'd lick our wounds. Tomorrow I'd deal with this new lust for blood and go speak with our resident vampire.

Once the decision was made, I actually felt kind of good about staying. Though I wouldn't exactly call them friends, I knew more people in this town than I had after living and working in Indianapolis.

I flipped on the radio, rolled down the window for Ramble, and we drove through the snowy, Halloween night, letting snow in the car and listening to Led Zeppelin's "Ramble On."

About the Author

J.J. Russell lives on a small farm in Downeast Maine with her husband and two adventurous dogs. When she's not writing, you can find her growing veggies or out on a trail running (very slowly). Check out her author page at www.JJRussellWrites.com and sign up for the newsletter to hear when new books are released and to get free short stories for characters in the Artemis Necklace universe!

You can connect with me on:
- 🌐 https://www.jjrussellwrites.com
- 🐦 https://twitter.com/JJRussellWrites
- 📷 https://www.instagram.com/JJrussellwrites

Also by J.J. Russell

Want to learn how Vianne wrangled her hellhound companion and fought against vampires to obtain the Artemis Necklace? Experience her introduction to the world of the supernatural in the first book of the Artemis Necklace Series, *Suck It.*

Suck It: The Artemis Necklace Series, Book 1

I'm Vianne Vanator, and I'm an alcoholic. And, apparently, a vampire hunter.

Turns out I'm the descendant of a famous vampire hunter. However, without a magical necklace, I don't have the same abilities my ancestor did to annihilate bloodsuckers and other supernatural beings that go bump in the night.

The problem is, I didn't know any of this until vampires tried to kill me, a vampire hunter saved me from them only to then kidnap me, and I accidentally made a deal with a hellhound. Not exactly the day I expected when I went to work this morning.

If I want to continue having a pulse, I'll need to stay one step ahead of the vampires and beat them to finding the Artemis Necklace. Luckily, I'm being helped by a pushy hellhound (who might also be okay with ripping me to shreds) and a veteran vampire hunter (who, ahem, kidnapped me).

Yup. This is gonna go great.

Suck It follows Vianne as she learns about her family's history as vampire hunters, comes to terms with a world full of supernatural creatures, and discovers that many of those creatures want nothing better than to see her dead.

Made in the USA
Middletown, DE
12 September 2024

60227182R00181